Possessive Puckboy

Also by Eden Finley and Saxon James

Puckboys

Egotistical Puckboy
Irresponsible Puckboy
Shameless Puckboy
Foolish Puckboy
Clueless Puckboy
Bromantic Puckboy
Forbidden Puckboy
Possessive Puckboy
Stubborn Puckboy
Charming Puckboy

POSSESSIVE PUCKBOY

EDEN FINLEY & SAXON JAMES

canelo

DK | Penguin Random House

First published in the United Kingdom in 2025 by Sadenverse Books

This edition published in the United Kingdom in 2026 by

Canelo, an imprint of
Canelo Digital Publishing Limited,
20 Vauxhall Bridge Road,
London SW1V 2SA
United Kingdom

A Penguin Random House Company
The authorised representative in the EEA is Dorling Kindersley Verlag GmbH.
Arnulfstr. 124, 80636 Munich, Germany

A CIP catalogue record for this book is available from the British Library.

ISBN 978 1 83598 526 7

Printed and bound in Great Britain by Clays Ltd, Elcograf S.p.A.

Look for more great books at
www.canelo.co | www.dk.com

FSC
www.fsc.org
MIX
Paper
FSC® C018179

CHAPTER ONE

PARKER

It's been six months since my life fell apart. I'm not talking a little blip or an overdramatic flair of bad luck. No. Every little piece of my life has unraveled. First, I sold my company, then my dad died, then I gave Mom a bunch of money, and she disappeared on a years-long trip around the world, leaving me stranded and alone. Okay, not *alone* alone. I'd had a boyfriend. A nice boyfriend. A boyfriend I thought might be a husband-type person at some point down the line, but then he left me as well.

Workaholic. Right. Well, sorry, but you don't get to be as successful as I am without putting in the work, and maybe that meant he was neglected sometimes, by accident, but what am I supposed to do? I wish that was a rhetorical question, but I actually don't know the answer. People and dating don't come easily to me.

But six months later and not much has changed.

You'd think being a twenty-six-year-old billionaire would mean the rest of my life is set. I appreciate that my mom and I will never have financial worries in our lifetimes, and hopefully, neither will my kids. My kids who don't actually exist yet. Because to have kids, I'd like a partner to raise them with, and while money *will* get me a partner, it's not the type of partner I want.

And that's all led me to here: in a luxury suite in Ball Arena, overlooking the same ice I used to watch from the nosebleeds.

The crowd around me goes wild as Colorado scores the first point in this game. It's still preseason, but Colorado fans are passionate, and considering I've been coming to this arena since I was a kid, I suppose I can count myself in with them.

Dad was a hockey player for Colorado, but he only made it two seasons before an injury ended his career before it could take off. He wound up working in an office up until he died, but he still took shifts driving the Zamboni, and when he wasn't needed, we'd watch the games together. I've been a season ticket holder since I was five.

Now, I have an entire suite, and it's only me.

Dad would have loved for me to follow in his footsteps, but no matter how much I tried, staying upright while skating isn't something I managed to master, and it's sort of a basic requirement for making it to the NHL. Or even a high school team.

It also didn't help that I preferred to have my head in my laptop, coding a new game or working on building a life-size robot so I had at least one friend.

Ah, the trauma that was my adolescence.

The door to my suite opens, and I glance over at Brendan Murray, the team owner.

"Parker," he says, his deep voice a warm memory from my childhood. He owned the team when Dad played for them and was an owner who was actively involved in the sport and his players. The older he's gotten, the more he's pulled away, until here we are.

Like a switch has been flipped, I put a halt to my whirlwind of thoughts and channel the super-professional grown-up exterior I always have to work to maintain through these meetings.

"How did it go?" I ask.

When Brendan had mentioned at my father's funeral that he was looking to sell, it was the one light in a very fucking dull few months. The process wasn't as simple as throwing money at him either. I've had to go through background checks and interviews. Had to make sure there was no pushback from the other owners. I needed to draft a business plan and prove I have enough assets not only for the sale but to keep the team going if their season takes a dive. I've engaged a broker who specializes in the buying of sports teams, and I'm ready for them to open the team up for sale because I'll outbid anyone who tries to take this from me.

As long as I have approval to even try. Which is hopefully the news Brendan is bringing me now.

"You've got the green light," Brendan says. "Given that you're local, who your dad was, and my glowing recommendation, it's unlikely things won't go your way."

Relief sweeps over me. As much as I'd like to give them a figure and be done with it, for a high-profile team like Colorado, I'm not the only one with interest. Unlucky for anyone else, I'll bankrupt myself to buy this team if I have to. Brendan isn't making it widely known that the team is for sale because he doesn't want to disrupt the way things are run here, but he's open to offers. Thankfully, it's valued at a much lower number than what's in my bank account, so it shouldn't come to that, but it was Dad's team. The one I've always rooted for, and while I didn't expect my software company to explode the way it did, it feels serendipitous that I made the sale right before Brendan decided he was done. Right at the time where I had all this money to burn and a memory of my father to cling to.

My gaze returns to the ice where the lines have changed, and I narrow in on one player.

It's also serendipitous that my home team happens to be the same team that *he* plays on. The man who started my stupid nickname in high school that I was never able to shake.

The man I might have had the most stupid high school crush on that maybe hasn't completely stayed in high school.

Connor Kikishkin.

Mr. Hockey Captain. Mr. King of the School.

I still vividly remember the day I'd been talking to his little brother and he'd shoved me into a locker and warned me to stay away. It was that same day he'd altered my last name—Duchene—to douche. And that had stuck.

For all four years of high school before it followed me to college.

It wasn't very inventive, and some dumb jock probably would have gotten there eventually, but if Connor hadn't singled me out that day, would anyone have known who I was? If I was another nameless, faceless nerd, they wouldn't have had any reason to know my name.

But they did.

Because of Connor.

So while I'm buying this team first and foremost for Dad, to honor his memory and try to keep some kind of connection to him, I can't deny that having Connor Kikishkin's career in my hands holds a certain appeal.

All I've dreamed about since high school is stepping into my reunion and showing all those dumb jocks who bullied me mercilessly for four years how far I've come. That I succeeded where they couldn't.

But if I'm honest, it doesn't feel like I've come all that far. I've spent the last five years with my head in a computer, working my butt off, building an empire, and now that I've taken a step back and remembered that the real world exists, there doesn't seem to be much waiting for me.

So if I can have one thing in this life that makes me happy, I'm going to give it to myself.

I'm going to own Connor Kikishkin.

And I'm not going to give him the satisfaction of knowing one of the reasons I'm here is because of him. In fact, I'm going to pretend I don't remember him at all.

"I know of two other parties that are planning to front up large sums," Brendan warns.

"You would say that though. The more I offer, the more you'll have to line your pockets."

"Not like you can't spare it. A billionaire at your age. Your dad wouldn't know what to do with you."

Pain slices through my chest. The whole reason I'd put my company up for sale in the first place was so I could throw money at the hospital to save him. He didn't hang on long enough for that to happen. Six weeks. He was here, and then … he wasn't.

"Trust me when I say you won't need to rely on food stamps for your retirement."

"For whatever it means, I hope your offer is successful. You were always a good kid, your dad was a good man, and this is your team—owned or not. I know you'll look after everything I've built here."

Everything, except for one man.

I shoot a smile his way. "Get that office ready for me. I don't plan on taking no for an answer."

CHAPTER TWO

CONNOR

Ever had that dream where you're back in high school and everyone is laughing at you, but you don't know why until you look down and you're naked?

I wish I was living that dream.

The man standing before the entire team is familiar yet almost unrecognizable, and his words sound like they're coming from underwater.

Something, something, introduce. Love hockey. Twenty billion something. New owner.

Our franchise was sold? To Douche? The Douche from high school?

He's not actually a douche. That's just what everyone called him because of his last name.

Memories of those days flood through my mind, racing on a loop and throwing me back to being king of the school and watching as my teammates … Shit.

If the ground could open up and swallow me whole right about now, I'd appreciate it, but that doesn't happen. Neither does our owner disappear when I try to blink him away.

I still remember that day clearly: the one where I saw Parker Duchene and my brother hunched over a schedule, heads close together. Smiling. Being … friendly. Overly friendly.

I don't know what came over me. I didn't know then, and I still don't know now. The closest I can get is figuring that while Easton wasn't out at that point, I knew he was gay, and I had to protect his future hockey career by getting in between him and the guy standing too close. Easton hadn't even confirmed his sexuality to me at that point, but I saw something I really shouldn't have on his laptop one day when mine had died, which was the giant tip he wasn't straight. Exactly like the one the dude in the porn on his screen had. One of the dudes anyway. Biggest mushroom tip head I've ever seen. Not that I'd ever taken notice of other dicks before then. I didn't say anything because I thought he should be the one to come out when he was ready. That, and all I could think about was what coming out would do for his career.

It's not like there weren't out guys in the league back then. Caleb Sorensen and Ollie Strömberg were well-known for being the first, but it was no secret that their careers weren't exactly smooth and scandal-free. Easton had the potential to be one of the greats.

No one could know about my brother, and I wouldn't let this scrawny, nerdy kid ruin Easton's life.

Even though that's the logical reason for what I did, something about it doesn't ring true in my gut. I can't pinpoint what it is, never could, but something came over me that day that told me I needed to separate them, so I did. I've had regret and confusion ever since.

I won't deny what I did was wrong. It was so wrong. I might play rough on the ice, but violence off it is never the answer, and I threatened it. I used it. I shoved this kid against a locker and told him to stay away from my brother.

And now, he's here.

The only question is why?

Am I really that self-absorbed to think he bought our team out of spite?

I want to say no, but …

Surely we've both grown in the last ten years. We're grown-ass men now, not stupid teenagers.

He finishes his speech, which I couldn't hear any of, and beside me, Easton asks, "Do we go say hi?"

I'd rather run in the opposite direction and keep running if I'm honest, but no. I'm going to be mature and take the high road. "I-I guess so." Look at me with all that confidence in my shaky voice.

I've got this.

Yet, as we approach him, I almost chicken out. My palms sweat, my heart beats erratically, and after my brother reintroduces himself, I pluck up the courage to reach out my hand to the dark-haired, bright-blue-eyed boy who's no longer a boy. He's … Fuck, I don't know what he is.

"Hey." I stumble over what to say. "Good to see you again. Parker." I must sound like a damn robot.

The team's new owner cocks his head as if he's confused, but his eyes hold nothing but contempt. "I'm sorry, have we met?"

I'm stunned speechless. That's how he's going to play it? Hey, fine by me. The less apologizing I have to do, the better. I'm still in the middle of groveling to Easton and my best friend, Knox, for being overprotective of both of them to the point they didn't think they could be together because of me. I don't need more penance added to my list of failures as a decent human being.

Parker hasn't lost his cold stare as he says, "If you don't mind, I'd prefer my players to call me Mr. Duchene."

My gut sinks because he's obviously still bitter about high school. He can pretend he doesn't remember me all he wants, but that's not what he's doing. He's here to be petty and probably vengeful, so the only thing I can do is grin and bear whatever he throws at me. Because if I lose it in front of him? I can say goodbye to the NHL and everything I've worked toward forever.

We, as players, rarely saw the last owner, and this will be no different. All I have to do is stay away from Parker Duchene, and everything will be fine. Great, even. Hey, if we win the Stanley Cup this year, maybe he'll give me a pass for my past actions.

One could hope.

-

Stay away from Parker, I said. It will be easy, I said.

Then why in the fuck is he here every fucking day? Taunting me. Making me think he has it out for me when he's still pretending he doesn't even remember me. Every time I'm on this practice ice, it's as if I can feel him staring at my back. Yet, every time I turn toward him, his eyes are elsewhere. He either has a sixth sense for when I'm about to look, or the threat of being confronted about one of the darkest moments in my life has me paranoid as shit.

The thing is, in high school, I was too busy focusing on hockey and protecting my younger brothers to have time to be a bully, but I can acknowledge that being the most popular guy in high school meant I didn't need to do anything to be part of the problem. Because I never stepped in. My teammates, the ones who weren't counting on being drafted or going pro … they did it for me. They saw me attack Parker? That meant he was fair game. I saw them do it to him? I didn't stop them.

And the sad truth is, I'm sure I had convinced myself that what I did was right because I was protecting Easton. My whole life, I was brought up to believe that was my only job: to protect Easton and Lachie with everything I have so that we could all make it to the NHL. With our parents working so much, all the responsibility fell to me, and I'd thought I was doing exactly what I was supposed to.

I achieved it all, but I'm starting to think I gave up a huge piece of me to do so. My empathy? My impulse control? That part of my soul that makes someone a good person?

It would explain why things with me and Easton are so rocky lately.

Easton asked for a trade to another team just to get away from me. After everything I've done for him, he says it's been too much. I've been overbearing, too interfering, and while we're getting better again and he's starting to live his own life, it's hard to switch that side of me off. He wants me to leave him alone, and yet, when I watch him leave the ice to head toward the locker room, I can't help that pang of protectiveness that stabs at me when Parker follows.

It's the same pang I felt all those years ago. Like this deep part of me doesn't want Parker near him.

I know Easton is way too invested in Knox to screw it up. He was willing to throw our whole brotherhood away for the chance to be with my best friend, so I don't need to follow them because Easton is a big boy. He can handle this.

And yet, I swear with all my being that before Parker disappears into the corridor, he turns and looks right at me. Challenging me.

I don't trust that guy, and even though Easton has told me to back off and not be that overbearing brother he hates so much, my feet don't listen to me as they head in the same direction.

My brain tells me to leave it and to turn around to let Easton handle him, but when I turn the corner into the locker room and see Parker Duchene basically cornering my brother at his cubby, a blind rage clouds my vision.

If he was baiting me, it worked because in the next second, I'm on him so fast even I don't know what is happening. But I do know I've fucked up. I've played right into Parker Duchene's hands.

Here I am, repeating past behaviors, with him shoved up against a wall. Doing exactly what my brother has asked me to stop doing. Why can't I help myself?

The death of my professional hockey career flashes through my mind while my forearm pins the new team's owner, and it would be one thing if this was the only time I've done this, but it's not.

With a smug look on his face, he says, "I see nothing's changed since high school."

That only confirms what I thought: he was lying.

Easton tries to pull me off Parker, but just like back then, I only have one thought running through my head.

What the fuck does he want with my brother, and what were they doing in here alone, standing so close? But most importantly, why do I hate it so much? Easton's had flings before. I've had nothing against those guys. But Parker?

I see him and want to scream that my brother is a taken man and he should back the hell off.

In fact, in the haze of rage, I'm sure I say that out loud.

"For fuck's sake." Easton finally pulls me off Douche. "You're doing it again. Back off, and stop being an overprotective shithead."

He's right, of course, but that doesn't make me feel any better about fucking up. Again.

Apparently, there's a huge difference between being a supportive brother and being hateable. And all I've been feeling from Easton lately is hate.

I'm too much and interfere where I shouldn't. I'm too obsessed with his and Lachie's lives that I don't have one of my own.

That's the part that gets to me the most. Because he's absolutely right. Between hockey and keeping my brothers from creating tabloid-worthy stories, I don't have a life outside of my best friend, Knox.

And now that he and East are frustratingly dancing around the relationship they both went behind my back to have, I don't even have Knox.

I have … hockey, a temper, and the occasional hookup with any girl who shows interest. Because I don't have time to think of having anything serious with another person. Only … now I do. I have time and the mental capacity to do what I want.

And I have no idea what that is.

Do I want a wife and kids? Yes.

But I also wanted to have a long hockey career, and now, thanks to my outburst, that's obviously gone out the window.

I keep ruining everything.

With nothing to lose, I ask, "What are you even doing here, Douche?"

"Real mature."

Surprising the hell out of me, East actually has my back. He gets in between us and glares in Parker's direction. "I could be wrong, but it sounds a hell of a lot like you bought this team so you can mess with Connor over some stupid nickname you were given when you were both young."

"I'm not here to fuck with him. I'm here to make his life a living hell." He straightens his jacket and walks out of the locker room, leaving me to deal with the reality that my past is here to bite me in the ass, and now it's not my brothers who need protecting.

It's me.

-

One restless night of sleep later, I wake up to my alarm with the urge to vomit.

I messed everything up yesterday, all because I couldn't control whatever that broken thing inside me is that makes me lash out when it comes to my brothers.

Mom and Dad worked their asses off to get us where we are. Dad worked two jobs, Mom worked full-time as a corporate lawyer, and so I was the one left to make sure Easton's and Lachie's homework was done, that their hockey gear was washed, and that they weren't being picked on by anyone at school or on their hockey teams.

When I was drafted and got a major signing bonus, I paid off all of our parents' debts, and they became my agent. Then Easton's, and now Lachie's. Mom knows contract law, and Dad knows hockey.

And I … know nothing outside of what I've done for the last fifteen years. I'm only twenty-six, and I feel like I'm a fifty-year-old parent with dependents who rely on me.

I'm single. I should be having the time of my life.

But I'm not.

I'm realizing I don't know who I am when fifty percent of my identity has been stripped away.

Easton and Lachie are adults. They don't need me. Knox doesn't need me.

No one does, and it sucks. Because I like being needed. It's a drug.

I probably shouldn't mention that. Especially not to a team therapist or anyone in the mental health industry because that can't be normal, can it?

Besides, my need to feel needed is the least of my worries.

We have a game today, and I have to walk into that arena and face whatever consequences Douche is going to give me. Whether it be official or personal. Because after admitting he bought the team to make my life a living hell, I have no doubt that he's going to follow through on that promise.

What's he going to do? Give me no ice time? Force Coach Macklin to make me a healthy scratch all season? Run me over with the Zamboni and call it an accident? Anything is possible.

My only hope of maybe moving forward from all this is if I go to the arena early, track down Parker, and beg for forgiveness. For yesterday and high school.

Groveling? It's so not me.

Then again, have I ever really had to do it?

No.

I force myself out of bed and get ready to head into the practice rink again this morning for a warm-up skate. I find Knox in our living room, either wallowing over Easton or freaking out about reffing his first NHL game tonight. I want to perk him up and say he'll be great, give him some reassurance, but nothing is positive and bright in my eyes, so I won't be much help.

"I made you your protein shake," Knox says and lifts one of his own.

"You're the best." Even my genuine words don't sound shiny and happy. I glance over at him, at the bags under his eyes, and I wonder if he got the same amount of sleep that I did. "You worried about tonight?"

"I know you've already said no to this, but can you please lose so I'm not accused of favoritism?"

I laugh. "I'll try my best."

With how much my head is not in the game and totally focused on the nerd from high school who's vowed to get his revenge, I might not even need to promise that. How can I concentrate on my career when I know someone is out there trying to destroy it?

If Parker wants to make my life a living hell, he's already succeeding. Hockey is all I have left, and if he takes it away from me …

I can't even think about that.

"What about you?" Knox asks. "How do you think tonight's going to go?"

"If I'm even playing? Not well."

"Do you really think Parker will pull you?"

"At this point, I'm expecting to walk in there and get put on waivers. He said he was here to make my life a living hell, and what better way than to take the one thing I have left?"

"The one thing?" Knox asks. It only takes a second for him to realize what I'm saying before he slumps. "You haven't lost East. Or me. Just because things are weird because I fell for your brother but can't be with him because of conflict of interest on the ice and he's mad at me and— Ugh, I'm not getting into it again. But just because all of that is happening, it doesn't mean you don't have us anymore. You have both of us. That will never change no matter what is happening between me and him."

He says that, but it doesn't feel that way at all.

I pick up the shake he made me and then grab my gear bag near the door. "I'll see you tonight. Hopefully. If not from the ice, then I'll be in the stands."

If I'm not squashed by that Zamboni.

CHAPTER THREE

PARKER

I swing on my office chair, feet kicked up on my desk, trying to keep the rolling frustration inside. When I bought this team, I thought it might keep me busy. Give me back that brain buzz I've lost since selling my company, but even though I'm the owner, there's not a whole lot for me to do.

My coaches coach. My managers manage. Public relations relate, the trainers train, the doctors doc. I shake my head because that's not even a verb.

But my point is that my players play, and all I do is own. Which apparently means jack shit.

Brendan Murray was a lot more involved in his younger days, but slowly, his ownership became more of a trophy than anything, and I'd thought I could replicate what he used to be. An involved owner. Someone who actually cares about his team.

Or most of his team. I care entirely too much about Connor Kikishkin, but not in a loving way. It's more of an I want to create a Pop! figure of him so I can get stabby with it kind of way. The rest of the team I actually want to see hoist the Stanley Cup.

Maybe I'll do everything I can to get the team to playoffs and, at the last possible moment, trade him out to a team at the bottom of the standings. It would kill Mr. Hockey King to see his brother with a ring and know he could have had that too. If he wasn't such an asshole.

Who still shoves people up against walls.

Truthfully, he had a point that I probably shouldn't have cornered Easton in that locker room. Actually, there's no *probably* about it. I'd been agitated already. This whole trying to get involved thing isn't working out the way I'd hoped, and I'd left the team trainers' office when they'd politely pointed out it would be a lot easier to do their jobs without me hovering.

I'd been sulking and heading back to my office to do exactly what I'm doing now when I'd seen Easton stalk off in some kind of huff. Fuck, he reminds me so much of his brother, and I try not to hold it against him since he's actually a decent person, but even the thought of Mr. Hotshot makes my blood boil.

In more ways than one, which I really, really hate.

Especially when I'd been pressed to the wall.

A flush of heat rolls through me again at the memory, and I face-palm at how much I hate my body. I can't even hold a grudge right.

Maybe I'd be smarter to offload the team to someone else and work on my next big techy plans. Make another couple of billion. Forget any of this ever happened.

But then I think of Dad and how he didn't ever get a chance to be proud of me for owning a hockey team like he never could have imagined doing, and all that work and those billions turn sour. My nonstop sixteen-hour days in the technology field are over.

There's a knock on the door, and I scramble to drop my legs off the desk and sit upright. I do my usual preparation of counting to ten so I'm not flustered. It's a real effort to steady my breathing and prepare for a professional conversation where I'm not some awkward loser but the most powerful person in this franchise.

Somehow, that doesn't help. Throwing my weight around on big decisions hasn't exactly made me feel like I'm anybody of importance.

"Come in," I call, dropping my tone a notch in an attempt to sound like a professional.

And when the door opens, the last person I'm expecting to see walks in.

A burst of anger, intimidation, and—fuck me—lust hits all at once.

"Mr. Duchene," he bites out.

Good to see I'm not the only one wanting to go for the throat. Honestly, it feels good that for the first time ever, I have his attention. That one moment in high school was all he ever gave me, and after turning my life to hell, he never once looked my way again.

Not in class. Not in the halls. Not even when his stupid hockey team was bullying me. Not when I'd go to every hockey home game and glare at him from the stands.

It takes me a second to remember I need to respond.

"Mr. Kikishkin," I manage and point at my chair across from me.

He doesn't have power over me anymore, but I'm struggling to remind my body of that.

Connor is classically handsome. Browny-caramel waves. Deep gray eyes. A square jaw peppered with stubble. But those things I can ignore. It's the gentle way his anger surrounds him, the way he holds himself like the tallest person in the room, how he manages everything in life with such extreme confidence—those are things I'll never have and will always crave. It pisses me off that I don't know if I want to fuck Connor or be Connor. I don't want to want either of those options.

"I, uh …" His jaw tics. "Want to apologize. For yesterday."

Of course he does. I could fire him in a heartbeat for that. I might not know much about where I fit in this team, but at least I know that. I also know that I won't. Because if I fire him, it means losing the chance to fuck with him again. But I'm not going to make this easy for him.

A long moment stretches out.

Somewhere from deep in that murky well of confidence that I apparently have inside, I smile. "So do it."

Connor stares at me. "Do what?"

"Apologize."

"I just did."

"No, you said you want to." My smile gets wider at his obvious discomfort. "I'm waiting."

The look he levels me with is maybe the hottest thing I've seen in my life, and I have to remind myself I'm a professional, not a pile of goo, damn it. He catches himself before he can say something inappropriate, but his face already said it for him.

Connor uses the most monotone voice I've ever heard. "I'm sorry."

"For?"

His teeth actually clack together. "I'm sorry for my reaction yesterday. I stand by thinking that you cornering a player is inappropriate, but I shouldn't have handled it like that."

"No. You shouldn't have." I ignore the inappropriate jab, even as my gut squirms with guilt. "I think you need some anger management classes."

"Anger management? Because I was looking out for my brother?"

First high school, now this? You'd think he'd grow up by now. "You can't keep using him as an excuse for your behavior."

"I …" Something behind his fierce eyes closes off. It should make me happy that I've clearly struck a nerve, but instead, I feel a twinge of curiosity. "Do you accept my apology or not?"

Do I? Of course I don't. It's in no way sincere and is only about saving his ass. It's as much of an apology as the one I got in high school. Which was none.

Only years of being ostracized. Years of having no friends because people were worried about becoming targets too.

I look Connor dead in the eye, anger finally taking over all the other bullshit. "I'll accept an apology from you the day you actually give me one."

"I literally did—"

"Don't you dare say that was an apology. That was lip service. That was a pathetic attempt at trying to save your career, and the fact you can't even swallow your pride for long enough to make it sound believable should be enough of a reason for me to bench you all season. Or send you back to the farm team. You clearly don't care about your career or this team if you can't even show a hint of humility."

His eyes have gone wide, and just when I'm sure I see something real—panic, vulnerability, fear?—his face morphs, and he levels me with that same furious glare he gave me a few moments ago. "I don't care about this team? Look who's talking. You bought us as a way to settle some high school grudge. This is everything I've ever worked toward, and you think it's a game to walk in here and mess with what I've dedicated my entire life to? Look, I'm sorry I called you that stupid name back then, I'm sorry people took it overboard, I'm also sorry for jumping to the wrong conclusions yesterday, but this is my life. My whole life." He's sitting forward, right on the edge of his chair, hands curled into fists.

The thing is, I did tell myself I was buying the team to fuck with him, but I'm either the least evil person in existence, or I need to read more supervillain comics because I'm low on ideas. Ideally, I'd ostracize Connor from his entire team and give him a taste of what being truly alone feels like, but I'd have no clue how to do that. Where to start. I like to pretend I'm tough and take charge, but I've yet to prove I can actually follow through on any of that.

I'm not going to say any of that out loud though.

Before I can give away that I'm in way over my head, I hitch that confident smile back up again. "Congratulations, Mr. Kikishkin. I very nearly believed you."

He storms from the room, and the second the door is closed, I fall forward onto my desk, head hitting the wooden top with a solid thunk.

Why the hell does he still get to me after all these years?

CHAPTER FOUR

CONNOR

It's amazing to me that my life could go from being a hotshot defenseman in the NHL with the world at my feet, random girls in my bed, and almost winning the conference finals last year to what it is now: a hot fucking mess.

I wish I could blame Parker Duchene for all of it, but I can't. My life was going to hell by the end of the summer, long before preseason started and he showed up.

I went from thinking my little brothers looked up to and admired me to having Easton be willing to do anything to get away from me. I thought Easton loved hanging around me, that we were more like best friends than brothers, but no, he wanted me out of the picture so he could steal my best friend. Not *be* my best friend.

Losing Easton's and my relationship has almost been like stripping away part of my identity, and with Parker now in my life, reminding me of what a shitty person I was back in high school, I can't help but think they're both right about me.

I'm an overbearing, overprotective asshole, and it's no wonder more people don't resent me. Or maybe they do and I'm blissfully unaware of it. I was when Easton felt that way.

And this is why I've decided to move out. To give him space.

Not only do I live in the same row of town houses Easton does, only a few doors away, but I'm put out on the ice a lot when his line is out there, and I even infiltrated his Queer Collective group even though I'm not queer.

Now that it's been pointed out to me, I'm amazed Easton hasn't stabbed me with one of his skates.

"What do you think?" the Realtor asks after showing me the third house for the day.

The first two were good, but this one is amazing. It's a four-million-dollar Georgian-style mansion in Cherry Hills that's all brick. It has six bedrooms and a pool house, and I'm the only one living in it. But hey, maybe I can pick some poor woman to become my wife, give birth to my kids, and then I'll have someone else to pressure and be overbearing with.

Ugh. I hate that's where my brain goes now.

"Connor?" the Realtor says, like I hadn't heard her. Because I still haven't answered her.

"It's the one," I say. It's more than the other two I've looked at today, but I've been living with cheap rent, or cheapish rent for a professional hockey player anyway, and I'm frugal with my money. I can afford this place … so long as Parker Duchene doesn't put me on waivers. It would be possible to get picked up by another team, considering my stats, but that same way of thinking that drove Easton crazy reminds me that if someone with my kind of stats is put on waivers, the rumor mill will start. And after Easton publicly punched me in front of the media during training camp, that would only add fuel to the fire.

I can see it now—the media narrative: If Connor Kikishkin can't even get along with his brother, how is he supposed to be a team player?

"Shall I put in an offer?" she asks.

I really have to think about that because it's a risk. But if Parker was going to push for me to get fired, he would've done it already. He's had plenty of chances, especially after the locker room incident.

Not my brightest or finest moment.

I've been on edge, waiting for the call or backlash to come because it was obvious he didn't accept my apology. But it hasn't happened. Which, in a way, makes me more annoyed.

I don't know what it is about him that makes me so … so … Ergh, I don't even know what I am toward him. I hate the guy for pulling all these weird emotions out of me. But I also can't hate him because I know what he went through in high school and feel somewhat responsible, even if I maintain, with his last name, he was going to be called Douche no matter what.

The smart business brain I got from Mom tells me not to buy this house. It's not out of my means, but something cheaper would be less risky. Yet, the lost part of me, the part that has thought it's been doing the right thing all this time when I haven't been, tells me to do something for me for once.

My whole life has been about everyone else. Looking after my brothers, keeping our parents happy, paying off their debt with my first big NHL contract. If I'm going to rediscover who I really am, what I want, and think about the man I want to become, I need to follow that voice in my head that says to jump in. Fuck the overly analytical guy who has strategy in every move I make.

"Put in the offer," I say.

-

All I can say is thank fuck I'm at the top of my game. Every game we have, be it away or at home, I'm on edge that Parker Duchene is about to walk in and blow everything up for me. He showed up at an away game to tell Easton he refuses to trade him. I wouldn't put it past the guy to show up across the other side of the country to watch my face as he says he's sending me to the AHL.

If I don't give him a reason to put me on waivers or send me down, he's stuck with me. That's my working theory anyway. Unless he wants to trade me, in which case, bring it on because I'd like to be out of his orbit as much as he would like me to disappear from his. I could let Easton move into my house and start again fresh somewhere else.

I'm thankful I thrive under pressure when it comes to hockey. The other team scores? I'm there pushing to follow it up with one of our own. We're down three goals? I set up Easton to get a hat trick and refuse to allow any more pucks to go near our goalie.

On the ice, I'm still a god. Off it? I'm realizing how messy I can be.

With my new mortgage and moving house, I'm learning who I am deep down. I'm that overly analytical guy who's opposed to risk, so buying that house on a whim? Not my most comfortable position to be in.

I'm not sure I'm even going to be able to enjoy living there. I thought Knox would move with me, but with him reffing in the AHL and NHL, he's constantly traveling, so he decided to move in with my brother instead so they could have valuable couple time when they're both in Denver. So I have this massive house, hardly any furniture, and no one to take this step with.

Every time a new piece of furniture is delivered, I can't help thinking, "I bet Parker would love to watch that get repossessed after he fires me." Or "I wonder if Parker is waiting for me to be happy again before he makes his next move."

And then every time I walk into this arena, run my hand over the cement walls of the back corridor—a ritual I started once and have to do before every game on my way in—I'm sure Parker is about to jump out of nowhere and take everything I've worked for away from me.

I don't understand why he's here, why he bought the team, or why I let him get under my skin the way he does.

He makes me uncomfortable.

Not because he's gay—hello, gay brother and bi best friend—but because … fuck, I don't know why. Maybe it's because he reminds me of a time when I wasn't as calculated as I am now. He's seen me at my weakest, at my worst, and he even brings it out in me.

All I know is the two times I've seen him close to my brother, I've hated it. More than I have with anyone else going near Easton. Which is another thing that reminds me of how Easton is right. I have been too involved in his life.

But even knowing that, there's something I still don't like about Parker being near Easton.

Make it make sense because my brain sure as hell can't.

Have I been raised with the notion that Easton is mine to give away, like a father figure offering their daughter to be married off in exchange for a dowry? Am I that possessive over my own brother? I wouldn't have said so, but the way Easton makes me feel when he says shit like I'm too "overbearing" makes me think I am.

Breaking that habit is harder than I thought it would be, but I've been trying.

I almost reach the locker room when I see Parker. He's at the end of the corridor, talking with Coach Macklin. His smile is a lot more genuine than the smarmy smirk he sent my way while I tried to apologize to him, and if I didn't know any better, I'd say his genuine smile proves he has a heart instead of the evil black sludge I know to be in its place.

That sludge is called bitterness, and it's my fault it's there.

He sees me coming, and I almost want to turn on my heel and run away like a child who's guilty of stealing a cookie and is avoiding consequences, but now that he's locked eyes with me, I won't give him the satisfaction.

I will, however, pick up my pace and try to get inside the locker room—to safety—before he can stop me.

I'm not so lucky.

"Kikishkin," Coach Macklin calls out.

Fuck. I want to keep walking and pretend I didn't hear him, but that won't work. It never does with him.

I turn to both of them, and Coach waves me over.

"What's up?" I ask as I drag my feet in their direction.

"There's a charity benefit being held this weekend, and Mr. Duchene bought us two tables to fill. Because it's the day before our next home game, I don't want to offer up too many players because these things have open bars."

My lips hitch. "Don't trust us enough to refrain?"

"You, I do. And Easton because of the leash you have on him."

I wince. Even Coach can see I've been too involved in Easton's life?

Out of the corner of my eye, I see Parker cock his head at my reaction, so I try to school my face into something more passive than the shame currently written all over it. He hasn't said anything, and I'm sure when he went to Macklin to ask for players to fill seats, I was the last person he wanted at the benefit, but of course, I'm going to say yes. The polite and image-conscious business brain makes me.

"Easton and I will be there," I say.

"And your parents," Coach says.

"Parents?" The thought of Parker in the same vicinity as my parents scares me because … well, what if he tattles on me about what I did to him in high school? I don't want my parents to be disappointed in me.

"Your friend Knox too," Parker says. "He's Easton's boyfriend, isn't he?"

I nod.

"That's five seats of the last ten," Coach says and rubs his chin.

"I can bring a date," I say and then immediately regret it. Because I don't ask women to charity events. I don't date. I hook up. There's a big difference. Dating implies I have the time or effort to commit to a relationship when I really don't.

I also don't have the skill to weed out who wants me for me and not for my money.

Parker frowns, and I'm curious to know why me bringing a date frustrates him when he's the one looking for butts to fill seats at short notice.

"Great. So then we only need two of the married players to bring their wives to fill the other four seats. The ones who are smart enough to know that if they drink, they'll be hungover, and I won't hesitate to make them healthy scratches if they look like a newborn foal on the ice at our morning skate."

"Can't wait," I say through gritted teeth. I go to turn and walk into the locker room when I realize something. "What's the charity for? You never said."

Parker sends that evil smirk my way once again. "The Bully Initiative. It's a fundraiser to raise awareness about school bullying and set up helplines and school programs to teach people how to handle that kind of situation."

I regret asking because now I know why I was singled out and why Parker would want my parents, my brother, and my best friend to come too. I have no doubt he's planning to embarrass me.

When I walked in here today, my biggest fear was being put on waivers. Now, that's all I wish for.

CHAPTER FIVE

PARKER

I'd been unprepared for Fred Macklin to invite the Kikishkins, but Connor just had to turn up where he wasn't wanted. As usual. It'll be good for him to see the sort of damage people like him cause though, so while I'm caught off guard having to be around him for a night when I wasn't mentally prepared, I can do this.

Turn it into some kind of punishment and make out like it was all part of my master plan.

Yes. I am that evil.

And not at all socially rusty after my years-long checkout from real life.

When I heard the charity still had two full tables to sell the night before the event, I bought up the seats, and only *then* did I remember I have no one in my life to fill them with. Asking Macklin, like it's some kind of Colorado-sanctioned event, was a really low point, but thankfully, the only person who will ever know that is me.

And if I can squeeze a few thousand out of Connor Kikishkin toward a charity that exists because of people like him, then I will.

He might not have been the one shoving me over or cornering me in bathrooms, but it was his team who did it. Him who put me on their radar. He was their leader, and if he'd told them to stop, they would have.

Who knows, maybe if I'd had a chance to make friends back then, I'd have people to fill the tables now.

I brace my hands on either side of the bathroom stall and take a long, measured breath. Count to ten. I can't stay in here forever. Technically, I could, but I shouldn't. And won't, obviously.

Tonight is going to drain my social battery quickly, and I'm glad I didn't put my name down to speak at this thing because that would have been a disaster. As much as I'd love to articulate the numerous horrible things I experienced in front of Connor, doing it in front of a room full of people would have guaranteed it came out as, "Ber, hum, uh, bully …"

I've trained myself to confidently talk software to hundreds, but it's all a facade. A thousand-times practiced facade that has me up the entire night beforehand.

I shake out my hands, straighten my shoulders, and then push through with the attitude that doesn't fit me well. In the back of my mind, I picture Connor moving through the halls at the arena with the exact same posture, but I push the image out again. No more thinking about that asshole unless it's for a grand master plan to turn his life to hell.

Which is something I'm totally capable of.

I button the front of my jacket, unlock the door, and then scrub the shit out of my hands at the sink. As nice as this bathroom is, it's like I can feel the germs crawling over my skin in here.

I leave, tucking the hand towel I used to open the door into my pocket, and confidently stride into the cocktail area, searching to see if everyone is here yet. Let them think I'm fashionably late. That's a thing important people do, right?

One glimpse of Connor Kikishkin has me stuffing my shaking hands in my pockets as well. This is not high school. We're different now. *I'm* the one with the power. Maybe my brain will remember that one of these days.

The first person to spot me from our group of misplaced jocks in a room full of former bully victims is Knox Addison, Easton Kikishkin's partner and Connor's best friend since high school. The only reason I'd suggested inviting him is because, from what I can remember, Knox was always nice to me, and I'd needed an ally. What I hadn't considered—and my anxiety decides to remind me of now—is that as Connor's best friend, he probably knows all about my plans to ruin a man he considers a brother, so this may have been a miscalculation on my part.

The nerves tighten so hard I almost forget to be confident altogether, but then I get closer, and Knox smiles.

The rapidly building tension eases away.

"Parker." He stands and pumps my hand in a friendly way. "Look at you, all grown up."

I try not to take that in a condescending way. "I hear time does that." And I'm trying not to resent that he's still almost a full head taller than me.

"Listen, I wanted to quickly thank you. I heard you might be the reason for my new career path, and I'm grateful."

"Ah. Right. Yes." I clear my throat, not really sure how to take someone's gratitude. In my mind, Knox is a good person. He wanted something, and I had the influence to help that happen. It's linear and not at all something that needs thanks for, but this is what I've always seen in him—he's a good person. And objectively attractive, so it would have been so much easier to have an almost decades-old crush on him instead of the asshole on his other side.

Pity Knox is so … levelheaded, I guess. Well-adjusted.

He'd never throw me up against a wall.

Jesus, maybe my billions should be going toward a goddamn shrink.

"Anyway, I really appreciate it."

"Anytime." I mentally slap myself because how many times is this kind of thing going to come up? Fucking hell, the night has barely started, and I'm already rattled. I normally don't drink at public events, but I think tonight, I'm going to need one.

"Mr. Duchene," Easton says, without the mocking hint I'm so used to being applied to my name. "That's my mom and dad, Kate and Michael."

We go over pleasantries, but all I'm doing is picturing smiling wide and thanking them for raising the man who made my life a living hell. Picturing really driving the knife in over what shitty parents they are. How it was their responsibility to raise decent people, and they failed. Then Easton continues.

"They're the whole reason my brothers and I have hockey," he says. "Dad really got us into the sport and worked two jobs to make sure we had everything we needed. Connor paid them both back with his signing bonus, and now they're our managers."

I didn't need all that backstory, and I get the suspicion that Easton only told me all of that as a "look how great and big-hearted my brother is" example.

But my gaze hasn't left Mr. Kikishkin. He got them into hockey. He worked his ass off for them.

I swallow thickly, all resentment toward them gone in place of the deep loneliness my own dad left behind. "Great sacrifices you made."

"Duchene …" Mr. Kikishkin rubs his jaw. "Wasn't there a hockey player by that name? Any relation?"

Now who's driving the knife in deep? "Yes."

I don't elaborate, and thankfully, at that point, Macklin suggests we find our tables. I lead the way, mostly to get away from them all, and before I can even get to our seats, I gratefully accept and down the glass of champagne that's offered to me.

Unfortunately, somehow on my detour to drinksville, in a room swarming with people, I end up next to Connor—and his date.

She has a real girl-next-door look to her. Tumbling brown curls, bright doe eyes that light up her face, and a curvier frame that's hugged by her dress. She's clutching Connor's arm like she's as nervous to be here as I am, which makes me want to warm to a kindred spirit, but I hate her instantly.

Maybe I can tell *her* all about how awful her boyfriend is.

"Mr. Duchene," Connor says, and this time, it has the bite I'm expecting.

"Mr. Kikishkin."

"For someone who hates me so damn much, it's nice to know you pronounce my name perfectly. Accented and everything."

Fuck off is uncomfortably close to slipping out, but I hold myself back. "You're one of my players, and I'm a professional." Plus, the number of times I heard it during high school and got irrationally irritated when it was pronounced wrong is burned into my memory.

"Alice," Connor says to the woman beside him. "This is Parker." I don't miss his smugness at using my name. "Only his property has to call him *Mister.*"

"Property?" she asks.

"He's the team owner."

"Oh, wow."

That's not an "oh, wow" like "oh, wow, he has a lot of money," that's the sound of someone who's feeling way out of her depth. I know because I've "oh, wowed" myself to an ulcer before.

Why can't any of these people let me not like them?

"Enjoy your night." I go to turn when there's resistance on my jacket sleeve, and I turn to find that Connor has grabbed it. Immediately, fire flares up in my gut, and I hate that it's not anger. Which, thankfully, makes me angry.

Connor gestures for Alice to head to the table. "I'll be there in a minute."

The room is full of the sound of people talking, so even with Knox right beside me, but his back to us as he talks to someone on the other side, he hasn't noticed the sudden tension.

"You got me to a bullying charity. Congratulations. I'll make a big donation and everything. Does this make us even now?"

I shrug out of his hold. Even? My anger echoes in my ears. Connor is here with his family, his friends, and a date he very obviously got at the last minute because it's that easy for him. He has his dream career, he's surrounded by love, and he's never going to give me the goddamn respect I crave from him.

And I hate that I crave it from him.

Yet some fucked-up piece of me revels in having his full attention.

"We'll never be even. But you can do one thing for me." I lean in to make sure he doesn't miss a word. "When whoever it is gets up to talk about their experiences and why this charity is so important, listen. Don't look away. Don't protect yourself. Maybe then, you'll start to feel even a fraction of what I have all my life."

Connor looks like I've drained the life out of him, and his voice isn't much better. "When are you going to let this go?"

I smooth out where his hold has creased the material on my sleeve. "That's up to you. I know you're not capable of an apology I'll accept, but I'll take cutting you off from everyone and everything you love as a consolation prize."

"You are so fucked-up."

"Yeah. And you made me this way."

CHAPTER SIX

CONNOR

Parker Duchene owns me.

He *owns* me.

He owns my career, he has power over my life, and I hate it.

Especially because it's like he's trying to do everything he can to make me snap again. In public. So he can fire me with cause and put it all over the internet that I was his high school bully.

Just thinking that makes my stomach churn because I've made it my life's mission to prevent bullying happening to my brothers. That act alone doesn't make me a saint though. That doesn't mean that I haven't made mistakes.

Parker Duchene happens to be one of those. A mistake I've made twice.

Hearing that I made him an angry little man looking for vengeance, it really does reiterate what Easton thinks of me.

Overbearing.

Interfering.

Asshole.

When those words came out of Parker's mouth, I wanted to get angry. I was close to doing what he's trying to make me do and punch him out, but he was the one who punched me. Right in the gut. With words instead of his fist.

I couldn't even stop him while he walked away, and I stood there for a good five minutes before heading to the bar, where I am now.

Coach wanted me and East here because he knew we wouldn't drink. As fun as being here sober sounds, I need something to settle my insides.

They're upside down and twisted, and I wish I could say it was Parker Duchene's doing, but if I'm really honest with myself, this all started when Easton asked for a trade to get away from me.

His own big brother.

Parker's right. I deserve everything he has in store for me. Unless I can give him a heartfelt apology that he believes.

And to do that, I'm going to need alcohol.

A lot of it.

I order some whiskey and drink it down immediately, and then order another with a wine for my date. She's about as interested in being here with me as I am with her, but when I'd asked around the locker room if any of the guys knew anyone who would want to go on a last-minute date with a hockey player to some bullying charity event, Munter said his sister Alice was a teacher and would love to come to a benefit like this.

She doesn't like hockey players because she grew up with Munter—enough said—and Munter would kill me if I hit on her, so while she's technically my date, it is definitely a no go.

I stay at the bar for a moment after the drinks are placed before me, trying to compose myself to somehow get through this night without letting Parker get to me.

That is no doubt going to be impossible, considering he's already under my skin.

I've just about plucked up the courage to go back to our table when a hand lands on my shoulder. I jump so high, thinking Parker's back for verbal sparring match round two, but it's only my brother.

He orders a Coke and then stares down at the glass of dark liquid in front of me. "Tsk, tsk, big brother. Won't that be bad for your image?"

Yeah, yeah, taste of my own medicine and all that other bullshit. "It's either this or threaten to kill our owner again. This time, where everyone can hear."

"I understand why he's doing this to you, but at the same time, he needs to be able to let it go. Have you apologized yet?"

"I tried! He didn't believe me."

"Well, did you mean it?"

I hang my head. "Not really."

Easton laughs. "Set your ego aside and go give him a genuine apology. Or are you still not sorry?"

"I'm sorry he had a hard time in high school? Does that count?"

My brother makes that annoying game show buzzer sound. "Wrong answer. That's not an apology. That's an 'I'm sorry you're hurt, but it wasn't my fault' apology. Try again."

"I'm sorry I'm the first one to use his last name against him and that everyone else followed, and now he hates me when I barely—"

Easton puts up his hand. "Nope again."

"You're annoying."

"Can't be too annoying. Duchene doesn't seem to have a problem with me."

No, he doesn't. I'm still not convinced Parker wasn't hitting on East when he cornered him in the locker room, but I also don't know why I'm so angry if he was.

Back in high school, when I saw them together, I thought I broke them up to save my brother's image. What if there was something else? Deep down? Maybe Parker Duchene is one of those souls I don't mesh with.

Instant hatred.

I know I need to apologize for real, but being wrong is new to me.

No, admitting I'm wrong is.

I down my second whiskey and then drink Alice's wine as well. "I need to go find him. I know what I'm going to say now." I think.

"I feel like I should stop you there," Easton says.

"What? Why?"

"What are you going to say?"

"That he's a bigger man than I ever will be, and he shouldn't waste his time on a selfish jock like me."

Easton side-eyes me. "Do you really believe that?"

"Yes."

"Con. Is this because of our fallout? Because I called you impossible?"

"I believe you used the word 'unbearable,' but … maybe. I'm obviously a shitty human. I just drank my date's drink."

"Come back to the table, listen to whatever speeches and crap they have coming up, dance with Munter's sister—but make sure your hands stay above the waist—and then tomorrow, before the game, if you still want to spout that crap to Duchene to see if he'll buy it, then go for it. But right now, you're too down on yourself to really be able to do anything genuinely."

Easton's probably right, but I hate this in-between crap. I still don't know where I stand with the team, with my position, and I have no idea what else Parker has in store for me. He said he wants to make my life a living hell, and he's off to a great start. If I have the chance to fix this and fix it now, I'm going to take it.

"I've got this."

I walk off to the sound of him mumbling something about looking forward to only having one brother from now on.

Please. As if Duchene will kill me. He likes torturing me too much for that. Keeping tight-lipped about me manhandling him, pretending he didn't remember me in high school, and now sending me here to a charity against school bullying.

I have to admit, as vengeance, it's a pretty good plan because it's impossible to anticipate what's coming next.

Parker is mingling with people I don't know, standing off to the side of our table like he stood to greet whoever they are. I don't want to interrupt, but at the same time, he looks like he would rather be anywhere but talking to them, even if it's with me, so really, I'm doing him a favor.

I put on my PR-trained smile, my charming voice, and say, "I'm so sorry to interrupt, but Mr. Duchene is needed." I take Parker's arm, and I can tell he's trying hard not to pull his arm out of the socket to escape my hold. "Hockey emergency," I say. "You know what us hockey players are like. All limbs and no brains."

Parker snorts. See, already off to a good start.

But when I actually drag him away and pull him into an alcove outside of the ballroom on the way to the bathrooms, he loses his professional facade.

"I'd be tempted to thank you for dragging me away from that conversation with those guys who want me to invest in a startup that will never get off the ground, but I have a feeling this conversation will be just as futile."

"Here is my genuine apology, and also, you're welcome."

He cocks a dark eyebrow.

"You're probably not going to like this one either," I continue, "but it is truthful, and it is genuine. I can promise you that."

Parker shifts his weight from one foot to the other and folds his arms. "Go on, then."

I take a deep breath. "I can't ever understand what it was like for you in high school, but I do know that my actions hurt you. For that, I can be sorry because that was never my intention. My only intention that day was to get you away from my brother. I didn't mean to hurt you, but I know that doesn't matter because the bottom line is I did. And for that, I'm sorry."

He looks contemplative, and I think for a second he's going to forgive me, but he's hesitating. He just needs that little push. That little bit more. And even though East says it's not a good idea, I go with exactly how I feel.

"That stupid teenager who acted before he could think grew up to be an asshole. I don't know how to be anything else. I haven't changed, and I think I've proved that. I am not worth your effort. You don't really want to be this guy, do you? Bitter? Vindictive? You bought a team so you could torture me? Don't you want to … let it go?"

And okay, with the way Parker's features turn into a glare so deep I worry it can actually penetrate my body and choke me, I'm guessing Easton was right.

In a turn of events, I'm not the one to lose my cool this time. I'm not the one pinning him. He's doing that to me.

I'm taken off guard, and my feet stumble, but then he pushes me again, and my back is more solid against the wall.

My body responds, itching for a fight, to maybe shove him back and reverse our positions and gain the upper hand. To be in control of this situation. But I am not in control.

I'm far from in control.

"Let me get one thing perfectly clear here," he growls. "I did not buy this team for you. You're right that you're not worth my time, but just so you know, I don't give a shit about you."

I can't tell if he's trying to get a rise out of me so I'll fight back and then force his hand or if he really hates me so much that he's trying to convince himself he doesn't care. "If that's the case, why are you bothering to make my life hell? Why are you making me so paranoid that every time I enter those back corridors of the practice facility or the arena, I'm going to be sent packing. You have the power to upheave my whole life, and you're holding it over my head. Tell me again how you don't give a shit about me."

"Maybe I'm teaching you a lesson."

"I'm a slow learner. What am I supposed to be learning exactly?"

Parker pushes off me and backs up. His skin is flushed, and he's breathing heavily. "That sickly feeling you get walking into the arena? That fear of being traded or put on waivers with the threat of the potential to change your whole life? Picture now if I actually did it, only worse. Picture how it would feel to have everything change because of one decision I make. One split decision to tell someone in the league that you're the hardest player to work with, you're uncooperative, entitled, and even got physical with me."

"You're that pissed off over high school you would ruin my whole life?"

"Don't you understand? That's *exactly* what you did to me. My life was hell. I braced myself every time I walked down the hall. I had no friends. I had nothing other than my love of techy things. All because of you."

"Oh, then I'm so sorry I gave you the opportunity to hone your skills and become a billionaire. So, so, so, sorry," I deadpan. Part of me is warning myself to shut up, but the other part of me is leaning hard into self-destruction. How does it make me feel? Fucking horrible. I can't even let myself think of this feeling lasting for years. The difference is I don't know if my life will ever get better, but Parker knows how his story turns out. Being rich and successful is what everyone dreams of.

"If you think money buys happiness, I don't think you've ever been truly happy a day in your life."

He walks away from me again before I can stop him. Only this time, I don't have an argument. Because he's right.

When I think of everything I have, all I can see is a brother who resents me, parents who put a lot of pressure on my shoulders growing up, a career that could be taken away from me at any moment, and Knox—my best friend. Who now belongs to my brother.

I have nothing, and I have no idea what happiness looks like for me.

CHAPTER SEVEN

PARKER

I'd planned to get so drunk I could go home and pass out, but as I watch Connor Kikishkin return to the bar after our words, I decide to enjoy the show instead.

When I bought this team, I didn't think it would be possible to hate Connor more than I already did, but after that conversation, it happened. I don't think I got distracted by his attractiveness once.

He struck a nerve, and while yes, I have very explicitly said I want to ruin him, that's not why I bought the team. For some reason, him unknowingly putting himself above Dad had made me see red. It'd also reminded me that what I'm doing to Connor—or what I'm planning to do—Dad would have hated it.

He loved the Kiki brothers, loved being a Colorado fan. I was tense every game we'd caught together in his last years and even avoided going, purely because I didn't want to see my own dad as obsessed with them as everyone else seemed to be.

I also couldn't bring myself to tell him the truth about Connor and what a horrible person he is because of how much Dad admired their skill.

Turns out I resent Connor for more than just high school. I resent the rift he caused between my dad and me, and now, I'll never get those years back.

A tiny voice in my head tries to remind me that those choices were my fault, but I'm feeding my anger, and it's working. For once, I can look at that broad back, at his swagger as he returns from the bar double-fisting whiskey, and actually hate him.

All that stuff with Dad and then him having the audacity to think he *made* me?

I'm so damn tempted to stab him with my butter knife that I shift it out of reach.

Dinner comes around, Connor keeps drinking, and my careful professional control wears away. We hear people speak about their experiences in high school, and I feel like they've split open my head and have started to pull my own memories out for display.

I stare at the table. I try to zone out. I'm not sad I came tonight, but I'm caught off guard by how uncomfortable this has been.

As soon as the last person leaves the stage and they announce that the dance floor is open, I politely excuse myself—not that anyone cares or even notices me go.

The second I make it to the bathrooms and lock myself in a stall, the instant safety that surrounds me is draining. I don't want to feel this way.

How different would my life have been if I'd taken after Dad? Would I have been one of those bullying hockey jerks? Would Connor and I have been friends?

I kick down the toilet lid and sit on it, face buried in my hands, like I've done countless times throughout my life.

The thing is, I thought I could face Connor now. I thought it would be different this time. That he'd see me as successful and admit that high school was high school and apologize for being a dick. In my imagination, we'd have a heart-to-heart, and I'd be freed of this resentment. But Connor hasn't grown up, and I'm unhappier than ever.

And sitting here, on this fucking toilet, makes me realize I've picked myself up only to plonk my ass back in high school again.

My rational brain knows that selling the team and putting distance between all this hate would be the smartest move. My lizard brain is yearning for Connor to see me as his equal. To validate that I didn't deserve what I went through.

"Quick, get him in here."

I freeze at the voice and the sound of people coming through the bathroom door.

"What are you … stop … leave me—" There's a groan as something heavy lands on the floor.

"How much did he drink?" That voice is familiar, and I get up to tilt my head near the side of the cubicle door, where I make out a sliver of Knox Addison through the crack.

Shit.

I straighten, hoping they won't come down to check this end cubicle, but before they can make the attempt, there's another loud groan.

"Wanna dance." The slurred voice is Connor.

"Then maybe you should have listened to me instead of getting wasted." And his brother.

From what Coach Macklin said, Connor is usually the one with Easton on a leash, so something has to be up for him to be taking control here. I don't think I saw Easton with a single drink all night.

"Want me to call a car?" Knox asks.

"Think it's late enough that I can tell Coach we're leaving?"

Silence. I creep forward in the cubicle again and glimpse both Easton and Knox in the mirror above the sink. Connor's out of sight, so I'm guessing he's on the disgusting floor.

"I can guarantee it'll be worse if we stay and Macklin sees his golden boy drunk off his ass," Knox says.

East grunts. "He'll bench him tomorrow for sure. After giving him a hundred warm-up laps in full gear."

"Sadist."

The thought of a very hungover Connor Kikishkin skating up and down the ice, trying not to hurl … I'm tempted to go and collect Macklin myself.

"Parker's fault," Connor slurs.

I freeze.

"Oh, shut up," East snaps.

"It is. I tried apologying. Didn't work. Bet he doesn't want one. Asshole."

"Exactly what was your apology?" Knox asks, sounding amused.

"Don't remember. But compy-compa-computers were his best friend because of me! He said that. Now, he's a billionaire."

Easton gasps. "Please tell me you didn't tell Parker Duchene that he's successful because of you? And somehow imply he should be grateful he was bullied?"

"Ah …"

Knox muffles a laugh.

"Not …" Connor tries again. "Not in *those* words."

"For fuck's sake." East disappears from the mirror, and I lean in even further to make out that he's crouched in front of Connor. "This is what I'm talking about. If it was me that did something so stupid, you'd lose your ever-loving mind. Why is it okay for you to act the way you do?"

Connor slumps right over onto the floor. "Yeah, yeah. I'm a shitty brother. The worst. Everyone hates me."

He's being immaturely melodramatic.

"For the last time, no one hates you," Knox says.

"Don't speak for me," East cuts in. "I kinda hate him."

I'm getting the feeling this is veering into personal territory, and it's not something I want to overhear. So I take that as my cue to unlock the cubicle and step out where they can see me.

"Me too."

Easton whirls around so fast he almost lands on his ass before pushing to his feet. "Mr. Duchene." His eyes couldn't get any wider.

Connor scoffs. "*Parker*."

It would be so easy to kick him while he's down. Literally. Right in the thigh.

My eyes narrow, and Knox quickly steps in front of me. "Don't listen to him. He … ate something funny."

"Was it whiskey?"

"No … it was, uh—"

Easton saves his boyfriend. "This weird fish thing he had at lunch. I told him not to eat it, but Connor's disgusting."

They all must think I'm an idiot if they assume I'll buy that.

"For the love of God, get your brother's head away from the urinal."

That makes Connor sit up. "Do what I want."

"This would be a good time to keep quiet," Easton snaps.

Connor boos. "Now who's telling who what to do?"

Easton turns his glare on Knox. "Shut your best friend up before I kill him. I'll do it. I will."

Even with that glare, the team owner right here, and his best friend drunk off his ass, Knox doesn't look worried. "There are no weapons in here, so I think Con is safe."

"I wouldn't be so sure about that," I say.

"Please, Mr. Duchene," Easton tries. "My brother, he's … going through some stuff at the moment. He'll be fine by tomorrow. I promise."

"I bought a winning team. I bought the Kiki brothers because I thought you'd be able to *give* me a winning team. This …" I wave a hand Connor's way. "Does not look like a winner to me."

"Because I'm a loser." Connor pouts. "I'm a big, egocentric loser, and nobody likes me."

I'm not sure what look crosses my face, but it makes Knox laugh. All I know is that if this image of Connor erases all the others I have of him, I won't be in danger of ever finding the guy intimidating again. "How much did he drink?"

Easton and Knox exchange glances.

And I … I realize this is it. This is my moment to actually ruin Connor. Fuck getting Macklin. I could easily cite his aggression toward me and then him getting blind drunk off his ass at a charity benefit as reasons to let him go. I could do it. Or hell, I *could* get Macklin and have him on his coach's bad side for whoever knows how long? I could even take a photo and leak it to social media.

I could do so many fucking things to make Connor's life hard, but I only stare at him. And he stares at me. And somehow, it makes a stupid lump form in my throat.

Revenge is supposed to make me feel good.

So why don't I want it anymore?

"Do it," Connor mutters. "Take away the one thing I have left."

One thing?

I look at Easton, who's glaring Connor's way, and then to Knox, whose amusement is finally gone, and he just looks sad.

There's something going on between these three.

"What does he mean?" I ask.

"Respectfully, Mr. Duchene," Easton says, "that's between me and my brother."

Knox looks away.

It becomes very clear, very quickly, that the rumored rift between them isn't as fixed as they're leading people to believe. Is Connor pissed that his best friend is dating his brother?

I'd assumed he was loving that the two of them were together. That he and Knox could keep a closer eye on East this way.

But then all the little snipes Easton has been sending Connor's way make sense.

Looks like I'm not the only one resenting Connor Kikishkin.

Easton shoves his hands in his pockets. "Look, if you're going to do something, can you do it already? Get Coach, punish him, whatever. If you're not, can you please go so I can get him out of here?"

My head is screaming at me to get revenge. That this is my moment. I'll come out on top.

Instead, I cross to the basin, wash my hands, and ignore them all as I leave.

Then I go in search of Coach Macklin, buy him an expensive not-on-the-menu drink for his amazing work with the team, and ask him about his strategy for tomorrow night's game.

Somehow, his back ends up facing the main doors.

Which is a total coincidence, of course.

Because I'm definitely not feeling the teeniest, tiniest bit sorry for Connor Kikishkin.

No way in hell.

CHAPTER EIGHT

CONNOR

"I don't think he's going to make it," Easton says. He sounds like he's underwater, and when the room comes into view, it's all blurry like it is when you open your eyes in a pool.

"Are we swimming?" I ask.

"Jesus. He's still drunk," my brother says. "How many times do you think a hockey player has been drunk during a game?"

"Plenty," my best friend, the traitor, says.

"I'm not drunk," I say, but it comes out exactly how a drunk person would say it. "I'm hungover as fuck, and it's too bright, and why did you two let me drink so much?"

"Ooh, and he just lost any sympathy I had for him." Easton disappears, and when I wipe the blurriness from my eyes, my best friend is staring down at me, arms folded.

I'm on Easton and Knox's couch, evidently. Have no idea how I got here, and ain't that the kicker? I drank so I could forget the conversation I had with Duchene, but the thing I can't remember is how I got home.

Figures.

"I'm worried about you," Knox says.

"Because I got drunk? Have you met me?"

"Because you got drunk the night before a game. That's not you."

"Yeah, well, I don't even know who I am anymore."

"Really?" Knox sounds skeptical. "Connor Kikishkin is having a massive existential crisis because his brother told him to stop meddling and someone from high school called him a bully?"

Knox doesn't get it. I'm not sure anyone will. Hell, I barely understand this new sense of … pointlessness.

"It's more than that," I say.

"How so?"

"Repeatedly being called a terrible person means I have to believe it at some point."

"I'm going to morning skate," Easton says, coming out of his bedroom with his gear bag ready to go.

"Wait, I'm coming with you." I try to get up, but nope, that's not going to happen without Easton's entire town house spinning.

"You should skip it and rest up for tonight. Unless you get a call in between now and then telling you to stay home because you've been benched."

My eyes widen. "Did Coach see how drunk I was?"

"No," Easton says, and I relax in relief. "But Parker did."

Fucking fuck fuck shit. "Where's my phone?"

"Why?" Easton asks.

"I've probably already got the call to say I'm being released from my contract." But when I find it in my pocket, battery almost dead, there are no notifications, no nothing.

Easton rubs his chin. "If Parker was going to say something, he would have last night. If he was going to fire you, he would have after you attacked him in the locker room."

"It sounds like he's keeping you around on purpose," Knox says.

"Considering he says he hates you so much, it doesn't make sense," Easton adds.

"Except it does." I run my hand through my hair. "He says he didn't buy the team to ruin my life, but he's sure hell-bent on doing so."

"Stay here and hydrate," Easton says. "I'll tell Coach you got food poisoning and hope Parker hasn't told him otherwise, or I see me taking your punishment for you, and I don't want to puke on the ice this year if I can help it."

"The season's still young," Knox says.

"Will you be here when I get back?" my brother asks. At first, I think it's to me, but then I remember Knox has to leave today to fly to Austin to ref an AHL game.

"No, but I'll be home tomorrow," Knox says.

They kiss goodbye, and I turn away at their affection. It's still weird for me to see that, but I'm not mad at it like I once was. I don't have a right to be because it's not my place.

It's not.

My place isn't with my brother or my best friend.

I used to think it was on the ice—no, I was *certain* of it—but now, I can't help thinking my place is in the woods, away from everyone I've ever unknowingly hurt. I could become a hermit and have rocks for friends.

Though Miles Olsen says his pet rocks hate me too. Mainly when me or Easton score on him, but still. Even the rocks hate me.

I flash back to last night, to Parker shoving me and the disdain in his voice as he told me I'm experiencing the same thing he did all the way back then, and as much as I want to lay blame on me being young, stupid, and everything he says I am, I think it's time I own it. Properly.

I need to stop putting the blame on everything else, accept that I was an asshole—no, still am an asshole—and then take steps to change those behaviors that seem to come naturally to me. And I should start by forcing my dumb ass up and get it to the team's morning skate. If I vomit on the ice, I vomit.

This time when I sit up, the room still spins, but at least it rights itself before I have to lie down again.

I stand, and it turns out I don't have to wait until I reach the ice.

I run to the bathroom and vomit up the entire contents of my stomach.

Usually after a puke, the hangover goes away, and I'm all good. Not this time. If anything, I feel worse.

Okay, becoming a better human can come later today. No matter what, I'm going to be there for the game.

-

I've made it. I'm at the arena.

Sure, I'm in the bathroom throwing up for the tenth time today, but I'm here. I'm also starting to think I might have food poisoning on top of the hangover because I shouldn't still be throwing up.

"Dude." Easton appears behind me. "You're still going? How do you have anything left in your stomach?"

"I don't," I croak. All I'm throwing up is the Powerade I've been drinking to try to rehydrate.

"Still not good?" Coach Macklin's voice comes from the door to the restroom.

I tense and then try not to dry heave again. Guilt shoots through my body, stabbing me in the gut and making me want to vomit again.

Coach asked me to go to the benefit because I'm not supposed to be like the other idiots on his roster. I'm the levelheaded one.

Or, supposed to be. Maybe all my levelheadedness comes from the need to be. The need to look after my brothers. Maybe I'm naturally as big a dumbass as Lachie.

"Roberts," Coach says.

I look back at Easton, who puts his hand to his ear to gesture that Coach is on the phone.

"Get your ass down to the arena. You're up." In the next second, I hear, "Kikishkin, rest up. You're scratched tonight."

I'm part relieved and part freaking out that this is going on the long list of things Parker can hold over my head.

As if the mere thought of his name summons him, his voice appears next. I'd be embarrassed about being on my knees in the middle of a restroom, but apparently, he already saw me like this last night in a restroom much more disgusting than this private bathroom for the team.

I'm guessing the charade is up now. No more food poisoning excuses. He's about to tell Coach every—

"You got the food poisoning too, huh?" Parker asks. "It had to be something at the benefit last night. I was sick earlier but am okay now."

I turn and land on my ass, meeting his eye.

"Same with me and Knox," East adds. "Nothing says romantic like vomiting and shitting all over the place."

I am so fucking confused.

Why are the two people who hate me most in the world covering for me?

Easton, I get. He might say he hates me or how I behave, but deep down, I know he still loves me. You know, being brothers and all.

But Parker?

I'm hoping that even though our conversation went terribly last night, maybe he is beginning to accept my apology, but the cynical voice in the back of my head is telling me he's only doing it so he can add this to his torture log of how to hold my position on the team over me.

"Easton, you go get ready to hit the ice," Parker says. "Coach, get everyone in hockey mode. I'll take care of Connor."

I silently scream at Easton not to leave me, but we don't have a telepathic bond. When he and Coach disappear, leaving me completely alone with Parker, I can't help but ask, "When you say take care of, you're not meaning in a take him out back and shoot him kind of way, right?"

"I feel like that would be giving you mercy, and I'm taking enjoyment from seeing you so miserable."

For whatever reason, that makes me laugh.

"Come on. Up you get." He moves toward me, and I flinch. "I'm not going to hurt you. I was going to help you up."

I frown. "So you can push me back down again?"

"Only in my fantasies." Parker's tone is dry, almost detached, when he holds out his hand, and I take it this time.

His palm is warm and soft, and when he helps me to my feet, our hands linger until he drops his quickly, like I zapped him with an electric shock.

"You can come watch the game with me in the owner's suite."

I have no clue what's happening, but the anger and hatred he was spewing at me last night seems to be missing.

My gut lurches. Fuck, don't think of the word "spewing."

Parker's at the door of the bathroom when he says, "Coming?"

"I have one question."

"What's that?"

"Why?"

"Why, what?" He's losing patience with me. "Why is the sky blue? Why is hockey? Why is life? How philosophical do you want me to go here?"

"Why are you being nice to me when last night you looked like you were willing to murder me and pay off every single person at the benefit to help bury my body?"

Parker's lips look like he's trying to hold back a pitying smile. "Again, that was just another one of my fantasies. I …" He glances away. "Other than saying I bought this team so I could get some petty high school revenge, you made a good point last night. You said I shouldn't waste my bitterness and anger on you, so today, I'm going to try not to."

I narrow my gaze. "You're going to poison me in the suite, aren't you?" I gasp and step back. "You already did poison me, and that's why I've been sick all day."

He rolls his eyes. "Fine. Stay in here and miss the game."

I have a choice here. I could stay here and feel sorry for myself, go home and feel sorry for myself, or go up to the owner's suite with Parker and try to get on the right path with him. If all of this being nice shit is legit.

"No, I'll come up. I'm just going to make sure you eat and drink everything before I do. Just in case."

This time, his smile does come out properly, and my gut swoops. It's the same smile he wore back in high school, talking to Easton, and I don't think I've seen it again since. All the air is pushed from my lungs, and I'm frozen for a moment in time, asking how something so simple can steal my breath.

Or maybe that's still the hangover.

Before I can take a step toward the exit, I'm hunched back over the toilet and throwing up some more.

CHAPTER NINE

PARKER

The fact that Connor thinks this is what nice looks like is telling. I'm doing the very bare minimum here, and he's acting like I've had a lobotomy.

But I'm *trying*, damn it. The bitterness still clings to me like a glove, but where I thought revenge might make me feel better, it's only made my life worse, so I might as well change tack. The realization last night that Dad wouldn't be happy with how I'm acting really hurt, and I'm tired of hurting. I'm tired of being alone and trying to fight for myself in a world that doesn't give a shit.

So Connor can win.

Maybe if I accept that, things will finally be easier.

He's heavy on his feet as we enter the expansive suite, the huge size constantly reminding me I have no one to share it with.

"Wow." He goes straight to the fridge and helps himself to a bottle of water. "This is … compensating for something?" He gives me a cheeky look I'm sure is supposed to make me weak at the knees, but I remind myself to ignore it. Which is a lot harder to do with the blood rushing to my cheeks.

I hold my teeth together so tightly I'm going to end up with a headache later and then head out into the seating area. I sit in the very middle of the front row like I do every game. Rows and rows of empty chairs stretch out either side of me, and I sit here and watch as the crowd starts to file in. I almost forget about Connor completely until he takes the seat right on the end of this row.

He could have sat anywhere, but he had to pick a spot in my periphery, so now I have that anxious pressure to say something to him with no idea what words to use. He might be feeling the same way, but knowing him, he's probably as comfortable and relaxed here as he is anywhere. The arena is his stage and all that.

I cross my arms and lean back, trying to show that I'm as relaxed as he is while being very much not as relaxed as he is. This was a stupid idea. In an attempt to not be a dick and rethink how I was behaving, I've massively overswung it.

Connor slides down in his chair. "Why are there so many lights?"

"Wait until the pregame festivities begin and they all start flashing."

His pathetic sob makes me look his way. His elbow is propped on the armrest, hand cradling his forehead as he looks my way. "I thought you weren't going to be mean anymore."

"Stating a fact isn't mean." Like giving him basic common decency isn't nice. "But it's going to take practice. You're really underestimating how much I want to hate you."

"Get in line," he says dryly.

I glance over again, and this time, he doesn't look ready to hurl, but his bloodshot eyes are watching me, like he's daring me to ask why.

It's not my business, but I can't say I'm not curious, especially after last night. Plus, if he's talking, it means I don't have to.

"Who else hates you?"

He looks away and mumbles, "Everyone."

Really informative.

He continues, words falling from his mouth rapidly like he can't stop himself. "Apparently, I ruin people's lives. Yours, Lachie's, Easton's, Knox's—even though he's too loyal to actually say the words. The real kicker is that my parents are the ones who raised me to look out for my brothers, and now they're backtracking on that really fast. *Oh, we meant make sure they're not walking into alleyways that have homophobes lurking.* That's not what they said. Between the long hours and the stressful time off to watch us play, it was always *thank God for you, Connor*, and *your brothers are so lucky to have you, Connor*, and on and on about how they can rely on me and how I'm doing such a great job. And now that they have the time to be parents again, suddenly, I'm overstepping, and it's my fault my brothers resent me."

And I thought I had issues.

That sounds like a lot to be dealing with, but there's no way his brothers hate him. They're his family. And he's … Connor Kikishkin. He has an entire team at his back. An unshakable best friend. Those three brothers would kill for each other. "Why are you telling me all this?"

"Dunno." He kicks the barrier in front of himself. "Maybe so you don't feel special in hating me."

"Believe me, there's no danger in that. I don't think I've felt special a day in my life."

"Not even when you sold your software for a cool twenty B?"

"Especially not then." The ache behind my sternum increases, and I utter words I've never spoken out loud. "I didn't want to sell it."

"What? Then why did you? Was it like a push-out kind of thing?"

"It was a *my dad's dying and I need to free up all of my finances to save him* kind of thing."

He's obviously not expecting that, if the way his mouth drops is any indication. "Damn … Is … is he okay now?"

My hands are shaking. "I didn't sell fast enough."

I pointedly don't look at him because seeing sympathy from someone like him might kill me.

He shifts a few seats closer. "I'm so sorry."

"You didn't kill him."

"No …" Connor takes a deep breath. "I'm really, actually sorry."

Something about his tone catches my attention.

"For … everything. No excuses." He screws his face up. "Talking to you and then hearing all those people recount their horror stories of high school. That's why I drank so much."

"You felt guilty?"

"I should have said something. Put a stop to it."

I give him the driest look I can manage. "You, Mr. Hockey Star, really think you would have stood up for the scrawny kid who talked about coding and had serious skin issues?"

His face falls. "No, I don't think I would have. I didn't even know it was going on half of the time."

"That's very privileged of you."

"Yeah … I guess. And I know you probably want more from me, and if I have to get on the floor and grovel, fine, but this is as genuine as it gets. I fucked up. I should have done better, and even if it wasn't directly from me, not standing up for you was me supporting it anyway. I'm sorry I didn't listen when you tried to tell me that, but I think … I don't *want* to be a bad person. It's taking me a minute to realize that I am."

I'm hit with the most overwhelming urge to cry. I keep my shit together, but it's there. This … I don't know? Relief? It catches me so off guard I have to look back out at the ice again. All my life, I thought if I could just get an apology, everything would be better, but I'm not sure how things can be better when the other person is hurting. Not that I *should* care. But I do.

Still, getting an apology at all proves that maybe Connor really does want to be the good guy he says he does.

When I've got myself together enough to face him again, he's only a few seats away. "Thank you."

His smile is part grimace, but it still counts.

I'm tempted to tell him that I bought the team to be closer to Dad because he used to play, that he thought Connor and Easton were going to get Colorado the Cup, and he couldn't wait to see it. But while I might not be on his list of haters anymore, we're not friends, and those aren't even thoughts I've shared with my mom. The one and only person I have to talk to.

"This place would be awesome for a party," Connor says out of nowhere.

"Sure. I'll invite all of my zero friends to come."

He makes a *pfft* noise. "There's no way I believe you don't have friends."

"Okay."

"You're a billionaire."

"And?"

"Fucking buy some."

This is another one of those moments where I want to snap at him, but this is the closest I've felt to another person in a long time, and isn't that all kinds of fucked-up? "Call me screwed in the head, but I'd sort of like to know what a real friend feels like one day." Maybe I could have had one in college, but by that point, I was way too closed off to bother trying. At work, I kept a professional distance. And now, here I am.

"Does it make you feel better to know that I don't have any either?"

"No, because as dramatic as you're being, Knox and Easton were still there when you needed them. No matter what they think of you. Your parents showed up last night with no notice. You pulled a date out of thin air, even if she didn't look exactly thrilled by you." I sigh. "You have friends. You're clearly … going through something."

"You can say that again." His face contorts like he's about to vomit, but he pulls himself together. "Is it possible to have a midlife crisis in your twenties?"

"My entire life has been one big crisis, so what would I know?"

"I think I'm lost."

I cross my arms even tighter. The players have just taken the ice for warm-ups, and Connor is watching them with regret. "Why are you telling me this?"

"I dunno. Maybe because I don't have a single other person I can talk to. You opened up to me, so I'm trying to be real here. Knox is biased now he's dating East, and Lachie's going through that stage where he doesn't care about much except hockey and reaching the legal drinking age."

"So he can take after your drunken footsteps?"

Connor scrubs at his face. "That's what I used to think. That my brothers loved me and wanted to be like me."

"Shocking for you."

"Fuck off, Parker."

His constant audacity, I swear. "I'm the team owner, we're in my box, and you still can't show me the slightest bit of respect?" I'm not angry. It's … good to know.

"Trust me when I say that calling you Mr. Duchene is never going to be said with respect." His hangover at least seems to be lessening its hold because Connor looks mad. "You know what, don't worry. Everyone else expects me to bottle it up, and I think I'm stroking out to assume you'd be different."

"Fine. Talk."

He lets out a hollow laugh. "No way, man. You'll probably find a way to use it against me down the line."

"You're such a baby. I might not have said it explicitly, but I accept your apology. Spill your damn heart out to me for all I care. No one else is here, and after tomorrow, my grudge will be gone, you'll be back to focusing on hockey, and neither of us will have to acknowledge each other again."

"Really?"

It kills me that he so easily wants to forget about my existence, but this is reality. "Really. So get out whatever you need to."

"I don't even know where to start."

"Fine … why do you feel lost?"

"I've had this image of myself for so long. I'm the levelheaded brother, the protector, the bruiser, because I thought that was my role. Now that I've been told they're my worst features, I'm beginning to question if I was born that way or if it was taught. How much of it is real? Do

I like playing hockey, or do I only think I do because my dad pushed all three of us kids into it? Are hot dogs really my favorite food, or is it because Mom and Dad said they're all I would eat as a child? Am I really commitment-phobic, or is it that I haven't had time for a relationship? And if I want a relationship now, who is my type? Nearly all the WAGs are blonde bombshells. Do I like blondes? Or am I more of a brunette kind of guy? I know nothing about myself."

"Maybe you're not into women at all?"

It's a stupid throwaway comment that makes Connor stiffen.

"I'm straight."

"Not my point." I try again. "I'm just saying, maybe none of those things are true, and maybe they all are. Instead of clinging to being this guy who jumps to assumptions and throws people up against walls, why don't you let it all go? Start over."

"Start over?"

"Yeah. Figure out who you are."

He props his elbow on the armrest and leans his head into it again, but this time, it's the side closest to me. He's three seats away, and those three seats feel minuscule, considering he's looking me right in the eyes and we're talking. Actually talking.

"And if it turns out I'm every bit the possessive guy who acts first and thinks later?"

The image of us in the locker room flips so that I'm in East's position and Connor is pulling someone off me in a possessive, jealous rage. It's a struggle to keep my voice even when I say, "Then you have to find someone who'll appreciate being possessed. And some people really, really like it."

CHAPTER TEN

CONNOR

For the entire first period, it's hard to focus, and I don't think it has anything to do with the hangover.

Parker Duchene decided sometime last night to stop being a dick. And here he is, doing it. How does he flip a switch so easily?

Why can't I flip my switch and be an understanding and caring guy without going overboard? Why is it that when Easton is flattened against the boards, I can't let go of the urge to go down there and beat Baarsey until he bleeds?

Protect your brother at all costs. Mom's voice rings through my head, and I can't help asking if it's because anytime Easton or Lachie were hurt, I'd have that at the forefront of my mind or if it has always been instinctual to act.

They were my brothers, and it was my job to protect them.

Was I reading into what our parents taught me? Taking it to a level I wasn't supposed to? Or was it a natural progression?

I hate that I'm questioning every thought now. Every gut instinct.

Parker laughs, and when I look over at him, he's staring at me. "You look like you want to kill Baarsey."

"It was a cheap shot that was borderline at best. If Knox was down there, he would've called it."

"The refs right next to the action disagree with you there."

I huff.

He laughs again. "You really do have this ownership-type relationship over Easton, don't you? Should I be worried about rumors of brocest and inappropriate behavior?"

"If there's any brocest, it's between Easton and Knox." I shudder. "It's still weird seeing two guys I consider brothers make out."

"That's one less thing for the franchise to worry about, then, but all I can say is, I kind of see where Easton's coming from."

"Yeah, yeah, everyone can see it. Even me now that it's been pointed out, but the issue is not knowing how to stop that side of me from coming out. How did you do it?"

Parker cocks his head. "Do what?"

"Decide to stop hating me and then just stop. When Easton and I got in that fight on the ice and he asked for a trade, I promised I'd stop, but … the instinct is still there, and it takes a conscious effort to squash it down."

Parker looks down at where the game is on a short re-icing break. "Maybe it's easy for me because I know the anger I've directed at you has been misplaced."

"Has it though? Like you said—"

"Don't get me wrong, I hated high school, didn't like my life much, and I fully blamed you for that. I thought I wanted to see you with no one, like I've always been, but now you're telling me that's how you feel, and … it's not the victory I'd expected it would be. Besides, my anger toward you isn't because of that. Not completely. It's because my dad died before I was ready to let him go, and it's easier to be mad at someone else instead of him. Or the medical field. Or cancer. If I'm focusing all my anger on you, it takes away the pain of being angry at someone or something that can't fight back."

Fuck, that's heavy.

Parker turns his head to me, his eyes glassy like he's holding back tears, and it would be so easy for me to break down and cry with him. Over what? Anything. Everything.

"I bought the team because my dad loved hockey. He loved this team. It was the one he played for during his brief career with the NHL."

Oh. Ohhh. Yup. Looking back on our last conversation, where I accused him of buying the team for some silly vendetta, it's looking a whole lot petty from my side of things.

"It kind of sounds like we both need a friend," I say.

Parker almost chokes on his spit.

"And I know that sounds ridiculous, considering our past and what you've put me through this season already, but I'm just saying—" I gesture around the empty owner's suite. "I'm lost and have no one. You're grieving and have no one. And maybe if we can both swallow our differences, we might be able to move on from our misgivings. You can begin to heal after your loss, and I … I can figure out who I am outside of being Connor Kikishkin, eldest Kiki brother who is a bruiser on the ice and a possessive asshole off it."

This time when he looks at me, it's with a smile on his lips, and the lights of the arena make his wet eyes sparkle. "High school me would be very interested to know that if I gave it ten years, Connor Kikishkin would ask me to be his friend."

"High school me deserves a kick in the teeth. We should time travel together and go back to our old selves. You can tell yours that even though you have no friends, you have billions of dollars, and crying in an owner's suite is a lot more comfortable than crying in the nosebleeds. I can tell past me to pull his head out of his ass and at least try to be a decent human being."

"Sounds like a plan." Though his smile fades, I do get the sense he's being genuine.

We stare at each other, not speaking but somehow saying everything.

We're both sorry.

We're both hurting.

And it's not fair to take it out on each other.

"And so you know, you have grown up to be a decent person."

I wish I could believe him, but with the rift between Easton and me only getting bigger and repeating the same mistakes with Parker that I did in high school, it's really difficult. "I'm not, but I hope to be one day."

"And that's how I know you're a decent person," Parker says and looks down at the ice again.

It's a scoreless game so far, one of those—dare I say it—boring games where no one can find the net on either end.

"How?"

"Because you care about being a decent person. A true narcissist wouldn't ever admit they're not perfect."

"So now you're calling me a narcissist?" I quip.

He holds his thumb and forefinger together. "Little bit."

That's probably fair. "I wish I could argue with you, but you've got me there."

"Nah, you'll be fine. Like I said, all you have to do is find that one person who likes possessiveness in a partner. Then, you focus all your toxic behavior on them. Win-win."

"I'd rather not be toxic at all."

Parker lifts one shoulder. "Eh, a little toxicity can be fun."

My gaze snaps to his, but before I can ask what he means, the horn of a home goal blasts through the arena, and he gets to his feet, clapping and cheering for my team. Our team.

And when he turns to me with soft eyes that remind me of that boy back in the halls of high school, something in my gut flutters again. Only this time, I know for sure it isn't hatred. Or being hungover.

I have no clue what it actually is, but I know that I like it.

-

Considering how wrecked I've been all day, I can't sleep when I get home after the game. I'm lying in bed, tossing and turning, unable to get comfortable.

Parker and I have made progress, and I'm understanding the guy a lot more, but … there's something about the words he said to me tonight that I can't get out of my head.

When I was asking all those hypotheticals like do I really like blondes or is it because hockey players are known for it, he said I might not like women at all.

In the moment, I got defensive and felt the urge to express my heterosexuality, but since that very second when the words came out, there was that little voice of doubt asking, "But are you?"

Easton didn't come out to us until he was in college, but I knew. He wasn't into girls the way I was, and when I saw him that day in the hallway with Parker, looking overfriendly and almost flirting, I thought he was going to fuck up his future because of it.

As we got older, protecting him from bullies became protecting him from his sexuality, and it's not until this moment that I realize I have no idea where that bias came from. Now, as I look back on it, I understand how it might come across. Especially to Easton.

Thinking he needed to hide who he was to ensure he got to keep hockey? Believing hockey was more important while I had all the hookups I wanted?

Loving my brothers so much that I didn't want to see them hurt sounds good in theory, but oppressing them to do it? Not okay.

And maybe it's been that line of thinking that causes me to quickly defend being labeled as anything but straight. Because in my mind, I have to be the straight one.

Have I ever thought of a man in that way before? No. But it's no different to asking me if I'd ever gotten drunk at a team-sanctioned charity event before last night. The answer is also no because I would never do something so risky.

What if I want to do something risky, damn it? Why do Easton and Lachie have all the fun?

And why do I keep replaying the look on Parker's face when he said all I have to do is find someone who likes my possessive side? The gleam in his eye, the small smile on his lips … the way his skin turned a shade of pink … or was that from the lights of the arena?

For whatever reason, when I think back on him saying that, I get the impression he meant *he* would like my possessive side, but that doesn't make sense because he still hates me.

He might say he's letting it go, or it's misplaced anger or whatever, but those feelings don't go away that easily. At least, I don't know how to let them go that easily. Usually. With him … yeah, I'm willing to let it go.

I thought he was here purely to get revenge, but he's not. He's here for his dad, and if it were my dad who was gone and I had an endless amount of money, I probably would've done the exact same thing.

I also can't get out of my head how he called me a decent person purely because I care about being one. I always thought I was a decent person. Loyal. And now, when I feel the world is against me, he tried to reassure me that I can be the guy I thought I was.

For whatever stupid reason, I like Parker seeing me that way. I wish I could've shown that from the second he stepped foot in our locker room—no, even before that, in high school—but the thing is, when your head is so far up your ass, you think everyone loves you.

I hate that I've hurt people close to me, but I think I hate even more that I've hurt someone I barely know. Who I never bothered to get to know.

If Parker and I have found a way to make a truce, then I'm going to make the effort to prove to him and myself that he can be right about me and that I can turn into a decent human being.

This revelation doesn't help me get to sleep, and the more I toss and turn, the more my sheets rub against my cock, making me realize it's been a few days since I jerked off.

As much as I want to, I don't reach into my pajama pants because I find it too weird that I'm rock hard while thinking about the heart-to-heart I had with Parker.

The two aren't connected. Sheets, friction, hard cock. It's basic biology. It's *science.*

Correlation doesn't equal causation and all that shit they taught us in high school.

High school. Where I knew Parker. Who's now my team's owner. I refuse to touch my cock.

I refuse to jerk off while Parker keeps jumping into my brain.

Though, the more I toss and turn, the harder my cock gets. By this point, I don't think I'll be able to sleep until I have some relief.

Fuck it. I strip off my pajamas and run my hand down my chest and hard abs.

I try to imagine what Parker's abs look like now he's grown up. He's still scrawny, but not like he once was. Does he work out? Does he—

Stop.

I wrap my fingers around my cock and focus on the sensation rippling down my hard shaft. So fucking hard. I close my eyes and throw my head back. I can't remember the last time I got laid, so this isn't going to take long. The quicker, the better. It's about release, not about anything else.

Or *anyone* else.

It's only me getting off. Like I have a thousand times before. Thinking of all the naked women. Porn. Them being turned out by some faceless dude I never pay attention to when I watch it. Though, that makes me ask why I never pay attention to them. Logic says it's because I'm attracted to women, therefore seeing other men in a fantasy situation is easy to tune out. But … what if … I haven't paid attention to them because I never thought I could? What if I thought my default setting was heterosexual, so I never even let myself think of men that way?

Parker's comment replays over in my head again. *Maybe you're not into women at all.*

And we're back on Parker again.

I slump back, the hold on my cock relaxing but not completely letting go. I'm too in my head to come, but I won't be able to sleep until I do.

Do I give up, or do I give in?

I'm Connor Kikishkin. I will step up and get it done. I start stroking again, fast. Hard. And all I let myself think about is coming.

Nothing else.

I'm not going to think about Parker. I'm not going to think about Parker Duchene. I'm not going to—

Without permission, his face appears in my mind, and in the next second, cum fills my hand before I can really register what's happening.

I still for a few breaths until the realization dawns.

I just jerked off over a man who, with one sentence, has made me question everything.

CHAPTER ELEVEN

PARKER

My bag is packed, ready to leave for the away trip today. I'm going on the team plane, still unsure if it's too weird and if it'll only mean getting in more people's way. The thing is, I could easily buy my own jet, but what's the point? I don't want a jet. The only place I'd fly is to games since I have nothing else going on in my life, and as far as I'm concerned, there's already a perfectly fine plane heading in the exact same direction.

This way, I have a day or two to explore the city before the game, and then we'll be off again. I'll use this time to visit more of the country, and hopefully, getting out of Colorado will help prevent this depressive fog trying to fall over me.

The only downside is the way I'm overly aware of being a mood killer. I don't want the team to even know I'm there. Maybe if I arrive early enough, I can hide in the back corner of the plane, and no one will even notice.

My phone lights up with a call, and I smile at seeing Mom's name. Last we spoke, she was boarding a plane to Australia, and while it hurts that the one and only person in my life is on the other side of the world, I'd never begrudge her. Mom needed to get away. I get that.

"Good morning," I say.

"I think you mean good night," she jokes with all the humor of someone on their first international trip. She and Dad weren't poor by any means, but between my school commitments and their work commitments, the farthest we ever made it for trips was Canada or Mexico.

"What time is it there?"

"Nine. We went out for an early dinner and ended up sitting at the bar and making it through a whole bottle of wine." She giggles, and in the background, I hear Aunt Caroline yell hello.

"I'm glad you're both having fun."

"It was so needed." She sounds good. Relaxed. But I know what's coming next. "I couldn't stay there, Parkie, you know that. It was … I just …"

"I know." Being home without Dad would have been too much. It's hard enough being in this city. Yet where she's running away from those memories, I'm clinging to them. Craving that closeness to him again.

"How's the team?" she asks, sounding less like she's going to break into tears.

"It's …" How much do I tell her? It's fucking weird because I've dealt with my high school bully, and he made the misguided offer to be friends. Awkward because I can't find where I fit. I know where my bank account fits, but I feel like I could offer so much more. Depressing because every game reminds me of Dad. Or … so lonely. "The team is doing great. We're in good standing."

"I suppose it's too early to know if you're going to make it to the playoffs."

"Way too early. And no jinxing anything."

"Sorry … sorry …" She laughs, and it's obvious she's tipsy. "You're okay, then? Over there?"

"Yes." I inject as much confidence as I can, otherwise I know she'll be on the first flight home. "This has been good for me." And that actually doesn't sound like as much of the lie as it was the first time I said the words.

"Good. We're going to go to bed, but we'll talk tomorrow?"

I mentally calculate the time difference. "We're flying into New York this afternoon, so I'll text you."

"Sounds good. Night!"

"Morning," I say to amuse her.

She's giggling as she hangs up, and I pull my phone away from my ear and stare at it. How can I be so happy for her to be out there getting on with life while so desperately trying to cling to everything from my past?

I brush the thought aside. I've got my plan, and maybe once we get to New York, I can go out. There are plenty of gay bars there, and I've missed human contact. If I need to hook up to get my hit of fake affection, it'll fill that loneliness for one night.

I glance around my home. It's a three-bedroom penthouse in Cherry Creek, and I only bought it because I'd thought things were getting serious with my ex. That we were moving toward the stage of living together and talking about kids. The whole place is big and clean, with its own outdoor area. A perfect family home. If I'd been looking just for myself, I could have bought a shoebox in Denver.

Too much money, too little brains, my dad would have said. He really didn't understand people who spent extravagant money on stupid things, and this penthouse is definitely a stupid thing. Moving out isn't an option now that I'm settled, so if I want the place to not feel so empty, I need to change that.

Maybe it's time I get a pet.

I check the time, and there are still hours before I have to leave for the airport, but that's another roadblock. I'm planning to travel a lot, and I don't want to buy a pet, only to leave it every few weeks. This isn't the first time I've considered a pet, but the list of cons far outweighs the pro of companionship. Pets are dirty. Most of them are dumb. Cats might be cute, but having that fur shed all over the apartment sounds like a nightmare. My cleaners come every day as it is; I really don't want to drag their team here in the afternoons as well.

Dogs are equally dirty, with too much energy, and while they might be willing to curl up in my lap, how do I sit there petting it, knowing it's full well probably trampled through its own shit at some point?

The thought of a dog in here makes my skin crawl.

Snakes are clean but terrifying.

Rabbits are adorable, but are they affectionate?

Ferrets are devil creatures.

And once again, I've successfully talked myself out of a pet.

So I'm back at square one. Huge apartment. No friends. Ready to board a plane full of people who wish I was literally anywhere else.

I spend the next few hours unpacking and repacking my suitcase instead.

The whole way to the airport, my anxiety creeps higher. It's been two days since I've seen Connor, and while I know that his whole *friends* suggestion came purely from the bizarre situation we were in, I'm still interested to know how he'll handle it. Will he ignore my existence, like I'd assumed would happen? Maybe try to follow through on his promise until the whole friendship is so forced and awkward that I want to die? Maybe casually throw me out a *hey* and then sit with his team and pretend like he can't feel my presence the same way I feel his?

Or maybe he really *won't* feel it.

Being invisible is my thing, and it wouldn't surprise me that while I've been obsessing over our conversation for days now, it hasn't crossed his mind once. It'd be typical of me to put more emphasis on a conversation than it deserved.

I got my apology. Why can't I be happy with that?

With my incessant need to arrive at places early in case I need a moment to find a bathroom and break down, I'm at the airport before anyone else and allowed to board early. I take the very back row, right in the corner, where I pull out my headphones and computer and make myself look busy.

Even if someone does see me jammed into the corner, they'll be less likely to approach, and hopefully, the headphones will make it clear I have no interest in what any of them are doing.

Instead, I focus back on playing around with some new ideas. The last software I designed was all about masking yourself online. Most people aren't aware of how this can be done, so I sold the memberships for cheap and made it as easy to use as possible, then marketed it as a way to keep your data safe. It took off, and while I hated selling something that I really believed in, with all my money tied to the business, I hadn't had much choice.

It also made me bitter about designing anything else until two days ago when I'd gotten the bug. Nothing has taken place yet, but I'm getting vague ideas, and I'm waiting for one of them to take shape.

A hand waves in front of my face, and I jump so hard I almost put my head through the overhead bin.

"What the hell?" I tug my headphones down and find Connor in the seat next to me. The sight of him does nothing to help with how fast my heart has taken off.

"I called your name twice, but you didn't hear me."

"I was wearing headphones."

"Didn't notice." He tries to look over at my screen.

"What are you doing?" I ask.

"Heading to a game. Assume you're here for the same?"

He's wearing loose gym shorts, socks with slides, and an oversized team hoodie. The casual look is way too good on him and not something I'd ever pull off in my life. Jesus, if I wore socks with slides, I'd wind up looking like some dad from the nineties.

"No, what are you doing here? In this seat? Right beside me?" I haven't had time to remind myself to be professional, and some of the real me is sneaking out.

"We're friends, aren't we?"

"Not really."

"But we agreed to be."

"Yes, but when we agreed to be friends, I thought that was more to make the whole conversation less awkward. Like when you go on a date that's barely okay and end it with 'I had fun, I'll call you,' knowing full well you're never actually going to call the person."

Connor blinks at me. "It wasn't a date."

"I know that." I scowl because, yes, Connor, you're straight. "I'm not talking about you and me like that. I'm talking about the fake-friend offer and now you sitting beside me. You don't have to do that. It's okay. I get it."

"Good." He eyes me. "Because I'm lost."

"You know what? Never mind. Carry on." I go to pull my headphones back up, but Connor tugs them down again. The accidental brush of his fingers against my jaw has my brain short-circuiting.

"It wasn't a pity offer." His dark eyebrows pull closer. "Are you saying you only said yes because you thought I was full of shit?"

"Ummm … kind of?"

He scoffs and goes to put in his earbuds, but I quickly continue.

"Because you're you. And I'm me. We don't have anything in common other than high school, and isn't that … weird?"

"Parker, you know absolutely nothing about me."

"You don't know that."

"Of course I do because, like I said, I know nothing about myself. If I don't even know anything, there's no way you could. So why don't you calm it on all those assumptions and … let it happen?"

Let it happen? Me? A chronic overthinker? "We are not the same person at all."

He smiles and reaches over to settle my headphones back on my head before putting his earbuds in. Connor turns his attention to his phone, and I'm so glad I chose the very back row because I think I stare at him with my mouth hanging open for the entire flight.

CHAPTER TWELVE

CONNOR

I'm having a bit of a crisis.

Not only the identity crisis but another kind. And it has to do with the man sitting next to me on this plane.

I wasn't lying when I said my offer to be his friend wasn't a pity offer. If anything, asking him to be my friend was asking for him to take pity on me.

Still, there's only one reason I hesitated to sit next to him when I saw he was on the plane, and it has nothing to do with being friends. It's because something happened after our talk.

That night in bed, I thought it was a random, horny moment where I happened to be thinking about Parker separately to my needy dick.

Yet, when I woke up hard again and reached for my dick, I thought of the night before, which only made me think of Parker again, and that weirdness settled over me again.

Especially when I went with it. Again.

I'd jerked off while thinking about Parker Duchene. Douche from high school. Technically, the person who now owns me and my career.

It's confusing. And mildly annoying. Because I can't figure it out. Just like I can't figure out who I am underneath everything.

Twenty-six-year-olds are supposed to have their shit figured out, aren't they? If it wasn't obvious before, it is now. I know nothing about myself.

Hence, sitting next to Parker on this plane.

Because it would be easy to ignore what I did last night, stay away from Parker, and turn my genuine offer to be friends into the empty gesture he thought it was, but if I do that, I'm still going to be in the same place mentally in a year from now. Confused, lost, with absolutely no self-awareness.

So here I am, not only wondering what last night was about but also curious if it's going to happen again.

It's entirely possible I'm reading into it. He said things that got to me. Like putting the seed of possibility in my head that, as he said, maybe I'm not into women.

I wasn't offended that he suggested it. I just thought out of everything I knew about myself, my sexuality was the one thing that was solid.

Apparently not.

Not that I'm flipping a switch now or suddenly into dudes. Or Parker. But I'm questioning everything.

Especially when Parker reaches over and puts a hand on my knee. For a second, I'm taken aback because what the fuck? Are my thoughts coming out loud?

But when I turn my head to ask him, he's glaring at me.

I take my earbuds out, and he takes his hand off my knee and moves his headphones to sit around his neck.

"Why are you so edgy?" he asks.

"Edgy?"

"Your knee hasn't stopped bouncing, and with all the respect I have for you, if you don't stop, I will throw you off this plane."

I laugh.

"It's cute you think I'm joking," he grumbles.

A few days ago, him saying I'm cute would've probably put me on edge. It still does, but not for the same reason. I let it sink in before testing something.

"It's cute you think I don't believe you." Was that … weird? Was it flirty? Am I flirting with a man?

I don't think so.

Flirting is more overt. This is me replying with a common phrase that he said first.

I think. I shrug it off. "I was laughing that you think saying, 'With all the respect you have for me,' when we both know that bar is not high."

Parker smiles. "True. I almost went with 'all the love in my heart' but didn't think it held a credible threat when … yeah, reasons."

"You could've said hate. All the hate in your heart."

"Unfortunately for you, I can't say I have any of that anymore. Bitterness? Yes, but hatred? Nah, I'll save that for people who deserve it."

"I wish I could say I didn't deserve it." How long is this guilt going to hang around? I want it to go away already.

"Maybe a little," Parker says.

"Hey, you were supposed to say, 'No, no, you've proved you're a totally okay guy now you're not a dickish teenager,' and make me feel better about myself."

"Will I ever win with you?"

I dunno. I'd say he's winning at something when it comes to me. I just haven't figured it out yet.

-

The usual buzz I get on the ice isn't there tonight. The thrill is replaced with something else. And it's not so much a bad thing, but where I usually love the competitiveness, the need for a win, and the glory of being one half of the high-scoring Kiki brothers, there's only one person I'm trying to impress, and I can feel his stare on me from wherever he's watching tonight. Perhaps the owner's box, even though we're away, or just a random suite. Either way, I know he's watching.

And it does something to me. Pushes me harder. Like if I can bring in a win for his team, then he'll … like me? Forgive me more?

There has to be some kind of logic in there somewhere. Deep down.

It's really weird to think that the only person I can confide in about the personality transformation is the kid everyone picked on in high school. It's weird to even consider him my friend. But the Parker who was in high school and present Parker are different people. Or maybe they're the same person, but no one gave him a chance back then because of how he looked. And because maybe I didn't consider what one little nickname could do to someone.

I need to make that up to Parker. I need to be the person I should have been back then. That must be why I'm doing this and why I've had more shots on goal tonight than a defenseman usually would.

Instead of setting up Easton to score as per usual, I keep sending slappers toward New York's goalie. But after numerous failed attempts, I should give up and do what I do best: make my little brother look good. The only thing is, I might not know myself well, but I do know I'm stubborn enough to not give up until I get at least one.

And in the next moment, my stubbornness pays off.

Our lamp lights up, and I score.

Fuck, yes.

I'm pulled off the ice from another shift, and after we take our seats on the back bench and pour water down our throats, another D-man, Hastel, taps the back of my helmet with his glove.

"You're thirsty for it tonight." And no, he's not talking about the water.

"Need to bring up my scoring stats," I say.

"Do you though? Your assist records are the best on the team, and that's including any of the forwards."

Easton's line is pulled off, and he sits on the bench in front of us, so I speak up loud enough for him to hear.

"Maybe I'm sick of letting my brother take all the spotlight." As soon as I say that, I hold my breath. I'm joking, and it's reflex to say shit like that, but with how rocky our relationship has been, I'm scared he thinks I might be putting him down or—

He turns and smiles at me. "It's about time you started pulling your weight when it comes to scoring. Just saying. Leaving it up to me all the time is exhausting."

I want to pat his head and tell him I love him, but in front of the team and where we potentially have cameras trained on us, I won't embarrass him like that. Look at me, I'm learning!

Things might be strained at the moment, but neither of us can say we don't want to get our close bond back.

From my goal, for the rest of my game, I go back to play as usual, and thanks to me, Easton gets one in the net, and so does Munter.

Leaving the ice with a three-point game puts me on a high, and when we reach the locker room and go through interviews, I'm tapped for the press conference. So is East.

And we're put on that panel side by side. Because of course.

"Easton, your big brother beat you to the first goal of the night. What do you think about that?" Of course that's the first question.

"With how much he was hogging the puck, statistically, he was bound to get one. So, good for him? I guess?"

Everyone in the room snickers.

"Connor, you did take more shots on goal tonight than you have in the entire season. Is this a new game strategy?" someone else asks.

"I was just feeling it tonight. My gut was telling me it would pay off."

And then comes the real question—what the last two reporters were trying to get to but were more subtle. "So the change of play had nothing to do with the rift between you two?"

Seriously, anytime Easton and I have been put in front of the media since our fight during training camp, this comes up.

Easton answers for me. "Everyone asks us that like we're going to change our response. Brothers disagree. We've moved on, and everyone else should do the same."

It might be true that Easton has moved on, but I sure haven't.

But I will. Eventually. When I work out how to turn my life upright again. When everything makes sense and I no longer have this divide inside me, pulling me in two different directions. There's the man I used to be, the man I want to be, and then in the middle, there's me. In limbo.

CHAPTER THIRTEEN

PARKER

After walking around New York this morning and then the team winning tonight, I'm in the best mood I've been in for a long time. Some of the fog swamping my brain has cleared out for the night, and everything doesn't feel so generally shitty.

The team will be out celebrating, and I sort of wish I had someone to celebrate with, but while I pushed things with them by catching a ride on the plane, I also know that team celebrations are for the team. Not me. So I won't be gatecrashing, especially when I know the only reason I'd want to go is to see Connor, and Connor will be busy riding the high of scoring tonight. Probably even hooking up.

So I'm going to do the same.

While I feel generally optimistic about the future, I'm going to go out, pick someone up, and hopefully find some of that intimacy I've been craving for the night. It's the only thing that could make today better than it already is.

I'm staying in the same hotel as the team, but where they have standard rooms booked, I'm in the suite. It sort of feels like the kind of thing a billionaire would do, and

I have to make an active decision to ignore how empty it is with only me hanging out.

I shower and manscape, clean myself up, then put extra work into getting ready. My normally fluffy black hair is tamed. I shave off the day's growth on my face, find some nice pants and a shirt, then cover my nervous sweat in cologne.

The thought of visiting a gay bar crosses my mind, and it's a toss-up between that and my hookup app. Both of them are pretty impersonal options. Maybe that can be my next project? A hookup app for people who don't want a relationship but also want a bit more than a quick fuck. A snuggle-bunny type of arrangement. Overnight boyfriends. Fuck like rabbits, then curl up and go to sleep before bouncing the next day.

I'd be as lonely on that app as I am anywhere else because I'd be the only person pathetic enough to use it. Sex should be enough, and I have to be grateful that I can find people who actually want to have sex with me now. Being a virgin until I was nineteen wasn't a fun time for me.

Instead of drinking alone in my room, I head down to the hotel bar while I decide what I'm going to do later. It's already busy, and being around people helps me soak up the company.

The tables are full, but there's a lone stool at the end of the bar that I slide into, order a drink, and look around. Once I got over being scared of people, they started to interest me. Why they make the choices they do, how they see the world, why someone would make the conscious decision to think they're better than someone else.

I don't only mean in high school with bullying either. Even here, with men and women both looking to find someone for the night, that choice comes from compatibility and finding someone worth spending that time with.

Or alcohol. Once people drink enough, the rest all goes out the window.

I turn to take another sip of my rum and Coke when a hand slams down on the bar beside me. I jump and almost choke, and when I'm sure I can breathe properly again, I turn to find Connor Kikishkin leaning over me.

He's standing close, body snugly cutting me off from the person on the stool beside mine, and my knee is touching his outer hip in a way that's making it hard to remember what words are.

He's still in his game-day suit, broad shoulders filling it out, top button of his shirt undone and showing off smooth skin. "Fuck me."

"What was that?" he asks, leaning in closer.

My face flushes as I realize I've said that out loud, but the noise of the bar has saved me. "I asked what you're doing here."

"The team was heading to the bar down the road, and I saw you sitting all by yourself."

For some reason, that reminder doesn't get me down. "Nothing new there."

"Come with us."

"There is no way I'm going out with a bunch of jocks."

"You own the team, man. They'll all be on their best behavior around you."

"Even more reason not to go."

He opens his mouth to push some more.

"That's a no. You don't have to do … whatever this is."

"This …" Connor says, waving the bartender over. "Is called being a friend. We'll get you used to it soon enough."

He orders two of what I'm having, and when he takes a sip, his nose scrunches up in a way that's wildly adorable for a six-foot-three wrecking ball. "What the hell are you drinking?"

"Rum."

"Isn't that for old people?"

Even though I probably shouldn't, I smile. "I'm beginning to think you don't know how being a friend works either."

"Fun. We can learn together." He holds his glass out, and it takes me a moment to work out he wants to do that cheers thing and not that he wants me to take it from him.

I tap my glass against his and manage to do it in a way that looks like I've done it before. "Shouldn't you be going with your team?"

"I have time for a drink with you first. After all, this was your win too."

"I don't think it works that way."

"Of course it does. Your team. Your win. It works the same for the fans. We play for everyone who can't and believes in us anyway."

"That was …"

"Not bad for a jock, huh?"

He needs to stop looking at me like that. All shiny eyes and wide smile. I'm so attracted to him it hurts. All this time I wanted his attention, I had no idea how tortuous that attention could be.

I gulp down the rest of my first drink, and Connor takes a sip of his without cringing this time.

"So if you won't come with me," he says, "what are you going to do? Drink alone at the bar all night?"

"Actually …" I tap the hookup app on my phone, and the options around here are many. "I was tossing up between a bar and a hookup. I think it's getting too late for a bar—I don't enjoy when everyone around me is blackout drunk—so I'll probably find someone on here instead."

Connor leans over my shoulder, way too close, and looks at where my phone is resting on the bar. "There are a lot of butts in those profile pictures."

"And abs. I like abs."

I have no idea if he's looking at me or not, but it feels like he is. Just seeing those mouthwatering pictures and having his scent surround me is making me antsy. At first, I'd wanted to go out for company; now, I really do think I need the sex as well.

After careful consideration, I tap one of the profiles that looks promising and type, "Pic?"

"What's that for?" he asks.

"You might want to look away."

"Wh—" A dick pops up on my screen, and Connor jerks back.

It's a real mission not to laugh as I check out what I have to work with here. If they're too big, I'd struggle to take him and actually get off, so I always check first. Looks like he'll do.

I'm writing back when this time, the feel of Connor watching me is too strong to ignore. I bravely look up, meeting his stare. A moment stretches out where I can't read his expression, but I can't look away from it either.

"I'm having one of those moments when I realize I've made assumptions again," he says.

"What do you mean?"

"Well ... you ... I guess I didn't picture you as someone who hooked up."

That makes me tilt my head curiously. "Why?"

"I dunno, you're being all … assertive. I'm not used to that."

"Well, as we've established, we don't really know each other, do we? Sex is a transaction, so I want to make sure I'm getting what I need before going ahead." Sexually, anyway. What I really need isn't something I can ask for on a hookup app. It's always part of the gamble, that we'll get off and he'll run, but sometimes they stick around. Usually, a promise of a round two will do it.

"And you need …" He nods toward my phone. "That?"

For some reason, his awkwardness is making me more comfortable. More confident. "A dick usually helps."

"Of course."

Then I say more than I probably should. "It might not be everything I want, but for a night, it'll do."

"Not big enough?" he teases.

Silly straight boy—everything is a measuring contest to them. "It's not all about size. But I wasn't talking about his dick anyway."

"Then what else would you want?"

I'm surprised he'd even ask that. For all his awkwardness, it's more that he's stumbled on this conversation and isn't sure how he got here rather than being uncomfortable. "Someone who wants to be around me would be a start. I'd even take someone who will spend the night. As for the other side of things … a guy who's a top, who—" I quickly cut off, veering on the side of unprofessional.

"Is a bit possessive?"

My eyes snap to his, and the teasing in his gaze lights me up. I didn't think he caught that when we were talking, but I obviously wasn't as subtle as I thought. "Can't give you all my secrets."

"Thought we were getting to know each other."

He's stupidly close, and it's getting to a point where I really, really need to go. "You don't need to know *that*."

The alert on my phone saves me.

The guy's in the next hotel over.

"Gotta go."

Connor's frown takes over his face. "We're not done with our drinks."

I choke mine down in one, trying not to worry about how I gulp or the way liquid dribbles from the corners of my mouth and down my chin. "I'm done. Now you can meet up with the team instead of having a pity drink with me." I go to turn around when something makes me stop. Before I can chicken out, I set a hand on his arm and add, "Thank you though. It was nice having someone to talk to."

Then before he can answer the patheticness of that with more pity, I leave. Out of the moody bar, across the brighter foyer, and into the busy New York street. It's cool enough that I probably should have brought a jacket, but in a few moments, I'll be out of these clothes anyway.

Joining some guy in his room sounds a lot less fun than sitting in the warm bar talking to Connor, but getting away was the smart choice. No need to scare off the first maybe friend I've ever had. I can't guarantee I won't be thinking of him the whole time though.

"Parker!"

I pause at my name and turn back, confirming that the voice belonged to Connor. He's jogging my way, perfect hair a mess, suit jacket tossed over his shoulder.

"What are you doing?"

He tugs me into the shadows between buildings. "Remember how I said I don't know who I am and you said I should try to figure it out?"

"Yes ..."

"Can I try something?"

My mouth is dry. "Ah ... yes?"

I'm caught totally off guard when Connor shoves me into the wall. Like the past two times, I go pliant, ready for his anger, that heated glare. But third time lucky, I suppose, because instead of a fist to the face, Connor's mouth crashes with mine.

I'm in shock for a few seconds, not able to comprehend what he's doing. He's kissing me. Not attacking. *Kissing*.

Shock and excitement spear through me. He smells like aftershave, and his lips move over mine with all the confidence he seems to unknowingly possess.

I arch my neck to reach him, mouth numbly following his lead, and when Connor's strong tongue sweeps into my mouth, I let out an unwelcome groan at the contact.

My whole head has gone fuzzy, lust pumping through my system, and while I might not know what the hell is going on, I do know that I don't want it to stop.

Almost as soon as I think that, Connor's mouth is ripped away with a loud inhale.

"Holy fuck," he mutters.

He stands there, eyes as wide as mine, his lips parted, and I'm left still trying to figure out if that actually happened or if my fantasies have evolved into full-blown hallucinations.

My fingertips meet my still-wet lips, and slowly, very slowly, it sinks in.

Connor Kikishkin kissed me, and now he's motionless. Quiet. I'm expecting him to lash out any minute and punch me, put this whole thing on me, and have a straight-boy freak-out.

But then he says something that is so not on the list of things I'm waiting for. "Don't hook up tonight."

He ducks his head and walks away, but if he thinks I'm not going to chase him after that, he has no idea of the effect he has on me. None at all.

CHAPTER FOURTEEN

CONNOR

Shit, shit, what was that?

Parker's calling my name, but it only rings in my ears.

I have no idea where I'm going or what I'm doing, but I miss the entrance to the team's hotel, so I keep walking. I weave in and out of people, my long legs able to move me at a quick pace.

I get a block before Parker catches up to me and another half a block before I finally stop. And the only thing to get me to do that is the hitch in his voice when he says, "*Please.*"

It's busier on the street here than it was back there. Where I did something … something I never thought I'd do, want to do, or enjoy as much as I did.

I don't even know where the courage came from to do that. All I could think about in the moment was Parker's mouth on someone else's and the image of that dick pic on his phone.

When he said he was going to hook up, a voice in my head said, "But you can't." Like it wanted some kind of claim over him, which is ridiculous because Parker is allowed to hook up with whoever he wants. Just because I've had a couple of confusing thoughts over the guy, it doesn't give me any right to him.

He let me kiss him, but now that it's over, I'm realizing how inappropriate it was.

Before Parker can say anything, I beat him to it.

"I'm sorry. That shouldn't have happened, and I shouldn't have told you not to hook up. You should go. I'll be fine. I … I wasn't thinking, and that was inappropriate, and now you're probably going to doubly fire me, and—"

"Connor," Parker says calmly. He steps closer to me, and then someone bumps past him. "Breathe."

It's hard to do that with him around, but I try. As much as Parker will always be the guy I knew in high school first and my team owner second, what I did is sinking in, and it's not landing well. Perspective or not, he *is* the team owner. He owns my career. And Easton's. And I just kissed him.

"Come back to the hotel with me," he says.

The desire to kiss him again barrels into me because I couldn't process what I was doing the first time, but the fear of him thinking I now want more keeps me frozen to my spot.

What's going to happen if we're seen going into his hotel room? What does he think is going to happen once we get in there? Vulnerability isn't my strong suit, and right now, it's all I have. The seed of distrust that has always been there since Parker showed up in my life again rears its ugly head.

As if reading my mind, he adds, "We're going to talk. Or, more specifically, you're going to talk."

"I am?" I croak.

"You're obviously going through something, and like you said the other night, you don't really have anyone else to talk to because your brother and best friend are shacking up, so I'm all you have. This really isn't something you should hold inside."

There he goes, reminding me that he's a good person, and my overthinking makes me an idiot. I so desperately want to go back with him, but … I'm scared. No, not scared. Well, not of him. Maybe nervous. I'm angry that I've gone this long without even having an inkling that kissing a man might be something I'm into, let alone paying attention to what I want or need. Instead, I did everything my parents and brothers needed. There's a good chance if I go with Parker back to his hotel room and face all of these confusing thoughts, I'll only resent everything even more when I find out the truth.

That kiss turned everything upside down, but considering my life was already upside down, does that mean it's now the right way up? Or maybe my life is in the universe's tumble dryer at the moment.

"We'll just talk," Parker says. "No pressure."

I finally get the balls to look at him. His features are soft, his blue eyes empathetic. Or maybe they're full of pity. "And no getting in trouble for kissing the team's owner?"

"No one will ever know. I promise."

I slowly relent and turn back toward the hotel. "I really am sorry for doing that."

"Don't be."

I look over at him walking next to me. The tip of his ear is pink, and he's staring at the ground. The last thing I want to do is make him uncomfortable, so I try to be light-hearted as I say, "Now who's the one giving the pity friendship?"

His gaze flicks up to mine, and I get lost in his expression. It's no longer holding that tinge of empathy. His eyes are full of something else. Something I can't pinpoint.

We reach the entrance to the hotel, and I follow him into the foyer. We're silent as we head for the elevators, but as soon as the doors close behind us and Parker hits the button for his floor, he turns back to me.

"Just so you know, I didn't tell you not to be sorry for kissing me out of pity. I said it because you don't need to be sorry. At all. I'm not."

Butterflies erupt deep in my gut, and my cock stirs.

Our kiss was so quick that my dick didn't have time to register what was happening before a full freak-out happened.

"Y-you liked kissing me?" I ask.

He hates me. Or hated me. I was a terrible person to him. Why would he be okay with me throwing myself at him?

We reach his floor, and as the elevator dings, he says, "Saved by the bell."

It's not until we get to his door that I realize how this could be perceived by someone else. What if one of the team comes by and sees me going into the owner's suite?

None of those thoughts ran through my mind while I cornered him in an alley and kissed him, but this …

"Connor," he says again in the exact same way he did down on the street. He opens his mouth to tell me to breathe again, but I do it before he can tell me.

I take in an exaggerated big breath.

"Good boy." He opens the door and holds it for me to walk in first.

The suite is big. Big for New York, anyway. It has a sitting place, a kitchen, and a separate bedroom. It's a palace. It's probably the most expensive room in the whole hotel.

It's really difficult to see Parker as a billionaire. I thought I had wealth, but this is a whole new level.

My image of billionaires probably doesn't match at all with real billionaires though. I think of them like aging white guys from old money, but with the start-up boom, they're now everyday guys in their twenties.

"This is a nice place," I say.

"The best money can buy." His tone doesn't match his words. I think he's going for proud, but it comes across more … factual. Impersonal.

He walks over to the minibar and pulls out two wineglasses and a bottle of champagne from the fridge.

When he pours them and brings a glass over to me, I eye it. Not because I think it's spiked or I don't want to drink it. It just feels very … date-ish. And from the outside, this situation is pretty fucked-up.

Player kisses team owner. Team owner invites player up to his apartment. It's … inappropriate.

If Easton were in my position, I'd want to kick his and Parker's ass. I'd be pissed. Or old me would be pissed.

Even though I know it's inappropriate and I shouldn't be here, there's no way in hell I'm going to leave.

I take the glass and sip it.

He moves to the plush couch, but I hesitate because if I go sit next to him, will he think I'm asking for more?

I can't wrap my head around kissing another man, let alone doing anything else with one.

Either I'm really easy to read, or maybe he knows what I'm going through because he says, "You can sit anywhere you like. And like I've already said, we're here to talk."

I want to sit next to him. Hell, I wouldn't mind kissing him again so I could actually pay attention to his mouth, take my time, and feel everything. My heart was pounding too hard, my adrenaline spiking my veins with so much energy I was practically buzzing out of my skin. Kissing him left me with more questions than answers.

Maybe if I kiss him long enough, I'll find the answers I'm looking for on his tongue.

I take another deep breath and join him on the couch but make sure to sit as far on the opposite side as possible so there's no touching. Not even the casual graze of our knees or thighs.

I think that's what set this whole night off to begin with. While we were in the bar, I was casually leaning against him because there was no room. It made me think things that had never even crossed my mind before.

Like what it would be like to be that guy on the other end of his message. Pictured a wordless, nameless romp in a bed and then doing the awkward dance of trying to get Parker out of his room. Or are gay guys not like us straight guys who are taught it's rude to ask someone to leave? It's rude to kick out a hookup, but sometimes when you know that's all it is, it would be nice to say, "Thanks. Okay, bye." Maybe if you're with another guy, both there for the same reason, the awkwardness doesn't come. He just … leaves.

"What are you thinking about?" Parker asks.

How did my train of thought get me here? "You don't want to know."

"Actually, I do. Because that's why we're here. You kissed me and then freaked out, and I get the impression that hasn't happened before. Uh, with a man."

I shake my head. "It hasn't. You … You're the only one."

"Can I ask if it was a spur-of-the-moment thing?"

Yes. No. "It's impossible to answer that."

"I'll rephrase. Do you know why you did it?"

"I …" Ergh, I don't want to admit this. "For reasons I probably shouldn't have."

Parker's face falls, some of that leftover resentment shining through. "What do you mean?"

"All I know is from the moment I knew you were going out to hook up, I wanted to stop you."

"Because …"

I throw up my hands. "I don't know. And then out on the street, I wasn't really thinking at all, so I did what I thought would make you turn down the date. But the second I did it, I realized what a dick I was being. Because there's no reason I shouldn't want you to hook up."

"No reason that makes sense to you, you mean."

"Exactly. And now I feel guilty, and I'm worried that if anyone finds out, this is sure to be a scandal. I've spent my entire life trying to keep Easton and Lachie from jeopardizing everything, and here I am, doing something that is way worse than anything they've ever done, and the kicker is, I don't even know why I did it. I shouldn't have. I shouldn't have dragged you into my fucked-upness."

Parker sips his wine and then leans forward to put his glass on the coffee table. "I hate to break this to you, but I've been a part of your fucked-upness since high school. And out of everything that you've done to me, kissing me is by far the least problematic and the most enjoyable."

I can't argue with him there, and hearing that he enjoyed it as much as I did is a bit too much for me. "I still shouldn't have done it though. Not only because you own the team but because it was led by the old Connor taking what he wanted because his ego is big enough to think that just because you're gay, you might be into me and want me to kiss you. I took something because I wanted it, and I didn't ask for your permission."

"You asked if you could try something. I would've pushed you away if I wasn't okay with it." Parker moves in closer. "And if I'm completely honest with you, had you asked if you could kiss me first before taking me off guard, I might have come in my pants."

I burst out laughing.

"Wish I was joking. Do you know how long I've fantasized about kissing you?"

My eyebrows shoot up. "Y-you have?"

"I think the reason I hated you the most in high school is because other than that one time where you threw me against the wall and called me Douche, all I ever wanted back then was your attention, and you never gave it to me after that day."

I down the rest of my wine because it's hard to handle that. "What the fuck is wrong with me?" I slump down on the couch cushions.

"Only you can answer that question. Or a shrink."

I smile. "Thanks for the support."

"I'm not saying you have to have it all figured out right away. Chances are, you'll be lost for a while trying to change all your learned behaviors, but I need you to know that you can trust me. Confide in me. Things will get messier before they get better, and if you'll let me, I'll be here for you."

"No one will find out what I did?"

"Not unless you tell them."

"Will this complicate things for you and the team?"

Parker shrugs. "I don't know, but I also don't really care. I bought the team for my dad, and while I love hockey, it's not like I know anything about running a franchise. I'd rather make sure you're okay than worry about how the team is doing."

"Why though? Why …"

"Why do I no longer hate you?"

I nod.

"There are a lot of reasons. Because I've seen how you're struggling. Because you might be a late bloomer and haven't figured yourself out yet. Or maybe, just maybe, it's because I finally have your attention, and I'll do anything to keep it."

I speak before I think. "Even kiss me again?"

CHAPTER FIFTEEN

PARKER

I'm left staring at him like an idiot because even with everything we've talked about tonight, those were the last words I expected him to say.

"F-for … pity?" I'm confused.

Connor snorts and slides closer. "I never kissed you out of some sort of charity."

Right. No. He's figuring himself out, and I'm the only one he can do this with. That actually makes a lot more sense and means that I won't lose all respect for him—and for myself for wanting to do it anyway, pity or not.

Fuck, I want to kiss him, but he's still in that confused space, and I … I don't know what the best move is here. I have exactly zero experience talking someone through a big gay panic and even less experience supporting someone as a friend. But I spilled everything to him, and he's still sitting here, looking at me with big, sweet eyes, and I … still need to answer him.

"Umm … the thing is …"

He quickly slides back again. "I'm overstepping. I get it."

"No!" I cringe at how unintentionally loud that was. "It's not that. I have no experience with … all this."

Connor's eyes snap open. "You're a virgin?"

"*No.*" I almost roll my eyes at him. "This whole gay, bi, whatever guru thing. I always sort of knew who I was, so I have no clue what you're going through."

The slow smile he gives me skitters nerves through my gut. "I don't need a guru. I have my brother and Knox for that. All I need and all I'm asking for is a kiss. If it's a no, that's okay. I get it. But it should be a no because you don't want it. Not all that other stuff."

"I want it," I practically whisper.

"I think I should be clear that I only mean kissing. This whole thing is—"

"A lot. I know. Kissing is fine. Great, even." Just the prospect of getting to kiss him with it leading nowhere is making my head swim. I'd been ready to accept affection from just about anyone, but from him? I'd never even hoped this could be a possibility.

"Just kissing?" he checks.

"As much kissing as you need."

He tries to be subtle about his deep inhale, but then his eyes harden, and a determined look crosses his face. He's clearly nervous as he moves closer, but there's something in his eyes that tells me he wants this, maybe even as much as I do. A small part of me wishes I could be someone else. Someone hotter and bigger who could hold the attention of a guy like Connor Kikishkin.

But then I remember, for better or worse, I'm mostly okay with being me.

And it's this me that gets to kiss him right now.

He leans in, and I give him all the space he needs to take his time. It's fucking torture as his lips close the distance, and the second they're back on mine, that same high hits me.

I didn't imagine it. There's no way I could dream up a kiss like this.

His hand comes up to cup my face, the warmth covering my cheek, kiss still soft, hesitant, and I know, in this moment, that I'll never recover from being kissed by him.

His tongue sweeps over my lips, and I part them, letting him in. Other than his hand, we're not touching anywhere else, and somehow, it's perfect and torture all at once. I want to grip his hair, want to climb into his lap, want to press as close to him as I can and soak in his presence. But he said he's not ready for all of that, so I'll keep my ass planted on this couch, dick uncomfortably trapped along my right thigh, and enjoy the fact I'm getting this at all.

His kiss deepens, strong tongue taking the lead, hand slipping from my cheek to hold the back of my neck. The ownership in that one movement has me wrenching away.

"What's wrong?" His hand is still there. Still solidly, possessively, holding me in place and with only a few inches between us.

I really think I'm in danger of doing something I was only joking about before. "We said only kissing."

"Yeah …"

Of course he isn't taking the hint and is going to make me spell it out. "Connor … I am very gay and very attracted to you and very, *very* into the way you're taking control. Please let go of my neck."

His gaze drops to where his hand is, almost like he didn't even realize he'd done it. Typical. That Connor is *that* sexy when he doesn't even mean to be.

He swallows, thumb running from where it's resting under my ear and down my throat. Chills race down my spine.

"You like this?"

"Too much. And I'd really like to keep my word, so you're going to have to help me out here."

He releases me, and it's a relief and a disappointment all in one.

Before he can question me or probe more into my reaction, I jump in first.

"Did that help?"

"I liked it if that's what you're asking." He licks his swollen bottom lip. "I really liked it."

"Okay."

"So I guess that means something."

"I guess."

He hasn't moved back again, and when he stretches his arm along the back of the couch, it's close enough I could rest my head on it. Like a cat. I don't because I'm worried my self-control has done enough heavy lifting for one night.

Damn it's hard not to move closer though. It would take no effort to lean forward and press against his chest. To inhale that aftershave and his warmth.

But would that be too weird?

Experimental kissing feels vastly different from staying and hanging out. Maybe holding me a little.

"I really want to do it again," he admits softly.

"I really, really want that too. But maybe not now."

He nods quickly. "Sorry I ruined your hookup. You could have been getting some instead of dealing with my issues."

Maybe I'm weird, but if I was given a choice over where I wanted the night to go, I would have picked this. Hell, I kind of did. Connor asked me not to hook up, but if I'd wanted to, that wouldn't have stopped me.

The guy's probably blocked me by this point. I don't have a single part of me that cares.

"Actually, you probably saved me a whole lot of awkwardness."

"Really?"

I refuse to look at him. "I don't think he would have given me what I wanted."

"It's not like I am either."

"Actually, you're giving me something no one has in a while."

"A high school make-out session?"

I scoff. "We both know I didn't have any of those."

"Break my heart some more." Thankfully, I can recognize that's his mostly teasing voice. "If not that, what is it?"

"My ex and I broke up earlier this year."

Connor's face falls. "Was he a dick?"

The snappishness to his words is a surprise, but I don't hate it. "He was … fine. Nice. I thought we'd end up married and all that, but apparently, he didn't think the same. I'm a bit … particular about things."

"What type of things?"

"Normal things," I say defensively. "Like, don't throw all your clothes in an overnight bag for a week-long trip and hope you remembered enough underwear."

He makes a *pfft* noise. "That's common sense. Also, don't pack in advance because your clothes get all wrinkled. The less time in the suitcase, the better."

"Exactly. And who doesn't put their damn cup in the dishwasher once they're done with it? Don't leave your underwear lying on the floor. That kind of thing."

"You sound like a bit of a neat freak."

"*No*. My head gets messy enough that I don't need everything around me messy as well."

"You? Messy?"

"I hide it well," I say dryly. "But while all that was building up in me, my working too much was the deal breaker for him."

"Do you miss him?" Connor's full of the big questions tonight.

"No. Yes." I've never been more articulate.

"So you still love him?"

"No."

"But you miss him? He sounds like an asshole."

That's the thing. He really wasn't one. "I miss having someone." I don't want to say the next part out loud. "I love sex, but sometimes it doesn't hit that … that other side of me."

"You're not making any sense."

"I like intimacy, but that doesn't have to mean sex."

"You mean, like, blowjobs?"

I grunt in frustration and bury my face in my hands. Then, with my whole head feeling on fire, I murmur, "I like to be cuddled, okay?"

"Cuddled?" Of course Connor barely understands the word.

"Yes." I get the courage to glare at his confused expression. "When I'm falling asleep. I like it, okay? Sue me."

"I can't say I've thought much about that before."

"Maybe you should try it before you laugh at me."

"I'm not laughing." He holds his hands up in defense … while clearly holding back a laugh.

"Sure. What part about that sound trying to escape you would give me that impression?"

It finally gets out. "I'm down if you are."

My head snaps up to meet his gaze. "What?"

"Cuddling." His lips twitch, and he holds out his hand. "Show me what all the fuss is about. I don't think I'm ready for anything else, but cuddling, I can do. Or maybe I can't. I guess we'll wait and see. Maybe I've been a closeted cuddler this whole time, but because society says it means more and could give my hookups hope of being the next Mrs. NHL Player, I've never risked it."

I'm numb as I take his hand, and he pulls me to my feet. "Explain to me what's happening here."

I watch in shock as Connor unbuttons his shirt. "Do you have a T-shirt I can borrow?"

He might as well be speaking in another language, though, because as his abs are revealed, my brain goes offline. Then the fucker flexes them.

"Stop." I cover my eyes. "Check the drawers. There's something in there." Don't make me think after having those incredible abs burned onto my brain.

The sound of the drawer sliding open reaches me. "You actually unpack?"

"Weird, remember?"

"Nope. If you're weird, I'm weird too, and I refuse to let Easton and Knox be right about that. Unpacking stops *the wrinkles. The wrinkles, Parker!*"

My name from his lips in a playful manner makes this whole situation even more surreal.

Material hits me in the face, and I pull my hands away to find a T-shirt. Is this actually happening?

I pass him to grab some sleep shorts, then disappear into the bathroom to change. My heart is hammering so loudly I can hear it in my ears, and after I'm done washing my face and brushing my teeth and make it back to the bedroom, Connor's already in my bed.

Connor Kikishkin.

Is in my bed.

He flicks the covers back. "Come on, then. Don't make this weird."

"Everything about this is weird."

But I climb in beside him anyway because it's either that or stand there and let my knees give out.

He's bare-chested, which is totally unfair.

"What happened to borrowing a shirt?"

"Yeah," he draws out the word. "None of your stuff fits me."

Makes sense.

He lets the blankets drop over us, and I roll over onto my side. A moment later, Connor's large body curls around me.

I almost forget to breathe. His scent is strong, his grip is tight, and even though I'm probably going into cardiac arrest, it's worth risking death for this.

However temporary.

He's holding me, and for a moment, that loneliness in my heart settles.

CHAPTER SIXTEEN

CONNOR

Okay, I could get used to cuddling. It's like a warm blanket and a lot more comfortable than it probably looks.

Somehow throughout the night, we became a tangled pile of limbs, and now, as I'm slowly waking from a coma of the best sleep I've had in a long while, I'm on my side, one arm over Parker's chest and my top leg in between his. He's on his back, but his lower half is turned toward me with his leg over my hip.

Last night, I wasn't so sure I was ready for more than kissing. Kissing him has been like an out-of-body experience, as if I'm watching myself do it instead of experiencing it. I wanted to keep kissing him, but I also didn't want to push because I wasn't sure how much further I could go.

This morning though, as I feel his morning wood against my thigh, I want more than kissing.

He's still sleeping though, and I'm sure he wouldn't appreciate me rubbing up against him, but *damn*, it's difficult not to. I'm just as hard, and if he were awake, I'm sure he could feel it too.

The thing is, while kissing him, *both times*, they weren't long enough for me to get hard over it. I liked it, it felt nice—not anything different than kissing a woman—but

I think I was too in my head both times to really think about taking it further. The urge to kiss him was strong, but it didn't have a chance to go beyond that.

Right now, all I can think about is how hard my dick is, and it's more than only morning wood.

It's being cuddled up to Parker all night. Holding him. Being pressed against him. I'm not sure if it's Parker-specific or man-specific, but I'm also trying to tell myself that I need to take this one step at a time. One runaway thought before another.

Maybe I don't need to focus on the questions at the moment or ask myself how long I've been repressing a potential attraction to men. It doesn't matter how or why, and I don't need to question it. At least, not yet. I'm sure a shrink will have a good ol' time telling me how the responsibilities that were put on me as a child made me repress a whole bunch of shit about me, but that's for future Connor to deal with.

Because it doesn't matter. Not in a big-picture kind of way.

Bottom line is I want to kiss Parker Duchene. Holy fuck, that's the weirdest sentence I've ever thought of, but it doesn't make it any less true.

I want to kiss him and … get off with him. However that might happen. Not going to lie, the thought of giving him a blowjob scares me more than anything, but I could probably handle touching him. Stroking his cock like I would if it were my own.

My hand shakes at the thought. I can't tell if it's because I want to do it, if it's out of nervousness, or maybe it's a bit of both.

I want him to wake up, damn it.

I shift, moving my mouth closer to his, but I don't kiss him. My breath is on his cheek, and it twitches, but he still doesn't open his eyes.

I run my nose up his jawline and whisper in his ear, "Parker?"

His eyes flutter, and then he's staring at me with a cute scrunch in his brow until it's like he remembered last night and what I'm doing here.

"You stayed."

"Turns out I'm really good at this cuddling thing."

"You are. I don't think I woke up at all last night."

"I was thinking ..." My lips skim over the spot below his ear. He trembles in my arms, and his hard cock digging into me only gets harder. "I'm really good at the whole kissing thing too."

He rasps, "You are."

"I'm wondering what else I might be good at."

Parker freezes. "W-what were you thinking?"

I have no idea. "I, uh ... All I know is I'm horny."

"I can relate." His hips roll, and as our bodies grind together, I can feel a wet patch between us. Not a huge amount, but enough precum to soak through his sleep shorts. The coldness of it against my thigh sets the rest of me on fire. "Do you know what you want to do?" he asks.

"Come," I say. "I ... I, uh, might be okay with hand-jobs? Maybe?"

He smiles. "You sound so confident about that."

"I'm really, really not."

Parker's hand runs from the top of my shoulder and down my chest. His light fingertips make my skin break out in goose bumps. "We don't have to do anything you're not comfortable with."

"That's the thing though. How do I know what I'm comfortable with and what I'm not? I do know I want to kiss you, and I want to come."

He blinks at me. And then blinks at me some more, and I get self-conscious.

"Is … is that not how this works? Like did I just use some gay code word for wanting to be hog-tied and fucked or something?"

He snaps out of whatever he was stuck on and lets out a small laugh. "That works good for me. Perfect even. But when you said those words, I had a weird flashback to high school and how I never thought someone like you could ever say something like that to me. I almost want to invent a time machine so I can go back and high-five myself. I'm working through my shock, that's all."

I can breathe again. "Okay, good to know."

"Don't you know all the queer lingo from your brother and best friend?"

Uhhh, if there was ever a topic to make my dick deflate, that would be it. "Not really. It's something we don't talk about."

His lips flatten. "Can I ask why?"

"I don't know. No, wait, I do know. Because I thought not talking about it would be more comfortable for me. With East, I was worried about his career, so he didn't care to hear what I had to say about it, and with Knox, he never really came out to me. There wasn't this moment where he said he was into dudes. He used to bring guys back to our place when we roomed together in college, but it was like an unspoken rule that we didn't talk about it. I didn't want to pry, and he wasn't open about it. I recently found out it's because he thought I'd assume he had a thing for my little brother—which he did—and he didn't want to ruin our friendship that way."

"Okay, I'm starting to understand more about why you've been completely oblivious that you might not be entirely straight."

Not entirely straight … Is that a label I could consider for myself? It certainly fits with how I'm currently feeling.

"What do you mean?"

"Statistically, if there's one queer sibling, there's usually more. People think it has to do with queer being genetic or what-the-fuck-ever, but I've always bought into the theory that when you grow up in an environment where you're free to live your true self, you're more likely to explore that side of you and come out—should that side of you exist. With you telling East that being queer will ruin his career and your friend too scared to come out to you, it's no wonder you never thought about it for yourself. You were too busy thinking your best friend was closeted and your brother's future was ruined. Why did you think Easton's career would suffer?"

"Because I know how to read the comment section on Pride night posts," I say flippantly. It's true, but I also know it goes deeper than that. "When all of East's issues with me being too overbearing and protective of him came up, I had thought it came from our parents. They said I always had to look out for him and protect him. I guess … I took that as protecting him from the negative comments and everything that's said online about the guys in that Queer Collective of his. I took it to a whole new level and built it up in my head. It's one of those things where I thought I was doing the right thing but might have gone overboard. It's been hard to take that step back from East, to let him live his life, but I know I need to squash that side of me down."

"I don't think you need to squash it down," Parker says.

"I don't?"

He licks his lips. "Nope. You just need to focus your overprotective possessiveness elsewhere."

Parker pushes up and rolls us so I'm now on my back and he's straddling my waist. While my dick had a small break because of an uncomfortable conversation, the second Parker's presses against mine, it wants back in on the action.

The notion that he's a man and not a woman isn't even a factor as I look up at his face. He was clean-shaven yesterday but now holds a rough stubble. I cup his cheek and run my thumb over it. I'd expect it to feel weird or different, but it's as natural as it would be with anyone else.

He turns his head and kisses the tip of my thumb. "If you want to stop at any time, let me know. You don't have to touch me or do anything you don't want to, but if you did want to, I won't stop you."

"What are you going to do?" I ask.

"I'm going to give you what you asked for. Kissing and coming."

I want to ask how, but he doesn't let me get it out. He crashes his mouth to mine as he shifts on top of me to slide down a bit.

This time, with his mouth on mine, I can feel everything, get lost in it all, and finally turn off my overthinky brain. I'm able to enjoy every stroke of his tongue, his taste on my lips, and sink into it.

And when he grinds against me? It only adds to the hotness of it.

My hands reflexively grip his ass as he moves, and I meet every rotation of his hips with my own.

Fucking hell, this might break me. It's like he's everywhere. All over me.

The hardness of his cock against mine has me leaking in my boxer briefs, and I suddenly wish they were gone. I want to feel his skin against mine.

Without thinking, I move my hands down to the waistband of my underwear and shove them down roughly.

Parker breaks his mouth away from mine. "*Yes*." He lifts up, discards his shirt, and then lowers his sleep shorts, where he's going commando.

I only get a quick glimpse of his cock, but it looks as desperate as I feel. The large mushroom head is red with a dribble of precum coming from his slit.

Then he's back on me again, and I get that skin on skin.

It's sticky between us, and I can't tell who's leaking more. Me or him.

We go back to how we were, him moving on top of me, me gripping his ass and using his body for leverage as I thrust upward. But this time, his head rests next to mine, cheek to cheek, while he puts his forehead on the pillow.

My brain fuzzes over as the need for release climbs. Higher and higher, I get closer and closer. I don't think I've ever come like this, except maybe when I was a teenager, but if he keeps going, there's no way I'll be able to hold back.

It's so … different. So much more intense.

"Fuck, Connor."

The deep sound of his voice makes me needy for more. Like the reminder of who I'm doing this with heightens everything.

Parker shudders, and I think he's as close as I am. My grip tightens on his ass cheeks, and each time our bodies come together, it gets harder and more frantic.

We're both breathing rapidly, and when he moans, I'm pushed over the edge.

I grit my teeth through my orgasm, the mess spilling between our bodies, and a few thrusts later, Parker joins me.

"Holy shit," he breathes. "Fuck."

He gets sweary when he comes, apparently.

He throws his head back, and the vein in his neck pulses in time with his heartbeat. Parker's still riding out his orgasm when I come down from mine, and I watch as his eyes glass over, like he's spaced out.

He's so goddamn sexy like this, and I had no idea I could even have that opinion about another man.

This is probably where I'm supposed to panic. Where I'll assume that if everyone found out about me, our family, the team, and anyone else in our circle could be ridiculed. I should be worried about that, but I'm not.

The only thing I'm thinking about is how mad I am that I didn't know this about myself sooner.

CHAPTER SEVENTEEN

PARKER

A full night of spooning followed by a mind-numbing orgasm?

Damn, I'm glad I chose to travel with the team. I send a dopey smile toward the ceiling as I catch my breath. Never in a million years could I have guessed that would happen, especially since I always thought Connor was straight. The weird revelation I had about my high school self still hasn't completely left me because how do you wrap your head around having sex with someone you've built up into a dream?

"Shit, I need to shower." Connor glances down at himself.

I follow his stare toward the sight of my cum on his abs. Is this real life?

At this point, I wouldn't be at all surprised to know that I'm actually dead and this is the afterlife I've conjured for myself. Literally no part of this feels real. Especially as Connor climbs out of bed, completely naked, and heads toward the bathroom.

He only gets halfway there before someone knocks on my door. "Mr. Duchene? Are you up?"

Connor whirls on me, eyes wide, as we both place the voice at the same time.

Coach Macklin.

I scramble into my sleep shorts as Connor ducks into the bathroom, and then I go for the door. "Morning."

"Morning." He looks tense. "Team bus is due to head off in five. Were you riding with us?"

Five minutes?

"Sorry, I lost track of time. I'll be right down."

I close the door right as Connor bolts out of the bathroom.

"Holy fuck, what time is it?"

"Ten."

"Fuck. *Fuck*."

I watch in a daze as he pulls up his suit pants, throws his shirt on, and grabs his jacket. When he reaches the door, he's careful to peek outside. The coast must be clear because he tosses me a quick "*see you down there*" and disappears out into the hall.

I'm staring at the place for way too long before I remember I need to pack.

This is the downside of unpacking that I never anticipated because I'm chronically early for everything. I pull on a pair of sweats and a zip-up hoodie, then thoroughly brush my teeth and throw everything into my bag.

I'm halfway out the door when something catches my eyes. Tangled in the sheets. Dark material.

Connor left his boxers behind.

I pick them up by the waistband, and of course, they're Calvin Kleins. I don't think I've ever, *ever* been left a slutty memento, and I'm torn between getting turned on or being grossed out. On the one hand, I bet they smell like him; on the other, there is nothing in this world that could get my face close enough to check.

At the very least, returning them will give me an excuse to talk to him once more.

I hate that I don't have time to shower, and my hair is a fluffy mess, but Connor is going to be worse off than me because all our cum this morning ended up on him. It's probably my imagination, but I swear I can still smell him on my skin.

I shiver as the elevator takes me down, remembering his weight wrapped around me. That heavy thigh between my legs. He might be only beginning to realize his attraction to men, but this is something I've been aware of for a very, very long time. Thick thighs, big hands, the scrape of stubble. I don't know if Connor is coincidentally ticking all of my boxes or if he created those boxes because of my unrequited crush, but I know last night and this morning will never be topped.

There's no point trying.

From now on, every man I ever meet will have to measure up to Connor and will fail.

It's probably time to accept that I'm destined for a very lonely life.

I hand off my luggage to the driver and climb on board the bus, where bored, impatient hockey players are waiting. Some of them have their faces stuck in their phones, but the ones who don't glance my way.

Lots and lots of eyes. Lots and lots of jocks. Being surrounded like this isn't something I've experienced for a long time, and I hate the way it immediately makes me want to shrink in on myself.

Then I catch Easton's eyes, and he smiles. "Mr. Duchene. Slumming it with us, huh?"

"Seemed economical."

Munter turns my way. "But aren't you a billionaire? Shouldn't you have people driving you around and opening doors for you?"

Flores slaps him on the back of the head. "Inside thoughts."

"That would imply Munter thinks," Easton adds.

The three of them laugh, and I awkwardly hover there, not sure if I should laugh with them or slink away and find a seat.

Coach Macklin saves me with his booming voice. "Anyone seen Kikishkin?"

"Right here." Easton raises his hand.

"Not you. Your brother."

"Since when is he late?" Surprise crosses Easton's pretty face. "Just leave him in New York, Coach. The better Kiki half is all you need."

Macklin glares his way, and I make the mistake of meeting Easton's eyes as he ducks down, like hiding will save him from his coach's wrath.

Easton's gaze narrows slightly. "You wouldn't know where Connor is, would you?"

Alarm bells shout in my mind, and the urge to stutter all over myself rises. I can't give Connor away like that, and I'm reminding myself to play it cool when he continues.

"If you killed him, I'm probably going to have to defend his honor, and that sounds like a lot of work for me."

"Fucking finally!" Macklin shouts.

Connor jogs onto the bus, cheeks flushed and somehow looking hotter than ever.

He's jeered by some of his team, and I quickly find a spare seat before he looks my way. Tisdale is beside me and sleeping, and Connor doesn't even notice me back here as he takes the seat beside his brother.

The whole ride to the airport, all I can see is the back of his head, and I watch it wistfully. What we shared was in the past, and he'll never know what it means for me to finally feel seen. I'm fully aware that guys like me don't get guys like him, so I know what happens from here. He goes on to explore his sexuality, and I get to be content with the knowledge that I helped him get to that point.

I'm one lucky man.

We get to the airport, and I catch up with Macklin as we head inside.

"Sorry about this morning."

"No harm done. You weren't the only one we were waiting on."

I'd apologize for that too, but if he knows it was my fault, he'll know what happened between us, and that isn't something anyone can know. Connor was right. As the team's owner, the imbalance of power is heavily in my favor, even if I don't feel anything close to powerful, ever.

Macklin sighs. "Something's going on with Connor Kikishkin."

"What?"

"Just a hunch. Normally he's one of the dependable guys, but I get the feeling something's off. Even if he does go and do something stupid after a game, he's still normally on time for the bus."

Wow. I think this is the first time ever that *I'm* something stupid. I don't hate it.

"I was also thinking about the night after the benefit. Where he was sick all day and I had to pull him from the lineup."

"It was food poisoning," I say. It definitely wasn't my fault for taunting him into thinking he could lose his job.

"Mm. Maybe. Then there's the fight between the Kiki brothers during preseason."

My heart rate picks up because I can't help but think the only reason Macklin is suspicious is because of me. Me coming back into Connor's life has caused him to have some existential crisis, and it's affecting the game he is paid millions to play. "They seemed close on the bus," I point out, but it's a weak argument.

"Shit. I shouldn't be talking to you about this."

That brings a flicker of annoyance. "Why not?"

"It's not something you need to worry about."

"Considering this is my team, I'd say everything is something I should be worried about."

"Yeah, but gossiping like a preteen doesn't help anyone. He played a great game last night. In the end, that's all that matters."

I'm getting the distinct impression he's trying to put me back in place. That position slightly out of the inner circle where I don't have to worry about the intricate workings of the team. I just have to keep throwing my money at them.

That same crippling feeling of being left out and ostracized by peers claws at my throat. I've experienced it my whole life, and while I know the power I hold here is from a financial advantage, I don't want to be known for only that. "Actually, I care about my players on *and* off the ice. I know Brendan did things one way, but I want to be involved. That means talking through concerns, being part of strategy meetings and—"

"What would you know about strategy?"

He doesn't ask in a mean tone, but I feel inferior anyway. "Not a lot, honestly. Dad taught me what he could, and I know a fan's perspective, but that's the point. I want to learn. I want to know how my team runs. I want to shadow people as they work and know the organization inside and out."

"So do it. No one can stop you."

"I'm also acutely aware that people don't want me around."

Understanding lights up behind his eyes. Macklin stuffs his hands in his jeans pockets. "Want to know what I think?"

After this conversation? I'm scared to. But I force myself to stop being chickenshit and nod.

"I respect you because you're professional and you don't get in my way. You also really care about the team—or at least winning—otherwise, you wouldn't be making it to all the games. Not many owners do that, so it gets you immediate points in my book. But you're young, you're rich, and you're kind of hard to approach."

"I am?" Me? Is he sure he's talking about me? Parker Duchene?

"You intimidate people. Not me, but I don't think anyone does. The others … yeah. You're a hard guy to read."

That's not my impression of myself at all. It's hard to shake the timid guy I was in high school and the closed-off guy I was in college, but I've been working on it. Most of the time, my brain is a rambly mess, and I'm trying to control it when I'm around other human-type people.

"It's hilarious that you think people are scared of me when I'm literally scared of everyone."

"I would never have guessed that."

Really? "I'm five foot nine. I think I'm the shortest man around this team."

He cracks up laughing. "You forget the skates add height. But when you walk in, wearing your suits, with that pissed-off expression on your face, telling people to call you Mr. Duchene … trust me when I say your height doesn't factor in."

None of that would have ever occurred to me. Here I was, trying to be professional and grown-up, and all I've done is terrify my staff.

"How do I fix it?" I ask.

"Loosen up." Macklin runs his eyes over me. "This. This morning. This is good. No suits, you're chatting, and you don't smell like disinfectant." He cuffs me on the shoulder. "Sit next to me on the plane. I'm good at telling people things they don't want to hear. We'll have you a true Colorado boy yet."

I know enough not to point out I literally grew up there. Macklin wants to help. He's also not scared of me. This is a good start.

And sitting next to him on the plane means that I don't have to deal with finding an empty seat and being disappointed when Connor doesn't fill the one beside me.

It'll also take the pressure off him feeling like he needs to.

CHAPTER EIGHTEEN

CONNOR

From the second I sit next to Easton on the bus to when we get on the plane, my brother eyes me. Not in his usual glare or with the air of annoyance our rift has brought between us but with … suspicion.

It could be paranoia, but it could also be that *he knows*. Somehow.

I'm not ashamed of what happened with Parker. I don't have that voice in my head telling me if it got out, it would be the worst thing in the world. Yet, when Easton and Lachie would hook up with men, that was all I could think. I realize this makes me a major hypocrite, but it was because I didn't know then what I know now.

Nothing about what I did with Parker in bed this morning should be shameful. Because it's not. It's natural and no different than being with a woman. Sure, the logistics of it were different, but the outcome was the same.

Actually, if I'm being completely honest with myself, it was more intimate than anything I've ever experienced before. I can't say why because I don't know. Just like I don't know how I got here. It's as if the shackles of responsibility were taken off, and now, I'm the one who's wild and free, and … it makes me take Easton's side in our fight.

If I tell him or anyone else what happened and they responded with warnings of being careful, I'd feel unsupported too. I'm getting better at shutting off those instincts toward him and Lachie, though I'll acknowledge East gets the brunt of it because our lives are more intertwined than with Lachie's. But even though I've seen the light or whatever—a come to Jesus but not so much Jesus, more like dick, moment—there's a part of me that will always worry and want to protect them. Because they're my little brothers. Despite that, I'm hoping my newfound experience of what they've actually been through will give me pause the next time I go to butt in.

"So," Easton says once we're up in the air. "What happened to you last night? You said you were coming out with the team, but you never made an appearance."

I don't want to lie to my brother, but at the same time, it's not like I can tell him I hooked up with the team's owner, who's a man and technically someone who could ruin me if he wanted to. Especially can't say any of that in front of the rest of the team.

"Wait until I couldn't escape to bring it up?" I sit up and look around exaggeratedly. "Think they have parachutes on this thing?"

"Just saying, you didn't show up for team celebrations, arrived late to the bus, and you smell like cum. Either you hooked up early last night or didn't shower after jerking off for the first time in like a year. At least, that's the only reason I can think of why the stench would be that strong. Keeping it inside that long isn't healthy, bro." East is so casual in his delivery, and he's not even looking at me while he says it. His head is in his phone.

My lips part, and I go to say something—anything—but all that comes out is a noise that is in no way, shape, or form a word.

Easton breaks his gaze from his phone finally and pierces me with his gray eyes, which are a lighter shade than my own.

I still don't have the right words, so I settle for any words. "It was a hookup, and she didn't mean anything."

"Sounds like a lie, but okay." He goes back to his phone.

I'm starting more and more to understand my brothers. Because I want to tell East what happened. Hell, I wouldn't mind getting his or Knox's opinion or thoughts on it. On why I'm so confused when the answer is obviously simple: I repressed every single aspect about myself for the sake of everyone else, and now, I'm discovering things that I never questioned before.

And now I'm in this place where I realize I'm not straight, that I'm probably bi like Knox, but that makes me question why I was never attracted to Knox or why, when my brothers came out to me, it didn't even cross my mind?

Why was it this one nerdy boy from my past that seemed to flip that switch?

I think back to that day in high school when I saw Parker and Easton talking. Possibly even flirting. I've always maintained that I stepped in because I didn't like the way Parker was interacting with East. East had a future, one he shouldn't screw up. But looking back now, is it possible that something, somewhere buried deep down, when my subconscious said "mine," it was not, in fact, talking about East?

Could something inside me have put a claim on a person without even interacting?

The way Parker smiled that day flashes across my memory and tugs something deep in my gut.

I have to tell myself to stop trying to figure it out because it's not going to be as easy as saying, "Oh, I rubbed up against another dick this morning until I came, so obviously, I'm queer. Where are my rainbow pom-poms?"

Or maybe it is that easy? I don't fucking know.

What I do know is if I was going through this as an adolescent and I had someone older than me telling me to squash it down, don't draw attention, and think about the type of future and career I want? Yeah, I would be in prison for murder. So how East only snapped this year is beyond me.

Who knew Easton had the patience of a saint?

And like every other life lesson being shoved in my face of late, they all lead to one conclusion.

I turn to my brother. "I know that things are still patchy between us and that I've probably been mopier about it than I should be, but I need you to know that I am deeply sorry for everything I've put you through since you came out. I thought I was being supportive, but I wasn't."

He hits the Off button on his phone to put the screen to sleep and turns to me. "Okay, what happened last night?"

I put my finger to my lip and glance around the plane again. Everyone has their heads in their own business, and the engines are loud, but … "Not here."

"Then where?" he asks. "Us going into the bathroom together is going to look incredibly incestuous."

"Is Knox home?"

"Flew out this morning for a game tonight."

Fuck.

"But by the time we get home, we should be able to video call. We have a date set up before his game, but … I get the feeling this is more important than sex."

I screw up my face. "I still don't need to know any of what you two get up to in the bedroom, thanks. So long as he's answering that video call fully clothed, I'm there."

"Of course he will. We're not animals."

Yet, I don't miss the way he picks his phone back up and frantically types out a text to Knox.

-

A few hours later, Easton and I are on my couch, side by side, with my laptop open on my lap. We're in my giant, empty house—though at least it's furnished now—and on a video link with Knox, who's in his hotel room.

I'm proud of my best friend for chasing his dream of reffing in the NHL, but it also sucks that he's not around as much anymore. That was going to happen either way, but with him and Easton being together, even when he is back in Denver, I don't have him the same way I used to.

I'm not going to be selfish when it comes to Knox though. If Knox is Easton's happiness, they deserve to have as much time together as possible to make up for the years of bullshit I put East through.

"Sooooo," Knox says. "Should I be worried that both my Kikis want to speak to me? At the same time? You haven't killed each other, so there's one of my concerns gone, but I have about a billion more. Which one of you is being traded, who hit who, or which one of you was swapped with me at birth and I've actually been having sex with my biological brother all this time?"

Both Easton and I screw up our faces.

"What is wrong with you, dude?" I ask.

"I don't like to agree with Connor, but I do on this one," East says.

"Stop keeping me in suspense," Knox whines.

"So … I hooked up last night."

"That isn't anything new." Knox lowers his voice. "I'm missing out on seeing Easton naked for this."

"It, uh, wasn't with a woman." I so desperately want to say who it was with, but that bombshell can come later.

"I knew it!" East shouts.

"You did?" Knox asks him.

"With how much he smelled like cum this morning, I wouldn't be surprised if he says his first foray into the gay world was with a bukkake celebration."

Do I want to know what the fuck that is?

East turns to me. "Wait, this was your first time, wasn't it? Because if you've been hooking up this whole time while ridiculing me for—"

"Yes. First and only. And surprising. Because I had … I didn't …" I take a deep breath.

East puts his hand on my shoulder and grips tight. "It's okay."

"No, it's not. It's messed up, and it has the potential to ruin—"

His grip tightens to the point of pain. "If you go into all that bullshit again that you spouted at me, just look at what coming out has done for me. I am—"

"I didn't mean it like that this time, but that's one of my issues. I'm realizing that I might not be the most … empathetic? Sympathetic? I dunno, the one where I can't relate because I've never been through it, and now that I have all this confusion and I'm unsure where this attraction came from, I can see how one-track-minded I've been. It's always been about hockey for me, and so I pushed that onto you and Lachie. And now …"

My best friend hasn't said anything, and when I force my gaze back to the screen, his lips are pursed.

"What?" I ask. "What are you thinking?"

"Why do you think hooking up with a man is messed up?"

I run my hand over my hair. "It's not the man part that's messed up. It's who it was."

I can see by the image on the screen that next to me, Easton's face has dropped. "Ohhhhh fuck."

"What?" Knox asks. "Who was it?"

"You and Parker were both late for the bus today," Easton says.

"You slept with your team's owner?" Knox screeches.

"No! Well, yes, but not in a problematic way. I've never deep down seen him as an authority figure or someone who can ruin me, even though he wanted to. I've always seen him as that guy in high school. The one who didn't deserve to be treated like dirt—"

"We never treated him like dirt," Easton says, waving a finger between him and Knox on the screen.

"It's messed up because he sees me as the guy who made his life hell in high school, and now … now we're …" Kissing and snuggling with morning orgasms. Remembering that should feel so … so … right. "I don't know what I'm doing."

"You need gay sex tips?" Easton asks.

I hold up my hand. "Nope. Not from you. I mean, in general. With life. Am I really bi, or am I having a quarter-life crisis? Is Parker doing this to mess with me more, or is it real? Do I love playing hockey, or is that all a lie I've told myself for years too? Every time I find out something new about myself, it makes me question everything else."

Both Easton and Knox look sympathetic as they smile. But they're both smiling.

Easton pats my back. "Welcome to the queer space. I'll need to make your membership card, but don't worry, it'll say, 'We're all overthinkers here.'"

That's … somewhat reassuring, I guess.

CHAPTER NINETEEN

PARKER

Hooking up with Connor should cover my urges for a good two to four business *months*, but somehow, I want sex more than ever. Usually I'm too busy with my face stuck in a screen, working long hours, to give sex much thought, but sex with Connor is quickly overriding everything else.

Sex with him is also very much only in my head at this point, and I'm getting to the arena late because I'd lain in bed, jerking off and thinking about our one brief hookup. Real life is so much better than fantasies, and those memories will keep me company for a very long time. It's not only the sex that has him constantly popping up in my mind, but I'm trying not to think about the other stuff. About his identity crisis, and the cuddling, and how he's quickly becoming more of a real person than the high school fantasy I had of him.

I like the real person.

Which is where I'll get myself into trouble if I don't get my head screwed on right. I'm the team owner. He's a player. Even if that wasn't wildly inappropriate, I need to give him space to work out who this new side of him is.

Yes. *I'm* giving *him* space. That's what I'll continue to tell myself so when he's nothing but professional and detached, I'll know it's because it's what I want.

He can end up with any person on the planet after all, but he'll never take my memories from me.

I climb out of my car, feeling ridiculous dressed in Air Jordans, Nike sweats, and a matching hoodie. It's like what a lot of people I used to work with wore into the office, but I'd always preferred suits. They were like my armor.

This also may or may not be the same outfit I saw Macklin wear the other week, so if we can ignore how they're glaringly brand-new, at least it should help me blend in.

With the jocks.

Keg stand. Fist pump. Gatorade.

I blow a dejected raspberry as I cross the underground parking lot and step into the elevator. It was a toss-up between coming here and maybe finally going and looking at pets, but I thought it was better to get this over with before I chickened out.

I have no idea if Macklin and the team are at the practice facility today or here at the arena where our headquarters are, but I will find someone around, and I will be the relaxed, easygoing team owner.

My talk with Macklin on the plane gave me a lot to think about, and I'm feeling a lot more comfortable around him now—hopefully, he feels the same. In a choice between approaching him or the GM Galecki, I'll choose him any day. Galecki scares me. He hasn't done anything but be professional and shake my hand so hard my fingers almost broke, but that was terrifying enough.

I'm walking down the corridor, trying to come up with a way to not sound like the uptight asshole I apparently am, when voices come from one of the meeting rooms up ahead.

It's Macklin and some of the team, and when I'm about to step inside, I spot Connor and duck right back out again.

"Mr. Duchene?" Macklin stops me.

Shit.

I force a smile onto my face instead of aiming for professional and step right back in again. "Morning," I say, pointedly not looking Connor's way. I don't want to have to see his gorgeous face, and I definitely don't want him to be plotting how to avoid me. I will play things totally cool and let him know I'm totally cool and everything is very, very cool between us.

By making it clear there's no us at all.

"We were talking Dallas and Walter's weakness on his left side."

It takes me a second to place Thompson Walter as their goalie. "Hasn't he had three shutouts in a row?"

Munter thumps his forehead with his palm. "They're gonna kill us."

"With that attitude, they will." Macklin turns to me. "The odds of him getting a fourth are as good as zero. Dallas is having a good year, but I'm done with those cocky sons of bitches and their showboating."

"We'll show them what a real team looks like," Connor adds, and I very nearly look at him but catch myself before I can give in to the urge.

"And so you know," Macklin says, approaching me and speaking low, "before games, we motivate. We don't point out how well the other team is doing."

My cheeks burn at such a stupid error. It had been an observation, but I really should have stopped and thought first. Hockey players get all up in their heads over everything, and it's counterproductive to psych my team out when the more we win, the more I see myself claiming the Cup in Dad's name.

"My mistake," I say. "But like you said, no chance for more. We're on a streak too. We've got this in the bag." The whole room fills with groans, and my face gets hotter. "What? What did I say?"

Out of everyone, Easton is the one to answer. "Dude-uh-chene. Duchene. Mr. You just jinxed us. It's like you're trying to make sure we lose."

Fucking hell. I should have stuck to my suit and apparently intimidating presence. I don't even know what the fuck this is, but I'm doing it wrong.

"Sorry. I have to head out. Good luck this weekend."

I turn on my heel and leave, wanting to stuff my fist in my mouth and make sure nothing else escapes. Maybe I should pay some worldly, social extrovert to follow me around, and then I can pass them a slip of paper with what I want to say, and they can make it sound good.

It wouldn't be at all weird. At least, not for a tech billionaire. We're known to be eccentric.

I really should have gone pet shopping.

I'm about to turn into the next corridor when heavy footsteps sound behind me, and someone grabs my arm.

"What are you—oh."

It's Connor, and with how determined I was to avoid looking at him, having him right beside me, grinning like that overconfident jock that he is, is like a blast of cool air. His gray eyes are soft, and his hair is still slightly damp, but I have no idea if it's sweat or from the showers.

"You ran out of there fast."

"I was afraid if I opened my mouth again, whatever I said next would somehow exhume Lord Stanley."

He laughs, and it doesn't sound mocking. "You're giving yourself a lot of credit there."

"I'm only going off your reactions."

"We're hockey players. We're superstitious. You should know this."

"I didn't think mentioning very reasonable odds would set you all off though."

He throws a look back down the corridor, sees we're still alone, and leans casually against the wall beside me. "I don't need to get a skate in until later. Did you want to hang out?"

It takes me a second to realize that, no, he actually said that. It wasn't my imagination. "Hang out?"

"Unless you have work to do."

"No work. But … why?"

"Why not?"

That didn't answer my question, and I'm still confused. It's my turn to look around. "It's okay, you know."

"What is?"

"You don't have to be all nice and friendly because we had se—"

He slaps his hand over my mouth, the other holding the back of my head as he checks the coast is clear. Again. He's almost laughing when he pulls away. "Keep your voice down."

"Sorry." Between our dynamic and him being closeted, I should have known better. "All I'm saying is, it's okay for us to go back to being …" Not enemies, but … "Professional."

"When were we ever professional?"

I crack a smile. "That's true. But it's not too late to start."

"I'd rather stick to being friends, if that's okay with you?"

For the first time since he said that, I think he might actually be serious. "R-really?"

"*Yes.*"

"Why?"

He plants both hands on my shoulders and ducks his head to meet my eyes. "Parker Duchene, I actually think you're really fucking cool."

I glance over my shoulder to see if there's someone standing directly behind me who also happens to be called Parker Duchene.

Connor shakes me. "Stop that."

I shake off my stupor. "Sorry, I'm trying to figure out what alternate dimension I stepped into."

"While you're doing that, what are *we* going to do for a few hours?"

"I don't know about you, but I was planning to go to the animal shelter."

"Really?"

I don't want to go into the whole loneliness, big place, blah blah blah, so I give the simple answer. "I've been thinking about getting a pet for a while, and I found a place that homes a huge range of animals. Everything from cats and dogs to snakes and lizards."

"If you tell me you want a snake, I'm going to think I don't know you at all."

"I'm not sure what I want yet." I know what I *don't* want, and snakes are firmly on that list. Trying to cuddle with one of them at night would prove difficult.

"Let's do it," Connor says.

"You're going to come with me?"

"Of course. I'd love to get a dog, but with how much I travel, it's not on the cards. Oh!" His eyes are bright when he turns to me. "Maybe you can get a dog, and I'll watch him when I'm home. We can co-parent."

He rambles about dogs on our way out of the arena, and I watch him with wide eyes, wondering who the hell this man is.

And not having the heart to tell him dogs aren't for me.

-

"Hi," a sunny man named Sam says as we walk into the animal shelter. He looks to be in his early twenties and has an overly animated face.

"Hey, I called earlier about adopting an animal."

"I remember you! Of course, I'll get Cherry up here to watch the desk, and I'll take you through."

A surly teen who does *not* look like a Cherry takes his place, and Sam leads us through some swinging doors and down a corridor.

"We pride ourselves on not turning a single creature away. We've got the teeny fur creatures and the edgy amphibians and all the usual suspects. It kills me that people can so easily say goodbye to these sweet souls, but that's why I do what I do."

"I've never had a pet before," I confess.

"Oh, you'll love it. Bit of work, but they bring a place alive, I think. Do you know what you're after?"

We reach a room lined with glass cages set into the walls and small animals inside some of the boxes. "No clue."

"A dog," Connor says.

"Not a dog," I quickly say. "Unless it has no fur, doesn't slobber everywhere, and won't run into things."

Sam smiles. "Why don't you tell me what you do want?"

"It needs to be clean," I say immediately. "Probably small enough that it can travel with me. A smart animal that won't ruin my things is nonnegotiable, and …" I'm dying inside as I say the next part. "Something affectionate."

I can feel Connor watching me, but Sam's eyes soften. "Cuddly one, are you?"

My whole face is burning. "Do you have anything like that?"

Sam sets his hands on his hips and looks around the room. "Cute little pygmy goat out back might be a bit big to travel with. Doubt they'd take them in cargo."

"It won't be going in cargo. It will be traveling with me."

"That could work." He looks hopeful, and I hate having to bring him down.

"Don't goats chew things?"

"Not all goats." He shrugs. "But this one's a bit of an asshole. A hamster is cuddly. Kinda smart."

"Can they be toilet-trained?"

"Yes …" He runs his eyes over the walls. "We don't have any young ones though, so it might be a bit more of a challenge."

Well, this is going downhill fast. "Do you have anything that *is* toilet-trained?"

"Cats and dogs. Oh, and—hmm, maybe not."

"What?"

"Well …" Sam wanders over to one of the walls and points at a cage. "We've had this guy for six months now. Hasn't been much interest in him."

I approach and lean in to look at … "Is that a rat?"

"Yup." Sam crouches down and quickly unlocks the cage to pull the little creature out. "Super fucking smart. This one came to us already toilet-trained, very curious, and was clearly handled since he was a pup because he's very, very cuddly."

"There is no way in hell," Connor says from beside me, but then the little thing pokes up its head and turns its pink eyes on me. It's got a long face and a cute little nose that twitches in my direction.

I crouch down too. "Aren't rats dirty?"

Sam puts the rat on his shoulder, where it immediately tucks its head into his collar. "Common misconception. They're about as clean as an animal gets. Look after themselves like cats do. Like I said, this one is litter-trained, and he's very smart. On some quiet days, I come out and make a little course for him."

A rat had never crossed my mind, but there's a reason they're used in research. Rats *are* smart. This one is clearly affectionate, it's small, and if he's litter-trained …

"Can I hold him?"

Sam plucks the small animal off his shoulder and hands him over. I cradle him in my hands, not sure if I'm holding him right, and he pushes up onto his back legs, nose twitching again toward my face.

It's actually … kinda cute.

"You can't be considering this," Connor says, sounding close to laughter.

Sam shoots him a look. "I think guys who own rats are hot."

I glance up, meeting Sam's eyes, unsure if he's actually flirting with me. His steady smile confirms that, yes, that's exactly what he's doing. Even if it's only so I'll get the rat, I can't wrap my head around him doing that when

Connor—basically the hottest man alive—is standing *right* there.

A loud thump breaks our eye contact, and I glance up to find Connor's large hand on the empty glass cage above my head.

"You're going to get Florida's mascot?"

"I ..." I look down at the creature still watching me. "I think I might."

"Fine. If you want a rat, we'll get a rat."

"*We*?" I ask.

"I always wanted to be the parent of a sewer dweller."

Sam strokes the rat's head. "He's never been in the sewers a day in his life. The rate of people owning rats has been rapidly on the rise because they're such easy pets."

"Easy is what I need," I admit.

"What *we* need."

I shoot a confused look Connor's way. "What do they eat?"

"A lot of fruits and vegetables. Grains. That kind of thing," Sam answers. "I can print out an info sheet for you."

"No need. I'm already googling it," Connor says, hurrying to pull out his phone. "We'll need a cage."

"I'll need a cage."

"*Our* baby will need a cage."

I have no clue what Connor's doing, but when I look up again, his jaw is set, and he's gripping his phone hard. "Are you okay?"

"I'm great. We're buying a scabby little mutant baby."

Sam gives him a flat look. "He can hear you."

"He's a rat."

"They're very smart." I pretend to cover his little round ears, and he scrubs his face against my hand. "Aww ..." I melt. That makes my mind up immediately. Look at me, so starved for affection that the slightest hint of it has me buying a rodent.

Connor leans over my shoulder to look at it, trying to stop his face twisting in disgust. "Adorable."

"Isn't he?"

Sam's flirty smile is back. "You both are."

"Right," Connor snaps, tugging me by the arm back to my feet. "Wrap him up. We'll take him."

"Wrap him up?" Sam echoes.

Connor rolls his hand. "Whatever it is you need to do."

"There's paperwork, and we'll organize a cage and some printouts. I'll have to get the rat daddy's details as well."

"You can have mine," Connor cuts in. "I'm buying him."

"Adopting," Sam corrects with an edge to his voice. "And I'll need the details of whoever the animal is living with and registered to."

"That will be me," I say before Connor can cut in again. But there's something about the way he's behaving, how unsettled and off guard he looks, that has warmth forming in my gut.

"He'll be living with us both," Connor corrects. "We're sharing him. Can't wait. I've always wanted a rat to stink up my house and piss in my bed. It's the dream."

It's a struggle not to laugh. "You can try to say it again without clenching your teeth."

Connor's still glaring Sam's way.

"Can you give us a moment?" I ask Sam.

"Sure." He takes the rat, places him on his shoulder, and walks away, the little thing turning back to watch me as he goes.

"It has red eyes," Connor says straight away. "It's a demon."

"But did you see the way it snuggled into me? I love him. I'm getting him."

Connor's face softens. "If that's what you want. I guess I'm getting us a rat."

"Me a rat."

"Never in a million years did I think I'd own a rat."

"Good thing you won't be."

Connor slings an arm around my shoulders and steers me toward the door. It's a real struggle not to swallow my tongue. "What will we call him? Devil? Evil incarnate?"

"How about rata*kiki*?"

"I will end you."

"It has a nice ring to it."

"We're not naming our baby after me."

"*My* baby."

He's being fucking ridiculous.

"And stop being a dick to Sam."

"I'm not being a dick to anyone." He lets me go, and as I walk ahead of him, I catch him muttering, "Sam needs to keep it in his pants."

My gut gets warmer, and thankfully, Connor can't see the way I'm smiling.

I could get used to this friend thing.

CHAPTER TWENTY

CONNOR

"Want me to drop you back at the arena while I take this little guy home?" Parker asks as we get into his car and he places the rat on my lap.

Watching that Sam guy openly flirt with Parker made old Connor resurface. I wanted to put Sam in his place, but the thing is, flirting with Parker is his place. It's his right. I have no claim over him.

My inner possessive caveman doesn't understand that though. "I still have time. I want to see where Master Splinter will be living. I need to make sure it's suitable."

Parker side-eyes me. "One, that's not his name, and two, are you trying to get an invitation to my place?"

I smile and hope it comes across as charming. "No, I'm inviting myself over. There's a difference."

"The difference being my ability to say no?"

"Now you're getting it."

"I could pull rank and take you back to the arena anyway, you know."

That almost feels like rejection, but I pretend it doesn't get to me. "You could. If that's what you really want to do."

"Fine. Call me on my bluff."

Oh, thank God. "Besides. It's too risky making each other come if we're at the arena. People might see. Or hear you."

We almost run up the back of someone at a red light, and Parker has to slam on the brakes. His neck and the tips of his ears turn pink. "I'm not that loud."

"I want to dispute that, but I'm thinking you need to concentrate on the road." The traffic hasn't started moving yet, so I throw in, "And you are loud. And sweary. It's really hot. Experiencing it only once would be a shame."

Parker shifts in his seat as the light goes green ahead. "You shouldn't be talking like that."

"Because we'll crash?"

"No. My poor Conishkin shouldn't be hearing such depraved things. He's only a baby."

I stare down at the rat in his cage, his red, beady eyes glaring at me, and even though I claimed co-parenting ownership with him back at the shelter, now without the threat of Sam hanging over my head, I don't know what to think of the little guy. Other than, "You cannot name him Conishkin."

"Why not? I'm naming him after his other daddy. Apparently. It's your first and last name squished together."

"Yeah, I got that, but no. Uh, I mean, I'm honored. But no, thank you."

"Would you be saying that if I'd gotten a puppy?"

I lift the cage to bring me face-to-face with the rat. He lifts his nose and gives me a good sniff, his cheeks and whiskers twitching. And fine, I might admit he's kinda cute. "When you get a puppy, I give you full permission to name it after me. This baby deserves a name that does him justice."

"What do you suggest?"

"Satan? Demon? Hell's butthole?"

"Conishkin is sounding better and better." Parker pulls into an underground parking lot of an apartment building in Cherry Creek.

"You live in an apartment?" I ask.

"The penthouse. Technically."

"Makes more sense. I guess I pictured you living in a huge mansion with servers and butlers and—"

"All that empty space freaks me out."

If that isn't a twist in my gut. "I understand that. I didn't realize how big my house was until I moved in. I thought if I filled it with furniture, it would feel less ..."

"Lonely?"

I was trying not to say lonely, but that's what it is.

Parker pulls into his double space, parking his Lexus LS right in the middle of both sides.

As much as it kills me to look at him and admit that he's exactly right, as soon as our eyes meet, I see the same emotion reflected back at me. He has it so much worse than me though.

He lost his dad, he has no siblings. All I'm dealing with is a very supportive family and best friend asking for space and to focus on myself instead of them.

"Where's your mom?" I blurt.

"After Dad died, she didn't want to live in their house anymore, and he worked so hard for so many years to support us, they never had a chance to travel, so she's taken my aunt on a round-the-world vacation. As much as I miss her, she deserves this time for her."

"You didn't want to travel with her?"

He blows out a loud breath. "This is a heavy topic to be talking about in a parking garage."

Parker gets out of the car, and I follow because he's not getting away that easily. That, and I have our demon rat baby. Who is most definitely not called Conishkin.

When we get into the elevator, Parker holds out his hands to take the cage off me.

"So, why didn't you go traveling with your mom?"

He slumps but covers it quickly by putting on an over-the-top smile and voice while looking at the rat. "There's my little Conishkin."

"Not his name," I sing.

"Who's my wittle Con-con Kiki?"

I sigh.

"You brought this upon yourself," Parker says. "You're the one who insisted on co-parenting something that you have absolutely no interest in. All because, why? Sam got a tiny bit too flirty with me, perhaps?"

Part of me is surprised Parker is calling me out like that, but the other part of me knows why he's doing it.

"Nice deflection."

The elevator spits us out on the top level, and Parker holds the cage in one arm while unlocking his front door with the other.

As soon as we're inside, I plan to keep at him about the mom thing, but the second I cross that threshold and see his amazing apartment, I lose all my words.

The hardwood floors, slate fireplace, modern furniture, and expansive balcony make me a jealous, jealous man.

He has a dark blue U-shaped couch, which is the only pop of color in an otherwise gray and wood aesthetic. I'm only in the entryway, and it already feels like more of a home than my giant mansion that I regret buying more and more every day.

"Can we swap houses?" I ask.

"After you told me how empty yours feels? No, thank you."

"Damn. Worth a try."

"Let's find you a place to live," Parker says to Conish— nope. Not his name. The rat. "Do you not love our baby at all?"

"Of course I love him." And I can say that without squirming now. Yay. Maybe in a year, I'll be game enough to hold him too.

"What I can't understand," Parker says as he puts the cage on a side table next to his couch, "is if you don't even like rats, why are you insisting that he's ours and not mine?" He cocks his eyebrow at me.

"Why are you here, watching over the team, when you could be across the world having fun with your mom?"

He huffs. "Would you want to go on an around-the-world trip with your mom for months on end?"

Well, when he puts it that way … no. "Maybe not for the whole time, but for part of it, yes. Have you even been overseas? You have all this money, and as much as I love this apartment, it's an apartment, and you could do anything in the world. I understand buying the team to honor your dad, but do you actually want to be a part of it?"

"Okay, it's time for Conishkin to have some outside time." He unlatches the cage and puts his hand out for the rat to climb on. He does immediately and runs up Parker's arm and sits on his shoulder.

I step closer to him. "Park—"

"I'm around the team so much because it reminds me of my father, and it might sound silly to someone like you, but when I'm watching the team practice or play, I feel closer to him. Every time the Zamboni comes out to resurface the ice, I expect to see my dad sitting in it, for him to give me a wave. It's hard when I realize that will never happen again, but being in the hockey world … it brings him back to me. So, no, I didn't go on Mom's vacation because where she finds the memories heartbreaking, they bring me comfort."

Now, don't I feel like a complete ass?

"Shit, I'm sorry." I step forward to hug him. "That makes total sense, and I didn't think about it that way."

As soon as our bodies collide and I lower my head to bury into his neck, rat me holds up his little … paw? hand? Whatever it's called, as if to push me away.

"Okay, maybe his name really is Conishkin. He's already showing possessive tendencies over his daddy." I meet Parker's gaze. "Because you're right. With that Sam guy, I …" I grit my teeth. "I thought he was hitting on you, and I couldn't help myself. I might not know a lot about who I am deep down, but I do know that once I see something as mine, it's as if this possessive demon comes out. I don't think I like it, if I'm honest. It's toxic, and—"

This time, Parker closes the distance, and little Conishkin lets us embrace. Parker's arms wrap around my back, and he glances up at me with his big blue eyes. "It *can* be toxic."

I go to say I want to change that part of me, but it's not going to be easy, when he cuts me off.

"But it can also be really hot under the right circumstances."

I frown. "Right circumstances?"

"Like when you're trying to claim your territory when another man tries to hit on it … wait, that's mixing analogies."

I chuckle. "You think you're my territory, huh?"

"You said it, not me."

I play back exactly what I've said to give him that impression, and— "Oh fuck."

"Mmhmm. You said, and I quote, 'Once I see something as mine.'"

"I didn't mean it that way," I say quickly.

Parker's grip around my waist loosens but doesn't drop. "No?"

What am I supposed to say here? Yes, I do have that voice in the back of my head saying he's mine, and I want to spend every moment together, and I want to see where this can go, but it's a bit soon to be getting all claimy.

Right?

But the more I stare into those blue eyes, the more I realize … it's got nothing to do with timing. It's how I feel.

"Okay, fine. Yes, I did. But—"

He cuts me off with his lips on mine, his tongue pushing into my mouth, and with the silent promise that nothing is going to stop this.

Until the very possessive and squeaky rat decides he hates seeing his daddies kiss and bites me on the shoulder.

I pull back. "Ouch. Motherfucker."

"What? What happened?" Parker asks, his eyes hooded in lust. It's a good look on him, and when my body responds to him now, it's not as weird or confusing as the last time.

"I'm not the only one with possessive issues." I rub my shoulder. "He might be small, but damn, his bite is hard."

"He didn't …" Parker says, sounding exactly like one of those parents who can't believe when their child does something naughty.

"Oh, he did." I take my shirt off and show off the mark. And yes, I am tattling on a rat. It's not bleeding, but there're two little teeth marks in my skin.

"Sam said he was affectionate." Parker takes Conishkin off his shoulder and places him in his hands. The emotionally manipulative jerkwad looks up at Parker with such innocence even I'd believe he didn't do it if I didn't have a throbbing shoulder.

"He is. To you. It's like he's chosen you. One look and bam, he fell, hook, line, and sinker."

"Sam did say rats are intelligent. He could see immediately what others take years to see." Parker flicks me a quick look through his lashes. "Even almost a decade."

He's right. My head was so high in the clouds in high school that being top dog and captain of the hockey team was all I cared about. It made me selfish, and now, I'm paying the price.

Because all this time, I could've had Parker in my life. If I hadn't cared about image and making it to the NHL, we could've had this back then, maybe.

I have a lot of regrets, but not getting to know Parker Duchene sooner might be my biggest.

I force a smile. "Okay, I'll give him that one. He's a much better judge of character than I am."

"Damn straight, he is. But it's time for him to have a nap." He puts Conishkin back in his cage and turns to me with fire in his eyes. "Should I give you a tour of the apartment?"

"Only if it ends in your bedroom."

"Done." He takes me by the hand, and any tour is canceled because he drags me down the hall, right into the master suite.

CHAPTER TWENTY-ONE

PARKER

Connor goes for my mouth as soon as we reach my bedroom, and I have to duck out of the way before he's successful. If he gets his mouth on mine, I'll forget everything. Including washing my hands.

"One moment."

He gapes at me as I duck into my bathroom. There's no wall between the bedroom and here, so I can see the exact way he watches me as I flick on the water and scrub animal from my hands. Conishkin might be considered clean, but he's still an animal, and there's no way I'm going to be able to do what I want to do with rat germies on my fingers.

Connor drops to sit on the edge of my bed. "This is a cool setup. Think after getting each other off, you can take a shower, and I'll lie in bed and watch?"

That tickle of nerves gets me again. I can't imagine how life would be to go through it with the confidence Connor has. Even though my sexuality has never been a secret to me, I still had a minor freak-out in the first break during college when I finally downloaded an app and acted on it.

I came out to my parents, and it was a minor shock to them, but they recovered quickly. I never once doubted that they loved and supported me. Yet, it *still* took me a lot of emotional labor to get to the point where I'm comfortable in my own skin.

Then here's Connor, always assumed he was straight, in an industry known for its toxic masculinity, and he's … taking off his shirt.

Oh my.

There're those abs again.

I dry my hands, turning to watch while I grip the basin behind me. He knows exactly what he's doing, and when his eyes hook mine, he lifts his hand and beckons me closer with two fingers.

There's no hesitation over a round two for me, and he seems completely into this, but I need to make sure. Maybe, if this happens again—and I'm trying not to get excited that it seemed to be what he was hinting at—I'd be able to believe it's actually happening. If I was confident about this whole situation, I'd already be kneeling between his thighs.

Connor casually reaches forward and pops his button.

I swallow thickly. "Umm … what are you okay with?"

"You moving closer would be a start."

I catch a laugh and finally push away from the basin. My dick is already getting hard, and even trapped in my briefs, I know Connor would be able to see it. These sweats don't do much to hide anything.

My pulse is drumming faster as I step back into my bedroom and approach him.

"That's better." His voice is comforting. Soothing.

When I'm close enough, he reaches for my hand and tugs me in. His hands rest on my hips as I stand in the place I'd hoped I'd end up.

"What are *you* comfortable with?" he asks.

He treats me like I'm breakable, but when it comes to gay sex, I have more experience than him at this. "I was once spit-roasted by random guys I met on an app. I think I can handle just about anything."

Pure shock crosses his face. "You … I'm sorry. What?"

My lips pull at a smile. Then I sink to my knees. "I want to suck your cock."

"Parker …" Connor groans. "Stop this."

"Stop what?"

"Stop confusing all my opinions of you. It's too …"

"Confusing?" I smirk.

"*Hot*."

I curl my fingers into his waistband and slowly pull his pants and briefs down. He lifts his hips to help me, and his dick springs out, hard, ready, tip swollen and red. My mouth waters at the sight. "I can act all innocent if you like?"

He quickly shakes his head. "Nah. Virgins aren't my kink. This is …" I swipe my tongue over his tip, and he chokes on his words. "Just keep going. Damn. You've got such a sweet face I want to see it deep-throat me."

Green light on the blowjob, then. I'm not going to make it easy on him, not when this is something I've hated wanting for so long. I used to hate touching myself to the thought of him. Used to beat myself up for not having an ounce of self-respect.

As I lick a stripe up the underside of his shaft and Connor lets out the most deliciously shaky exhale, I come to a very rational conclusion: self-respect is overrated.

If he wants to go all caveman over the first man he's ever been with, so be it. If he needs to explore this side of himself with me, he can go off.

At the end of the day, I get sex with my dream man, and that's a perfectly fucking fair trade-off to me.

I bury my nose in the crease between his thigh and his balls. His scent, sucking his balls into my mouth, running my cheek over his shaft … it gets me so horny I can't concentrate on anything but him.

The more of his skin that I feel, the more I want.

I wrap my lips around his tip and suck gently while I run my tongue over the smooth round head. He's a decent size, perfectly in proportion with the rest of him, and not obscenely big that if I ever end up bottoming for him, it won't be as uncomfortable as a colonoscopy. It's still a good stretch for my jaw though, and it's been too long since I enjoyed feeling this way. Since I let myself enjoy having a cock in my mouth. Since I teased and took my time. No hurry to get him ready and get us both off.

My entire focus is on making Connor feel good, for as long as possible, and I'm hopeful I'll get the same.

Maybe not a blowjob. I'm kidding myself to assume his confidence makes him an expert and ready to jump in on it all, but if I get to rub up against him again, I'll sleep happily tonight.

"More," he begs, setting a possessive hand on my head.

A sharp thrill races to my cock, and I give him what he needs. I sink down his shaft, slowly taking him all the way into the back of my throat, and he moans as I hold him there for so long I'm threatening my oxygen supply. I pull back when it gets too much and then finally give in to the urge to get him off.

I bob up and down, hand cradling his balls, sucking and licking so much that saliva dribbles out of the corner of my mouth. Instead of gripping my own needy cock, I run my hand over his meaty thigh, getting harder over the feel of the soft hairs under my hands.

He rocks into my mouth, cock nudging deeper, fingers twisting in my hair to grip tighter. The harsh breaths, small hums, and every other noise that falls from his lips torture my trapped dick, but I still refuse to touch. To give in.

"Take … take this off …" He roughly tugs at the collar of my jacket, and I quickly unzip the front and shove it off my arms. Then he pulls from my mouth and hauls me to my feet.

"What are you—"

Connor shoves my shirt up and tugs my sweats and briefs down so fast my dick flings out and hits my lower stomach. "Get on the bed."

I'm not about to question whatever he has in mind, so I kick everything off, then lie back, and Connor climbs over the top of me, straddling my waist. His balls rest over my cock as he jerks off fast. He looks close, breathing sharp and shallow, eyes raking over my less-than-impressive torso.

"Touch your nipples," he grits out. "You have such pretty nipples."

I reach up to flick my thumb over one, and Connor's thighs clench.

A second later, his hand stops moving, and he aims his cock at my midsection, emptying his cum onto my skin.

He takes a deep, steadying breath, then leans forward, lips by my ear, and rasps, "It's your turn to smell like us."

Then his hand closes over my dick.

The sudden contact has my eyes rolling back. His palm rolls over my leaking tip and smears precum down my cock, and I'm way too sensitive to take this. I'm glad our first time together proved I can last an acceptable length of time because he's barely touched me, and I'm scared I'm going to burst.

One of the things I've always noticed about Connor is his big hands. Unlike him, my dick, thankfully, isn't in proportion with the rest of me, and I'm a good size, but his hand makes me feel small. Swamped by his warmth. Completely surrounded by the rough skin and firm grip, and *fuck*. How is anyone supposed to survive this? Let alone me, who's been picturing this happening against all my better judgment for years and years and—

"Listen to you," he teases.

Shit. I hadn't even noticed the grunts leaving me as I thrust into his hold.

"No, no, don't stop." He kisses the hinge of my jaw, forearm holding his weight and resting above my head. "I want to hear you."

His words almost make me sob. I'm a self-conscious overthinker, with possibly the sexiest man alive hovering over me. I know I said I was experienced, but maybe I'm not so experienced with *this*. Sex where it actually means more than an orgasm. Sex with someone I've ached to have respect me. See me. Decide I'm worthy of him.

"That's it ..." he encourages, and once again, the sounds I'm making are completely unintentional. But I force myself not to clam up. I try to switch off that *shut up* cell in my brain and remind myself that I deserve to enjoy this. Whether Connor's wanting something regular or casual or maybe just this once more, I'm going to get everything I can out of it while I can.

"I'm so close," I tell him. "Keep doing exactly that." He squeezes tighter on the upstroke, and I'm panting hard. Desperately ready.

His lips slip from my jaw, down my throat, lightly sucking the spot right above my collar bone. I'm painfully hard, almost delirious with need.

And just as I think I can't take it anymore, my orgasm crashes into me. My balls throb with every wave of bliss that takes over, and Connor keeps stroking me through the high.

My limbs go slack. My harsh breathing breaks through my consciousness, and then Connor presses a kiss to my temple.

"I've decided I love watching you come."

My lazy smile takes over, and words slip out before I can question them. "Feel free to make it happen as often as you like."

"Is that an open offer?"

I hum my agreement, still not entirely checked in to what I'm saying.

Connor's fingers skim my stomach, rubbing our releases into my skin with soothing circles. "I think I've changed my mind about that shower."

It takes me a second to remember what he's talking about. "You don't want me to have one?"

"Nope. What I *really* want is to take you somewhere. Knowing you smell like me."

"You really are a possessive fucker."

"Yeah, but you said you liked it."

"I did." And I do. I really, really do.

The problem is I think I like it too much. Connor might look at me and think *mine* when he's horny, but we both know it's not reality.

Role-play is fun.

Until it isn't.

And I'm worried I might get too used to it too quickly because even the sticky tightness across my skin isn't enough for me to push the shower thing. I hate being dirty.

But for him, I already can't get enough.

CHAPTER TWENTY-TWO

CONNOR

Dragging myself away from Parker is next to impossible, but you know, hockey responsibilities and all that.

I go for my skate to keep warm for the home game tomorrow night, but as soon as I'm dressed and getting ready to head out, the thought of going home puts a pit of … *blah* in my stomach. It's so big and empty. Maybe if I swing by Parker's place, he'll invite me up. He might still smell like us. Though, my bet is he showered as soon as I left because he seems to be particular when it comes to washing his hands and having good hygiene. If anything were to come of us, that might be an issue, considering how disgusting my pads and gear are after a game. Or a practice. Or, really, just going near it. After years of sweat stench, there's no way you can get the smell out completely, no matter how many times you wash it. The franchise handles all that for us, but still. Hockey players are smelly.

It might be the deal breaker for him. Actually, anything could be a deal breaker for Parker. From seeing me as his high school bully to him being the team's owner and essentially in charge of my career to me being completely inexperienced when it comes to being with a man, I'd say there's no hope of this going anywhere.

I'm mostly okay with that. I think. I've never wanted more than a casual thing with anyone else, but there's no denying that I'm eager to get back to his place.

I can't get that blowjob out of my head. I want to know what it would be like to be in his position. Of course, I'd have no idea what I was doing, but that's not going to hold me back. Jerking him off wasn't any different than touching my own dick, but it's not like I've ever sucked my own cock. I'm not that flexible. I wonder if goalies can do that. I should ask. No, wait, I shouldn't. Not appropriate.

Though that does beg the question, is sucking your own cock considered gay? Jerking off isn't, but is that, like, a line?

Easton taps my shoulder from the cubby beside me, and I jump. "Are you okay? I was saying your name, but you kept staring off into space. What are you thinking about?"

"Blowjobs."

My brother looks at me as if I've grown two heads and then glances around the locker room.

Oh, right. In public and things.

My head's not on right because of Parker. All I can think about is Parker. All I want to think about is Parker. When he said I should focus all my possessive energy somewhere else, I don't think this is what he meant.

"From women," I add louder. I dunno. Am I supposed to want to hide what I've been doing? Old Connor would be screaming yes. Fuck knows I gave Easton and Lachie enough shit about it.

"I'm worried about you," Easton says.

"Hello, role reversal."

"Right? I don't like it. Stop making me care, damn you."

I shake it off. "I'm fine. Just still … thinking about stuff."

Easton leans against the edge of his cubby. "You know, Lachie's home tomorrow night. It's our first time playing our little brother."

"Is that tomorrow? I've lost track of the games. I just know where to be and when. Haven't really looked at the team's schedules."

"This is my point. You should be lecturing me about playing well but not making a fool out of Lachie either. He's a rookie, and it's two against one, and—"

"Fuck that. He needs to learn, so I say we go as hard as we always do."

Easton's still staring at me weirdly when he blindly takes out his phone and hits a single button. He puts the phone to his ear, and I can hear the faint ringing and then my best friend's voice as he says hello. "Connor's broken. What time will you be home tomorrow?"

"Should be morning. How is he broken?" Knox's voice is muffled but still loud enough for me to hear it.

"I think hooking up with *you know who* has made him … reckless." He lowers his voice. "He's talking about blowjobs and going hard against Lachie tomorrow night. I'm scared my big brother might … actually be cool."

Knox laughs, and I can't help it. So do I. If only I'd asked him the self-blowjob question. It's probably lucky I didn't. He might have collapsed.

"Tomorrow night after the game, all four of us should go out," Knox says. "All my queer Kiki bros together."

And that's what makes old Connor reappear. Pointing out that all three of us Kikishkins aren't straight. Am I queer? Turns out, yes, but I'm not comfortable with that label. I've been trying not to think about it because I know labels aren't necessary, and it's possible to change a lot. But the thing is, I do fit under the LGBTQIA umbrella, and so do my brothers.

I can only think of the bullshit the media will say when both Lachie and I come out.

Oh, look, carefree Connor is gone, and old Connor is back.

That didn't last long.

-

I don't end up going by Parker's place on the way home, and for the entire next day and the game against Lachie, I'm spaced out. I'm letting St. Louis' forwards get by me, allowing way too many chances for them to get shots on goal, and though I'm not the only D-man on that ice, our defense is struggling big time.

Can I claim I'm letting my littlest brother win because it's the first time we're facing each other in the NHL and it's still early enough in the season that taking a loss won't hit us too badly? I'm being a supportive brother! I'm only thinking about Lachie and wishing him all the success in his career. I'm definitely not thinking about how I want to get on my knees and suck my team owner's dick.

For my whole life, hockey and everything that comes with it has been my focus.

Now I have something else, and I can't seem to find that same need to make hockey my priority.

Okay, so it's been one game, and that's overly dramatic. I'm sure it's only because it's new. And because I'm worried about what the fallout might be. But if I learned anything from Easton over the summer, it's that I need to stop caring about what other people think of me or what the media might say. The media that spreads hateful things about queer athletes will never see it from our point of view, so I need to stop thinking we have to cater to those toxic sectors.

Aww, my first thoughts of *we* and *us* when referring to queer people and spaces. I really am embracing this. Go me.

While I'm praising myself on how accepting I am of … myself, Lachie skates around me and scores.

Oops.

"Thanks, big bro." He winks at me.

As tempting as it is to slam him into the boards to keep him in check, I'm too proud of him. He's having a killer rookie season, but it's a pity the rest of his team needs some work.

Yet, they're still able to take out the win against us.

I can't help thinking it's my fault.

"Excited for where we're going tonight?" Easton asks as we're redressing into our game suits to head out.

"Where are we going? I thought it was going to be us and Knox hanging out?"

"Oh, we'll be hanging out all right."

I don't like the way he says that. "You're not taking me to some place where we'll be naked and free-balling everywhere, are you? Because I might be discovering new things about me, but I can already say that would be a no."

Easton clips me on the shoulder. "I do not need to see my two brothers' hanging brain. We're just going to a bar."

Maybe I was reading into his tone earlier.

Except when we meet up with Lachie on our way out, he's wearing a shit-eating grin. "Aww, did my big bwovers get their asses kicked by the littlest Kiki to ever Kiki?"

"We're never going to hear the end of that, you know," Easton says.

"I know. But it wasn't my fault. I was distracted."

"Distracted with what?" Lachie asks.

We reach the players' exit and head out into the private parking lot, where Easton's car is waiting with Knox already in the driver's seat with the engine running.

"Probably the thoughts of blowjobs like he was at practice yesterday," Easton says.

"Blowjobs are amazing," Lachie says. "Giving or receiving."

Easton and I put our gear bags in the trunk and share a look. Lachie doesn't have his gear bag because it would've gone to his team's bus and to their hotel.

Easton nudges me, encouraging me to spill about the newfound side of me that likes men, but I worry that if I do, Lachie's going to complain about needing to stay in the closet longer because of the stupid plan that Mom, Dad, and I worked out. Three straight people—or assuming straight people—making plans for a schedule in which it would be okay to come out. Jesus Christ, what was wrong with me? How did I ever think that was okay?

Fuck it. We're all on our own timelines now.

"About that," I say and turn to Lachie. "I might have been distracted by thinking about giving a blowjob?" My voice squeaks at the end.

Lachie fights breaking out into a laugh. He manages to get himself under control before saying, "Interesting twist."

Easton puts his hand on my shoulder. "Hence where we're going tonight."

Okay, this time, I definitely heard it again. The "I'm about to walk you into a lion's den and love watching every minute" tone.

"Where's that?" Lachie asks.

"Only the campiest gay bar in Denver." Easton is way too excited about this, and as Lachie bounces on his feet, it's obvious he is too.

I swallow hard. Easton's going to push me into the deep end without a life jacket, and Lachie will be there to witness me drown.

Fun.

CHAPTER TWENTY-THREE

PARKER

Hrkp mr. 5her;s too mayn ddues grioopng my jukn

I stare at the message that's come through. I've just climbed into bed after getting home from the game and showering, and I assume, judging by Connor's completely incomprehensible text, that he didn't do the same.

I guess hockey players party hard, whether it's a win or a loss.

I stare at the message harder, trying to work out if it was something he sent on purpose, or if he sat on his phone. If he sat on his phone, it might be awkward to text back, but if he is drunk enough to be sending texts like that, it would make sense to check on him, right? As his team owner. The person who doesn't want his star player found dumped in a ditch tomorrow morning.

In English please?

I jump when, a second later, my phone starts ringing.

"I'm in a gay bar." His voice is borderline slurry, and he's doing that shout-whisper thing that drunk people do.

Warmth floods my cheeks. On the one hand, his voice in my ear is giving me some cozy, intimate vibes; on the other, he's out. At a gay bar. Where men are likely all over him. My teeth bury into my lip, and I remind myself this is good. Normal. He's cutting things off before I get mixed ideas and is taking the chance to explore his sexuality, which is exactly what he should be doing. This is a respectful phone call to let me know. Huge points for him. Very mature.

I can't make my voice believe me when I reply. "How great. For you."

"No, no. No. No, that's not the right idea. I'm here. But I don't want to be here. I need to go, but they kidnapped me."

I jolt upright in bed. "Who kidnapped you?"

"My brothers."

Relief sweeps over me. "How much have you had to drink?"

"Just … this … much …"

"You are aware I can't see you, right?"

"Maybe eleventy. Or twenty. No … Yeah. Twenty."

"Twenty *what*?" Dear God, do I need to confiscate his liver?

The line goes muffled as he talks to someone in the background, and then he's back, voice pitched low but still loud enough I can hear him over the blasting music.

"My jailers have gone to the bar. Quick." He hiccups. "Meet me out front. I'm gonna ditch out like a shadow ninja!"

The line goes dead, and I pull my phone away and stare at it.

I guess I'm getting back out of bed and going in search of my drunk … player. The one thing he is to me. And I'm definitely not moving quickly because I'm happy he's not out hooking up. Nope. That would not be fair of me.

I send him a quick text to send me his location and try not to constantly glance at my phone as I take the elevator down. There's every chance he got distracted in his drunken daze and has already forgotten about our call, but I'm not going to focus on that.

At least, I think I'm not, but I don't miss the breath of relief when his location comes through to me. I get in the car and take off.

My stupid hair is stupid and fluffy, but thankfully, he'll be too drunk to notice. Which leads me to a conundrum. If he's that drunk, I can't take him back to my house, but I also have no clue where he lives.

I guess I'll figure it out once he's in my car. Worst case, I have a spare bed. He can sleep there.

Only when I pull up on the curb out the front of the club, it's not only Connor waiting.

He dives in the front seat, stinking like vodka and looking like a sexy dream. "Quick. Before they notice I'm gone."

Before he can finish getting the sentence out though, my back door opens, and Easton, Knox, and the littlest Kiki all stumble and crawl into the back seat of my Lexus.

Did I mention I drive a *sports* car?

"Why is your car so small?" Lachie slurs, elbowing Easton in the ribs.

I watch in shock and also morbid curiosity as two hockey players and an even bigger ref fold into my back seat and somehow manage to get the door closed behind them. Easton is half on his brother and half on his boyfriend's lap, but they're *in.*

"Ah … seat belts, please?"

It takes Connor four failed attempts before I reach over and save him from himself. One of his giant mitts comes up and roughly strokes my cheek. "Sorry, baby, I might be too drunk to suck your cock tonight."

I don't think my eyes can get any wider as I stare at him … and Connor promptly passes out.

What the fuck have they been doing for the last—it's barely been three hours since the game ended?

"Address?" I call weakly to the other three, but Easton and Knox have their mouths fused together, and Lachie is looking at something on his phone.

Fuck me.

I guess it's back to my place, then.

-

I'm still tired when I wake up. By the time I got those four drunken idiots into beds that weren't my own, it was past three when I finally got some sleep.

And yet, judging by the heavy arm and leg wrapped around me, someone found their way into my room last night anyway.

I already know exactly who by his scent that still manages to be sexy beneath his *actual* smell of seedy brewery and booze sweat. By the heaviness in his limbs, he's still very asleep.

I slip out of his hold, unable to stop my smile at the way he grasps around in his sleep and eventually wraps the blankets under his arm. It was a real skill how quickly they managed to get drunk last night, and I wonder if the others are still passed out or if they made an early exit.

My money is on the early exit. No one wants to be caught in awkward conversation with the team owner.

Only when I walk out into my living room, I find I'm very, very wrong.

Knox is shirtless in my kitchen, standing next to my humming coffee machine, Easton is sitting at the counter with his head in his crossed arms, and Lachie is sprawled over my couch with Conishkin on his chest.

"Umm … hello?" That's a totally normal greeting for this very unnormal situation, isn't it?

"Morning," Knox replies, and all I get is a grunt out of Easton.

"You know," Lachie says like we were already in the middle of a conversation, "if you ever get sick of my brother, I'd date you just for this apartment."

I don't know how to feel about that. "Thanks?"

"Way to make yourself sound like a whore," Easton grumbles.

"Sorry," Lachie replies. "I couldn't hear you over the Connor coming out of your mouth."

"I think we all know whose mouth Connor comes in," Knox snarks.

My whole face goes hot. I have no idea what's happening here or what they think they know. Or do know. Fuck. "I … uh, I don't think—"

Before I can deny anything at all between us, Connor appears in nothing but boxer briefs and bed hair and walks over to kiss me on the cheek before joining Knox in my kitchen.

And now my face is even hotter.

"They know," Connor says.

I almost die.

"We won't say anything." Easton slowly lifts his head from his arms. "He might be an overbearing twat sometimes, but he's still our brother."

It's so weird hearing Easton call him overbearing because that's not the Connor I know at all. Sure, he has his possessive streak, but it's never once felt overbearing. The opposite, actually. Whoever Connor ends up with will never not feel wanted. Or like a priority.

"We won't *need* to say anything." Lachie sits up, relocating Conishkin from his chest and into his arms. "You're all Connor talked about last night. If I hadn't lost all respect for him a really long time ago, that would have done it."

Connor flips him off, and it's on the tip of my tongue to defend him when they both start laughing. *Laughing*. After being insulted. I do *not* understand siblings.

"I respect him very much," I say stiffly, mostly because I feel like I have to say something in his defense, but I'm confused if I should be defending or insulting him.

I guess now I know why hating him got his attention. The Kiki brothers are backward.

The coffee machine finishes, and Knox grabs out two more mugs. "You weren't saying that a few weeks ago."

"Well … no." I finally manage the courage to move further into my living room. "That was more of a—"

"He hadn't had time to adjust to my charming personality," Connor cuts in. "I'm an acquired taste."

"I'm still acquiring it," Easton says, making gimme hands at the cup Knox holds out for him.

Before they can start being mean again, I turn to Lachie.

"You have my rat."

"Yeah? I mean, unless it's someone else's rat. In which case I'm confused why you have it in a cage."

"No, no, it's mine. But your brother won't even hold Conishkin, so I wasn't expecting someone related to him to be cuddling with it."

"He's a good snuggler."

I eye him. "Exactly how long have you been holding him?"

"Fucked if I know. I liberated him from captivity last night, and we've been spooning ever since." And then, as if that isn't bad enough, Lachie lifts Conishkin to his face and covers the little rat's face in kisses.

Conishkin is cute as hell, but that's a line I will *never* cross.

"That's disgusting," Connor says, screwing up his face.

"Ehh." Easton rubs his stubble. "Lachie's used to picking up rats. At least the animal is probably cleaner than half the guys he sleeps with."

Before Lachie can reply, Knox walks over and holds out a coffee for me. I stare at the mug for a moment.

"This is for me?"

"Yeah?"

I take it and look around at the four of them. Knox joining Easton at the counter, Lachie still making kissy faces at Conishkin, and Connor leaning beside my oven, coffee mug in one hand and watching me steadily.

He's still looking slightly green, but he manages a smile.

"You feeling okay?" I ask.

"I'm getting there."

I move closer to him. "I swear I put you in one of the spare rooms about five times last night." He kept trying to sneak into my room, but a drunk Connor is about as stealthy as a herd of elephants.

His face falls. "Did you not want me there? I just remembered that you like cuddling, and now I think I like cuddling, and so I thought ..."

"I wanted you there," I say before he can start doubting. "But you were drunk. I didn't want you to wake up and think I'd taken advantage."

"Nah, you'd never do that."

He sounds so casual and confident about that, and it makes me happy to know that underlying the words, it means he trusts me.

"What'd you say this cutie's name is?" Lachie asks, breaking my attention from Connor.

"Conishkin."

He turns to me in horror. "No. You can't name this sweet little creature after ..." He nods Connor's way. "*That.*"

"Fuck you. He'd be lucky to be named after me."

That's a change of tune. "Good thing he is, then."

Connor looks torn between arguing the point and denying that's what his name is. I give him an innocent smile, and I swear his brain short-circuits.

"Frankie is a cute name."

I turn back to Lachie, trying to figure out if he's serious. "No."

"What about Gretzky?" Easton suggests.

"Stuart Little?" Knox throws out.

"Demon overlord?"

I backhand Connor's abs. "No. It's Conishkin. He already answers to it."

Lachie sighs and lifts the rat back up to his face. "I'm so sorry, little dude. I tried."

He keeps talking to Conishkin while Connor and Easton start bickering. Knox sips his coffee and scrolls through his phone, and I stare down at the coffee I'm holding.

A coffee I didn't make.

Other than the takeout types, I can't remember the last time someone made me a coffee. I'm sure my ex did at some point, but it's a distant memory now.

Not like this.

The steady conversation humming around me, Lachie's joy, and Conishkin's squeaks as they play, the warm taste of caffeine sliding down my throat.

I want to bottle this moment.

This brief flicker of time where my place feels full for the first time since I bought it.

How can Connor ever feel lonely when this is his life?

My gaze slides back to where he's standing. If I kept him, this would be my life too.

I'm too scared to even hope for that.

CHAPTER TWENTY-FOUR

CONNOR

Parker seems … overwhelmed? I think. I dunno. I'm too hungover to get a read on the guy. Not that I could read him the best before though either.

He's watching the four of us with a kind of bewildered expression, like he doesn't know how he's supposed to take us. That's probably fair. Us Kikishkins might be a hockey family, but we're far from a normal one. All three of us Kikis plus Knox grew up together. Practically in the same house because Knox's mom was always working, so he'd be at ours a lot. And yet, all four of us are so different.

East and Lachie know who they are. They've always known and always had that freedom. It's probably why they're so confident in themselves.

I used to think I was confident in who I was, that I was a good person. Parker and Easton, and even in a way Knox, showed me how I haven't been confident at all. I've been masking my whole life.

I approach Parker and rest my chin on his shoulder. "You okay?" I try to keep my voice low because I don't want the others listening in.

Only, out of the corner of my eye, I see both Knox and Easton are pretending they're not listening. They need to be more subtle than leaning closer toward us.

Lachie has no idea what's happening. He's chasing Conishkin around the apartment because he let him go, and now he's trying to coax the thing out of its hiding spot by pleading with it.

"If I lose you, your daddy's going to break up with Daddy Connor, and I don't want that to be my fault. Daddy Connor will fuck up on his own eventually, I promise. Then you and Daddy Parker can change that horrible name of yours and live happily ever after."

I lift my chin. "I can hear you, you know."

"I know," he calls out.

Third children are the worst. They have to be. It's science. To stop the world from overpopulating, the third child always has to be the catalyst to make parents stop reproducing.

"This is … weird," Parker says.

"Say no more." I turn to Easton and Knox. "Okay, time to go home now. Bye-bye."

"No, I didn't mean—" Parker's eyes widen. "You don't need to kick them out. I'm—" He's looking around frantically, worried about whatever imaginary backlash is coming, and I feel incredibly guilty and sorry for him that he has that reaction in the first place.

"It's all good," Easton says and stands from where he's still sitting at the kitchen counter. He finishes the rest of his coffee. "We can be a lot."

"It's not that," Parker says.

"Then what is it?" I ask softly.

"I'm not … used to this. Having people in my space. I don't have …" He takes a deep breath. "I don't have brothers. I don't have … friends. Wow, that hurts to say out loud. So this is weird for me, but good. I promise. You don't have to leave."

I lean in and speak low in his ear. "Not even for what I had planned for my day off? Let's just say it involves a lot of naked time. All good if you're into exhibitionism though."

A smile spreads across Parker's face. "On second thought—"

"Yup," Easton cuts in. "We're voluntarily out. I don't need to see that. Or think about it. Or—" He shudders and grabs Knox's hand. "We're out. Lachie, you coming with us or staying to be traumatized?"

Lachie's head pops up from under Parker's dining table. "What? We're leaving? But I just got him back." He holds the rat into the air.

"Up to you. Parker's going to introduce big bro to the world of gay orgasms, and I ain't gonna be here for that."

Parker's cheeks are aflame, and if I weren't so worried he'd take this kind of ribbing badly, I'd be all for it.

"You do know you're talking about your team owner like that, don't you? In front of him, no less."

Easton's gray eyes meet mine. "And just when I thought old media-image Connor was gone." He turns to Parker. "I'm sorry if my comments about your potential sex life were offensive. Here at Kikishkin Incorporated, we don't have personalities or make jokes, so we were as shocked as you that those words came out of my mouth."

Lachie's snickering to himself as he puts away Conishkin. I'm rolling my eyes.

"Go take your snark somewhere else," I say, making sure to sound every bit as bored as I am. If they even get a whiff of their comments getting to me, it'll make it so much worse. What else are brothers for?

Easton leaves without a word, Knox gives a casual wave, but Lachie has to part with one last jab.

"Have fun boning!"

The door closes behind them, and I slump. "I hate my brothers."

"No, you don't."

I'm bitter that he's right. "Fine. I love them, but I also hate them."

"That's closer."

"Okay, okay. I hate that I love them," I relent.

"There's the truth."

I wrap my arms around him from behind. "Are you really okay? I didn't mean for last night to happen."

"The getting drunk part or texting me to pick you up with your brothers part?"

"All of it. Well, no, the getting drunk part was part of East and Lachie's plan, and I didn't fight them on it, but they took me out to a gay bar, which I'm totally fine with. Or I thought I would be. But the whole time I was there, my brothers were asking me which of the guys they were pointing out were my type, so I welcomed the alcohol."

"Because you realized you were attracted to them all? It's a big switch to come to terms with." His words are supportive, but the way he ducks his head shows he's uncomfortable with me meeting other men or finding them attractive.

I shake my head. "None of them were you, so I wasn't interested."

Parker turns in my arms, and his gaze flicks up to mine. "What? Isn't that, like, putting all your eggs in one basket?"

"I thought the point of being with other men is there is no eggs?" I make the drum *bud-dump-ch* noise. He doesn't find it funny.

"That's a lot of pressure to put on me."

Shit. This is not going how I wanted it to. "Wait." I put my hands on his shoulders. "I'm not saying you're the only man I'll ever be attracted to or that you made me this way or any of that. All I'm saying is you make me feel things that I haven't felt with anyone before, and I want to keep doing what we're doing with no pressure on either of us."

His shoulders slowly lose tension, and then Parker presses his body against mine.

It sets my body on fire. My skin is sensitive everywhere his fingertips touch. My cock is trying to break free of my briefs.

I lean in to kiss him, but he screws up his nose.

"Seriously. Alcohol plus coffee breath is really difficult to find sexy."

"Okay, let me borrow your toothbrush, then."

This only seems to horrify him more.

"You've had your tongue in my mouth. What difference is a toothbrush?"

"Toothbrushes are used to dig out old bits of food and gross bacteria living in between your teeth. I've never once tried to do that to you with my tongue."

I throw up my hands in defeat. "Want me to go home, brush my teeth, and then come back? Do you have any mouthwash?" I pull him close again and try not to breathe all over him. "I want you. I'll do anything to have you."

Parker stares up at me, more confident than I've probably ever seen him. "I know a way we can both get what we want, and it involves no kissing at all."

He backs us up, and I don't fight him on it. When my back is against his kitchen counter, he runs his hand down my chest, and I tighten my abs so he can feel every ridge, every muscle as he keeps going lower and lower.

I'm about to ask him if he's going to give me a handjob while staring into my eyes with nothing but lust in his gaze and expecting me not to kiss him, but then he drops to his knees. My breath catches, which only makes Parker more confident.

I'm dying to have his mouth on me, but there's one thing niggling at the back of my mind. Okay, two things.

I grab his wrist and haul him back to his feet.

"What's wrong?" he asks.

"I want to make sure you're okay with this first. I realize we didn't really talk about it last time, and you've already done this for me without me reciprocating. I want to make sure you're not going to get some type of PTSD flashback of high school where you thought I was the enemy and being in that vulnerable position—"

That confident tilt of his lips is back. "You think giving blowjobs is the vulnerable position?"

"It's not?"

He pats my cheek. "Oh, my sweet summer child."

"I'm trying not to feel like you're being condescending here."

Parker takes my hand and pulls me over to his living room, pushing me down on his couch while he continues to stand above me. "I'm trying not to be condescending, and we can have this conversation if you need it, but is that all you're worried about? That I'll feel demeaned if I get on my knees for you?"

I glance down at my hands. "That, and maybe, you know, if you want me to—"

"Weren't you the one who said you want no pressure on either of us? It goes both ways. Besides, I love sucking cock, so you're really doing us both a disservice here."

"I wanted to make sure after …" I hesitate. "Everything."

"I actually appreciate that more than you know, and it only makes me more eager for this." Parker drops to his knees again, and the sight alone has precum leaking into my boxer briefs. My hips reflexively shift, placing my ass closer to the edge of the cushion. Parker leans in and mouths the damp material, humming against my cock.

I don't know why it's different with him, but it is.

I want him to be mine to cherish, to dote on, to own, but at the same time, I'm too worried about letting that out. About being too much. Too fast. So I hold back that instinct to unleash on him.

But damn, it takes nearly all of my focus to do that.

Parker takes his time, kissing his way up my thigh and dipping his fingers into my waistband without actually pulling them down.

My hips buck, and I lift my ass up so many times without getting anywhere it's almost as if he knows I'm holding back and is trying to get me to snap.

"Parker …" I whine.

"Mm?" He glances up at me, long lashes looking even longer at this angle.

"What are you doing to me?" I whisper.

"Showing you that I might be the one on my knees, but I'm in no way the vulnerable one here."

"I see that now." I *really* see that now.

Parker has me right where he wants me. Desperate. Trembling.

"Move so your ass hangs off the couch," he orders, and I do it, no questions asked.

He pulls off my underwear, licks his lips, but where I'm anticipating his mouth wrapping around my cock, he goes lower, sucking my balls into that wet heat.

I groan as he pulls off, licks his palm and covers it in saliva, and then goes back to mouthing my sac while stroking my cock.

It's almost over as soon as it starts, but I hold in there. I don't know how I fucking do, but I do.

His other hand runs up my thigh and then dips between my legs, massaging that sensitive area between my balls and my ass. He looks up at me, pulls his mouth away, his big pink lips swollen and covered in shiny spit. And then I feel it. His finger slips between my ass cheeks and presses against my hole.

I tense up immediately.

He pulls it back. "I'm not going to actually do anything. I promise. But if you trust me, I want to show you how sensitive that area can be. The only thing is, you have to be open to it. So you can say no—"

"I don't want to."

"That's okay." He goes to move his hand away completely when I stop him.

"No. I meant, I don't want to say no."

He smiles. "Oh."

"But I don't know how comfortable I'll be with it. I want to try though."

"Just to be clear," he says, "I won't actually go … in anything, if that helps you relax."

It does. A little.

I'm still coming to terms with liking a guy. Going near his dick, the thought of anything going inside my ass, it's all a bit outside my comfort zone, but I know it's only because I've never contemplated it before. Like anything new with hockey, if I get put with a different D-man, or our lines are played with and I'm used to having East and Munter on the ice together and then suddenly they're not, I just have to get my head around it, and then I'm open to trying anything once.

I think.

"Don't disappear on me," Parker says.

I reach for him to cup his cheek because I love the way he leans into my hand. "I'm here. And I want this. I want …" I almost say us. More. More of this. More of him. More … everything.

I can't ask Parker to do that for me though. Me. The guy who made his life hell in high school.

Parker keeps eye contact with me as his fingers trace over my balls and go behind them again. He doesn't lose that eye contact as he swipes over the sensitive skin all the way to my hole and then back again.

Every time his finger goes near my hole, I try not to tense, but I do. Stupid body not listening to what my brain says.

"You're not relaxing," Parker says.

"I'm trying."

"Okay, new tactic before I give up and will never bring it up again."

"Yeah?" I let out a shuddery breath. It does feel good, what he's doing. I don't know why it's instinct to shut it down whenever he gets close.

"Only focus on my mouth."

I glance down at his lips right as he leans in and sucks my cock into his mouth all the way to the root in one go.

"Holy fucking of fuck."

His shoulders shake, probably from laughter, but he doesn't pull off me. Nope. He doesn't stop sucking my cock until I'm so blissed-out I don't even notice that he's playing with my ass again.

He keeps his promise, not that I ever thought he wouldn't, and doesn't push inside, but the pad of his fingertip circling it is like a giant tease. Suddenly, my ass does want in on the action, and my hips try to take over, try to get him to press inside me.

My chest rises and falls with my heavy panting, and I throw my head back. "Okay. I'm open to it. I'm definitely open to it. God, I need it. Please. I need your finger."

Instead of giving me what I want, what I'm begging for, Parker buries his head in my groin and moves his hand away from my hole and to my balls, where he squeezes me once and then again.

I fill his mouth with my cum so unexpectedly I didn't even have time to give him warning, but he swallows me all down anyway.

My muscles ache in the best possible way, and then I slump against his couch.

He lifts his head and wipes his mouth, his expression so smug. "High school me would be shocked to know that Connor Kikishkin begged me to finger his ass."

"High school me would be shocked as well." I sit up, wanting to do something for him. I might not be ready to suck his dick, but I have done anal with women before. Or I could give him a handjob again. I was comfortable with that pretty quickly. "You need me to—"

I glance down at his lap, where his spent cock is peeking out from his wet pajama pants.

His smile is bashful, and his cheeks are a nice rose color. "I might have taken things into my own hands at the end there, but seriously, Connor Kikishkin begging for me might be the hottest thing I've ever witnessed."

My smile matches his. For some reason, his words make me bashful. Jesus H. Christ, I'm in trouble.

"I guess we'll have to make me begging a regular thing." Because I'm so not above begging if it gives me orgasms like that.

CHAPTER TWENTY-FIVE

PARKER

Conishkin and I sit at the front of the team plane.

I warned Connor not to be overly familiar when we were with everyone else, so he's sitting in the row behind us, and it makes my gut swim to know that I kissed him goodbye this morning.

Goodbye for, like, thirty minutes while we traveled separately to the airport.

The cloak-and-dagger secrecy is fun, I can't deny that—if I ignore how detrimental to our lives this whole thing would be if it ever got out. Connor let his brothers and Knox know, but while there's nothing seedy or abusive going on, we're both aware of how inappropriate our situation is. No one we don't trust can find out.

For now, all I'm letting myself focus on is the regular orgasms with a guy who's not only hot but also as affectionate as I am and that we're having fun while we do it.

"Is that … a rat?" Macklin asks, squinting at Conishkin's cage.

"Yep. I adopted him."

Macklin *hmpfs*. "What's its name?"

I freeze. When I'd named him Conishkin, I hadn't thought far enough ahead. If I tell the truth, it might open up questions about why. Favoritism accusations will be thrown around, and I don't want people paying too much attention to us. The last thing I need is for my first stint as team owner to be shrouded with controversy. That's no way to honor Dad.

"Nish." The warm voice over my shoulder fills me with relief.

I turn to where Connor has his elbow propped against the top of my seat. "Yes. Nish."

"He's our new mascot," Connor says. "If you ask me, I think *Mr.* Duchene secretly wanted to buy Florida and got stuck with us."

"I'm good with my choice." I use my most professional voice and ignore the way I want to smile. My unrequited high school crush has turned into infatuation when it comes to Connor, and considering it's reciprocated this time, I'm going to enjoy it. I'm going to lean into those butterflies and the urges to text. I'm going to enjoy the snuggles and the sex and waking up to him making me coffee.

Even if all this is temporary while he figures himself out, I'll never regret it.

"Mascot …" Macklin repeats. He must be used to hockey players' antics because he lets it go pretty quickly. "Lucky us."

"I'll keep him in his cage, don't worry." It's hard not to laugh over big, tough jocks being thrown by a tiny little rat.

Maybe I should have gotten a pet sooner. Like in high school.

It wouldn't have made me even more of a target at all.

I'm hit with a wave of Connor's familiar aftershave as he leans back into his seat, and those butterflies kick up again.

We land in Dallas, and I keep my eyes averted from Connor the entire time we're leaving the plane.

There has already been speculation about why I'm flying with them and not chartering my own jet, and if this ever gets out, I'm sure people will speculate it's because of Connor, but my money doesn't change the fact that deep down, I'm a simple guy.

Who bought a hockey team.

So maybe I'm bullshitting myself and I'm more extravagant than I like to think, but I'd prefer to go through life not being noticed, and a private jet doesn't scream anonymity.

I get friendly smiles and disinterested looks from the team as they pass, and at least they're used to me now. I might be back in suits because I feel more comfortable, but I'm still making an effort to be personable, and it's helping them be less scared of me.

Easton *definitely* seems less scared of me, given the way he looks me over as he hurries to fall into step with Munter.

Here I was, worried about Connor being the one to give us away when I should have been worried about his brother. Fuck. Imagine if people start speculating that I'm sleeping with *him*?

Our chartered bus is waiting to take us to the hotel, and as much as I want to text Connor and have him come to my room once we get there, I won't. I'm also not planning to join in the team dinner. They have a practice skate tomorrow, then the game tomorrow night, then back on the plane to Vegas the next morning. We have three away games before heading back to Colorado, and somehow, I need to go almost a week keeping my hands to myself.

I don't know how Easton and Knox do it.

Luckily, I have self-control. Allegedly. For the next week, I'll look after Conishkin and watch hockey. I've gone for way longer than that without sex, so this shouldn't be an issue at all.

Still, it's hard not to be disappointed when midnight comes and goes with no sneaky knock on my door.

After room service that looked on the undercooked side and a night with crappy sleep, I stare at my phone, debating if I should text him good morning. Does that muddy what we are? What if he's with someone from the team and they see?

I'm about to put my phone down when a text comes through with his name on it.

> Spooning a pillow isn't the same.

Hello, infatuation, and welcome back from that five-second vacation you took. My nerves take over, and I have no clue what I'm supposed to write back to that. "Being spooned by my pillow wasn't the same either" is less cute and flirty and more on the psychotic end of the spectrum. I badly want to type something that will make him smile as well, but I'm not good at this. I've had no practice, my ex wasn't overly affectionate or sweet, and being cool isn't something I've ever been. It doesn't magically change now that I'm getting off with a hockey god.

The illusion for him is going to burst very fucking quickly if I don't get myself together.

Only six days left until we're home!

I die the second I hit Send. Is that too presumptive? Too stalkerish? Six days, nine hours, and fifty-two minutes until we land and I can drag you back to my sex cave.

I drop my face in my hand. What the hell have I done?

His reply comes through.

But who's counting?

There. That's exactly what I was worried about. Now he thinks I'm obsessed with getting him back home, like I even have that right. Damn it, Connor, I have a hookup app, and I'm not afraid to use it.

I'm not a clingy idiot.

I'm not.

I'm typing back faster than I can think.

Not me. It was just a general observation. Six isn't a high number to count to.

And now, it sounds like I'm calling him dumb.

Damn. I guess I'm the only one who can't wait then. Six days and ten hours, in case you were wondering. ;)

Relief melts through the tension in my muscles. Then, another message quickly follows, and it takes me a moment to work out what I'm looking at.

It's a photo.

Of his abs.

Connor's abs.

On my phone.

I've been sent a million and one dick pics before, but never in my life have I seen something so sexy. My mind turns to an endless stream of *gah urg ma haahhhh* as I try to figure out if he sent the picture to turn me on, and if he did, does he know what I'm planning to do with that later?

That photo is mine now.

Thought it might tide you over until we're home again.

And just checking, when we are home, I'll be able to see those in real life?

If you play your cards right. Until then, I wouldn't say no to my own picture.

His … own picture? Of me? I glance down at my torso like abs might magically appear, but nope. Still scrawny and pale.

Are you sure you sent that text to the right person?

You're an idiot. Now show me that V.

That "V" is my hips, but it's not like I can say no, based on my lack of abs, when he already knows this about me and he's asking anyway.

So with a breath of courage, I hook my thumb into the front of my pajama pants, tug them down enough for a glimpse of pubes, then screw my eyes up and snap a picture. I text it to him without looking because otherwise I'll be here all morning, analyzing and overanalyzing. Maybe I should make plans to go to the gym today? Building muscle is something I could maybe get into?

I'm terrified to see his reply, but the second it comes through, I'm scrambling to open it. And it's one word.

Daaaaaaaaamn.

I don't think I've ever had a better message in my life.

CHAPTER TWENTY-SIX

CONNOR

It turns out being sexually frustrated is good for my game. My hits are harder, my risks are riskier, and my D game is on point. Mainly because my other *D game* is on pause.

I don't know what it is about having Parker on the road with us that makes it so much worse. Sure, his hotel room is only a couple of floors away from mine, so he's a lot closer than at home, but thirty seconds on an elevator might as well be cities away, seeing as we don't want to risk fooling around in the same building as everyone. He never said those words explicitly, but I got the message loud and clear when he said we shouldn't interact around the team. And on the road, I am constantly surrounded by teammates.

My growing want for him could be that I've never had this before with women. Not this need with any individual person. With them, I guess I always felt like if I got horny, I could go hook up with someone new because I'd never get serious with any of them. They were replaceable. Not in a discard them like trash kind of way, but in an *I don't want to give them false hope* kind of way.

Parker isn't like that. Parker is … irreplaceable in my head. Just like at the gay bar the other night, the thought of someone else doesn't do it for me. I can't picture myself hooking up with any other man. As for women? Right now, my only focus is on him. And hockey. Though, I'm not going to lie, ever since Easton pointed out all my flaws and I started questioning everything, hockey doesn't have the same shine it once had.

Not for me.

I'm hoping to get that purpose back one day, but it's like my mind doesn't know if I love hockey because I really do or because I was told to love it. Breathe it. Everything I've ever done for my entire life always traced back to the game.

Didn't go out underage drinking with high school buddies? It could ruin my future if I was caught.

Didn't give in to peer pressure to smoke or do drugs? It would make me sluggish on the ice.

Didn't explore these repressed feelings? Back then, there were more important things to focus on other than myself.

Or so I thought.

If I'd had the opportunity to figure this all out back then, maybe I would have realized sooner that hockey isn't the be-all and end-all. Other things are more important.

Like not being a dick to people in high school. Letting my brothers be independent of me and let them live their lives. Be happy about the man I'm becoming instead of being ashamed of the man I was.

I want to focus on the good things happening around me, and while hockey is going well for me, and I'm good at it … do I actually love it? I like it enough to keep going, but my priorities are changing. Working on myself currently outranks my need for hockey, but it's not like I can ask to take a break or even quit. If I do that and then realize hockey is my future, it would be really difficult to come back.

Something I don't love about hockey is how games like tonight, where yes, my hits were harder, and I did my job and we took out the win, I'm fucking sore. I'm way too young to be complaining about the bruises. That's like retirement-level bullshit.

As I'm undressing in the locker room afterward, my brother approaches and slaps my shoulder. I wince so hard he laughs.

"I'm surprised you're not bruised all over with how hard you were going out there tonight."

"I am bruised all over. Or it feels like I am."

"Aww, poor Connor need a big, strong man to kiss him better?"

I frown at him.

He tilts his head with a "Really?" expression across his face. "Relax. The guys can't hear me, and even if they did, they wouldn't know it could happen."

It's only then I realize I was frowning at the wrong thing. It should've been because his snark could out me to the team, but it was actually because Parker isn't big or strong. I thought he was saying I should go find a big, strong man … who isn't Parker.

Jesus, there really is something wrong with how gone I am over this guy already.

Is it because it's fun and new, and he's like a shiny toy? Is it because what we have speaks to that primal level of me that pisses my brothers off? Will it eventually piss him off?

I'm like a giant walking red flag of obsessiveness. Parker should be getting ready to fill out a restraining order.

"I don't care if the rest of the team knows I'm sleeping with a guy." This I say loud enough to catch a few stray eyes, but with Easton on the team, they don't have anything to say about it. If anything, their eyebrows just shoot up, and they move on. Because they don't care. I made sure they wouldn't care when East came out.

But for this part, I move in close and lower my voice. "It's who I'm sleeping with that can't get out."

Easton looks surprised as well, but I'm assuming for different reasons than the team finding out I'm queer. If Easton hadn't clued in to that yet, I'd worry about his IQ.

"You coming to this Queer Collective dinner with me, then?" he asks.

I rub my shoulder where I took out Dex Mitchell earlier. "Yes. I need to tell Dex that his body is like cement, and he should probably check to see if his bones are made of metal. Remind me next time we play Vegas that I'll let Dex get away with anything."

Easton laughs. "This could be fun."

It could. Or it could be a complete disaster where all I'll think about all night is Parker. Wanting to go back to the hotel and sneak into Parker's room. Wanting to see Parker.

Parker, Parker, Parker.

I need help.

-

When Tripp and Dex open the door to their apartment, Dex gets a confused scrunch in his brow. "You brought … your brother."

"So did you," East snarks, referring to when the couple were called the Mitchell Brothers because they were best friends and had the same last name but spelled differently.

Dex's confusion doesn't leave his pretty face. That's not queer Connor noticing he's pretty. He's just a pretty man in general. "I don't have a brother."

The poor guy.

I pat his shoulder. "It's okay, I'm seeing someone named Parker." Parker no last name. Like Cher. Or Zendaya. It's not the team owner. Nope.

"What does that have to do with bringing my brother?" Dex asks.

"No, I meant, that's why I'm here."

Dex still doesn't get it.

Beside him, Tripp sighs. "Just how hard did you hit my husband out there tonight?"

I shrug. "If the bruises all over my body are any indication, I'd say hard."

"Hockey is such a dangerous sport," East says. "Anyway, where's the alcohol? We have a win to celebrate."

"You have a win to celebrate," Tripp grumbles and then turns on his heel.

The three of us follow him, and I call out, "Hey, don't be bitter. Just be better."

Tripp flips me off.

Even the high I used to get from gloating isn't there anymore.

Figuring out who I am while stripping back all of my previously known likes and dislikes has broken me in a way I never saw coming, but I do want to keep going. I want to know everything about myself.

From competitive narcissist to … person who doesn't even like taunting? Who the fuck am I?

Tripp gets us drinks, and we go out onto their terrace.

The weather hasn't even begun to start cooling down in Vegas, even though half of Colorado is already seeing snow.

"Who's this Parker chick?" Dex asks.

I'm lucky my hand only reached halfway to my mouth before he asked, or there would be liquid everywhere from choking on it.

"Parker's a man," I correct him.

"Oh." His brow does the confused scrunch thing again. "Ooooh."

Now he gets it.

"It's new, and I'm not really telling anyone, but I know you've all been good to East since he came out, so I assume I can trust you?"

"Of course," Tripp says.

Dex nods.

"So, umm, yeah. I'm dating a man. I'm … bi?" I don't know why that comes out as a question, but oh well.

Dex lifts his hand to high-five me. "Woohoo to being obliviously queer!"

I hesitate to meet his enthusiasm, but hey, it's exactly what I was: too wrapped up in unimportant shit to see the real me underneath.

Tripp and Easton share a glance, one I sense is about me, but I don't call them on it.

I probably don't want to know what it means. I'm sure Easton's told the whole Collective how overbearing I am, and I'm trying to leave that all behind me and move on, so rehashing it now will only disappoint me and put me back in that bad headspace. I'm good where I am now. I still have a lot of work to do, but I'm no longer in denial.

"Ezra will be happy," Dex says. "The Collective is taking over the NHL. I heard the AHL has their own version of us now."

"Really?" I ask.

"It's amazing more and more people aren't scared to be their authentic self in this industry." For someone who is slow to pick up on things, Dex has a big heart and doesn't miss the important things.

I think about what he said and realize I'm lucky to be discovering this now, where so many have come before me that I don't have to fear backlash. Not from the important people in my life. My biggest fear is the news getting out that I'm involved with the guy who owns my career. It could be seen as a massive power imbalance, even though it's not like that at all. We're merely two people who might have found each other sooner if things were different.

If I wasn't hockey captain and he wasn't the computer geek.

"This Parker guy …" Tripp says. But then something knowing shines in his eyes, as if something clicks. "Wait. It's not—"

I stand in a hurry. "You guys got a bathroom I can go use?"

Tripp's eyes get even wider, but Dex is oblivious again.

He stands and gestures for me to go inside. "I'll show you to the master bathroom because our niece put her toys in the guest bathroom, and now we have to wait for a plumber to come out because we're in a high-rise, and she's messed up the entire line from that toilet to the next level down, so all it does it get backed up with so much shit. Like, literally."

"Got it. Master bathroom. That's all you had to say, man."

Once inside their bathroom, I take a deep breath. I don't actually need to go but make myself at least take a leak so I can lie to myself that's the reason I ran in here so fast.

I take out my phone and message Parker.

I think I messed up.

My phone rings a second later with his name. I answer and say, "Hey."

"At another gay bar, but this time, you fell into someone's mouth?" He sounds amused, but I can hear an edge in his tone too.

"No. I'm at Tripp and Dex's place, and I told them I was dating a guy named Parker, but it turns out Tripp isn't as dumb as they say he is, and I think he knows I was talking about you. He was about to flat out ask me, and I didn't want to lie, so I ran into their bathroom, and now I'm too scared to go back out there."

A soft laugh rings in my ears. "Is that what we're doing? Dating?"

I wince. "You know what I mean." I want to keep doing what we're doing, whatever it is.

"And that's why you think you messed up?"

"Yes. We're doing this whole sneaking around thing because of the team and what might happen if the league found out about us. I don't want to put that on you. Maybe I need to change your name. Peter—"

"What, am I eighty?"

"Parnell?"

"Con … you can tell your friends about me. Your brothers already know. Knox. And I'm sure your Queer Convention—"

"Collective."

"I'm sure a group of queer players will know the importance of the news not getting out. I actually trust them more than I trust East, if I'm honest. I swear every time he looks at me, his smirk is screaming, 'You've seen my brother naked!'"

I exhale in relief. "I … I thought you'd be pissed."

"Even if it did get out, I wouldn't be angry. Not at you. I'd be scared and stressed over the future of my involvement with the franchise, but I wouldn't be mad. I bought the team to honor my dad, and maybe … Maybe I shouldn't be so involved in it. Maybe I should go back to tech."

"You wouldn't be leaving Denver though, right?"

"No. Not Denver. Just the team. I'd still be the owner, but if I'm not so involved, then we won't have to worry about public opinion. Uh, that's if you even wanted to come out at some point. Or not—no pressure here to be ready for that. Or an actual relationship. Or more. Please tell me to shut up, or I'm scared I never will."

I laugh. "Parker?"

"Mm?"

"Shut up."

"Thank you."

When we end the call, I'm less worried about what Tripp knows and excited to tell both him and Dex about Parker.

The mere fact he talked about a possible future or relationship or coming out means he's thinking about me the way I've been thinking about him. It gives me hope that somewhere down the line, after I've figured my shit out, we might have a shot at being together for real. Like Easton and Knox. Tripp and Dex.

I've never wanted that before, but I've also never allowed myself to focus on a relationship. I've never allowed myself to do anything but focus on hockey. Not only my career but my brothers' too.

I head back out to fill them in without having to lie when voices in the kitchen make me stop at the end of the hallway. It's not so much the voices but the words they're saying.

"Are you sure you're okay with all of this?" Tripp asks. "I got the impression your brother was a bit of a homophobe, and now he's—"

Pain slices through my gut. Tripp may as well have stabbed me.

"He was never a homophobe," Easton says, defending me. Thank God. But he's not done. "At least, not intentionally."

Ouch.

I almost want to walk out there and make excuses for myself, but can I? Really? He's right. I had no clue what he was going through. And while what's happening with me and Parker is slightly different, the worry is the same. I didn't want East to face backlash, and I don't want it for Parker either. Weirdly, for myself, I'm not worried. Go figure.

East continues. "He and our parents have always been overprotective, so their misdirected 'need to be palatable gay to appease the straights' came from a good place. I always knew that, even if it was annoying."

"Look, I don't know Connor well, but I do know you and him got into a fight during preseason. It was all over hockey news. And of course we're going to welcome him with open, supportive arms, but I wanted to check in on you because I know your relationship hasn't been great since you came out. What if Connor decides he's ready to come out and doesn't go through nearly as many hoops as he put you through?"

If he thinks I'm not jumping hoops, doing what I have to do to be with Parker while protecting him, then he's right. He doesn't know me well at all. Then again, who does? Not me either.

"I'm actually happy that he's realized this side of him," East says, and my heart warms. "Connor has always had my back. Misdirected or not. And I actually hope he comes out and it's all smooth. Just knowing he understands now was enough for me to put all my resentment behind us."

"That, and I bet sticking it to his best friend every night helps."

"Little bit. But for real, when I finally snapped and showed Connor how he was actually hurting me instead of helping, he's done nothing but try to make up for that. I'm not sure if people can change who they really are deep down, but I know he's trying, and that's all I can ask for. I actually feel like I have my Connor back. The one from when we were kids. Before teenage hormones and the responsibility was dumped on him. He's my big brother, and I love him."

I peek around the corner, and Easton is smiling my way, sitting at a stool at their kitchen counter. Tripp is in the kitchen, and Dex is fixing more drinks in the background.

"Even if he's a big-eared, nosy bitch," East says.

I step out from behind the wall and throw out my hands. "All of that was bullshit, then?"

Easton shakes his head. "No, it was all true. I just knew you were listening. I meant what I said. I appreciate that you're trying, and I love that you've discovered this side of you and haven't run away from it."

"Yet," I say.

"Do you think you're going to run away?" Dex asks.

"No? Maybe?" I slump on the stool next to East's. "And you're right. I do understand now. More than anything. I told you to hold back with coming out because I thought it would put unnecessary heat on your career. I'm holding back because I know that sleeping with my team's owner will affect mine. And his reputation."

"I knew it," Tripp says. "He's hot. Good job."

"He's mine," I growl.

All three of them flinch backward.

"That escalated quickly," Tripp says.

"Connor doesn't do things in halves." Easton's right. I don't.

"I'm all in," I say.

Dex grins. "I bet he says that during sex."

East screws up his face, Tripp smothers a smile, and I laugh.

"Is it possible for any of the Collective to have a serious moment?" I ask.

Dex and Tripp answer in unison. "No."

Checks out.

CHAPTER TWENTY-SEVEN

PARKER

Connor must not have stopped by home first because I've barely set my suitcase on my bed to unpack it when there's a knock on the front door. I freeze like a deer in headlights, equal parts torn over answering and dreading the conversation we need to have.

When he called me from Tripp and Dex's place, he'd said we were dating. *Dating.* As in, possible boyfriend territory. But I'm refusing to get my hopes up because he'd dismissed it a second later. It was a slip of the tongue, and while I know that deep down, I still want to talk all that out. I'd wanted to immediately get into it on the phone before I remembered he was hiding in a bathroom and it probably wasn't the place to do it.

I shake off the urge to run hard and fast, but trying to calm myself only works to make me more nervous by the time I get to my front door and open it.

I swear Connor takes up my whole doorway. His face is scruffy with stubble that's longer than usual, but his eyes are bright, and the immediate smile that hits his face draws mine out as well.

"Hey." He steps inside, dumps his bag by the door as he kicks it shut, then swamps me in a hug.

For one brief moment, I forget about the potentially awkward conversation and lean into him. It's been a long, long time since I was given affection that I didn't have to ask for, and I'm still adjusting to how freely Connor dishes it out. His T-shirt has soaked up his body warmth, and I press my face to it, breathing in the crisp smell of laundry detergent.

"I nearly broke so many times and came to your room."

I force myself to pull back. "I'm glad you didn't. *Wish* you did. But that was smart."

A soft look crosses Connor's face that completely throws my thought process, but when he leans in to kiss me, everything hits at once.

"We need to talk," I say.

He freezes, leaning in halfway. "That's not good."

"No, no. It's … fine. Awkward and uncomfortable for me to bring up, but totally, totally fine."

"Fine, as in we'll talk and still be having sex after? Or fine, as in we'll talk, and then I'll get kicked out of your apartment?"

"The first one. Hopefully."

"Good." He grabs my hand and drags me through to my bedroom. "I'm a big fan of us having this talk. But in bed, with a whole lot less clothes on."

"Connor …"

"*Connor*," he mimics in a high-pitched tone. Then, he steps forward and begins popping the buttons on my shirt.

I try to give him my most serious look, but he just pushes my shirt from my shoulders before stripping off his T-shirt with a smug look on his face. My gaze drops to his abs, and I relent.

"Fine. You win." I quickly tug open the front of my belt. "We can get naked, but we're talking before sex."

"Can I at least have a hint what this is about?" He pushes down his sweats and underwear in one go, and I swear he's trying to torture me.

"Us."

"Still not sounding great."

As soon as he's naked, I set a hand on his chest and push him backward onto my bed. Then I move my suitcase, kick off my pants, and crawl up beside him. I lie on my front, propped up on my elbows so I can see him better. "I want to check we're on the same page with everything."

"Oh, yeah?" Connor rolls onto his side and runs a hand down the middle of my back. "With what?"

"Well … on the phone … in Vegas, you might have said it by accident or subconsciously or because you thought you had to, but you said we were dating."

"Yeah?"

"And what does that mean?"

Connor gives me a strange look. "Ah … we're dating? Seeing each other? Sleeping together?" He's such an adorable baby bi.

"The thing is, for queer relationships, that could be anything. We don't tend to follow the same path that heterosexual ones do."

"Okay …"

"So dating could mean that we're together. It could be open or exclusive. It could be just hooking up when the need hits us."

He's nodding fast, looking like he's trying to take in what I'm saying.

"For example," I mutter, not wanting to relive it, "my last boyfriend … I thought we were it."

Connor's hand on my back stills.

"I'd assumed we'd get married or whatever, but I could tell with the long hours I was working that he wasn't happy. We opened up the relationship for him to sleep with other men so he could get what he needed."

"That fuck—"

This is the hard part. "No, he didn't do anything wrong. We agreed that he'd keep it sex only and there'd be nothing emotional or affectionate. That was all mine. He kept his end. I didn't."

"Wait. *You* fell for someone else?"

That's almost laughable. "*No*. I wasn't honest. Open relationships are all about honesty. I thought I'd be okay with it, but the sharing gene didn't hit me, I guess. It hurt. I hid in work to avoid knowing anything about it, and he said it felt like he was dating a ghost in the end. It didn't work. And so as much as I'm probably going to break out in hives from this conversation alone, I have to be honest. If we're going to be anything other than you trying out sex with a man, I need …" Kill me now. "If we're dating. *We're* dating. No one else. Just us."

I'm staring at my tangled hands, inhale caught in my chest as I wait for him to reply.

Then he leans in suddenly, hand gripping my hip while his lips land near my ear. "Parker, if another man tries to touch you, I'll break every bone in his fucking hand."

My eyes are huge as I snap my head toward him. The intense look on Connor's face should maybe scare me, but it doesn't. In some messed-up ways, it makes me feel seen. Wanted. *Needed*. I think I could live the rest of my life with him looking at me like that.

Without breaking eye contact, he rolls me onto my back and settles over the top of me.

"When I say we're dating," he says, stroking my cheek, "I mean you're mine."

"Okay." I'm way too excited about that. "And you're mine too?"

"Yes. I'm still working myself out, but I'm having a lot of fun doing it with you. I don't want to stop."

I don't want him to stop. Ever. "I'm good with that." More than good.

Connor kisses a line along my jaw. "What have you done to me?" He sounds pained, and it sends a thrill through me to know I can get him so worked up.

"Me? You're the one scrambling my brain."

"I really hope you weren't lying about liking possessiveness because if you were, we're fucked. Tripp mentioned finding you attractive, and I wanted to rampage."

I take his hand, directing it to my cock. His big hand wraps around me, and my limbs turn to putty. "No lies. I need it."

He dips his head to suck on my neck as he moves his hand up my shaft with long, firm strokes. One of his knees presses my thigh up further, and my other leg parts with it. "I want to fuck you."

"Do it."

He grunts, teeth scraping my skin before he pulls back and pins me with his heated stare. "Show me what to do."

I direct Connor to grab the lube and a condom from my bedside drawer, and then I take the tube from him. He watches greedily as I pour out lube onto my fingers and ease him back so I can reach between my legs. "You need to get me ready first." I circle my hole with my fingertip, dick already leaking onto my stomach, and after a few seconds, when I'm relaxed enough, I press my finger inside. I'm ready for this moment, been fantasizing about it, and already it's better than I imagined.

Connor leans back so he can see. "You took that so easy."

"Experience counts for something. Plus, I'm super fucking horny."

"I'm super fucking horny, but I think I'd sob if you tried that on me."

My ass tightens on my finger. "Don't worry. I'm not much of a top. I'm perfectly fine if you never want to try this." When he frowns, I quickly add, "But if you wanted to, I'm not opposed. I'm only saying there's no pressure at all from me."

His exhale is heavy. "Yeah. I'm keeping you."

Those words give me a special kind of high. No one can promise forever, it's impossible, but I like that at least in this moment, he really does see me as his.

I press another finger into my ass, trying not to be impatient and rush things but needing to feel him inside me.

"C-can I?"

I stretch my fingers open, giving my body time to relax. "Lube first."

Connor quickly covers his fingers, then presses one inside. I swear his are worth two of mine, and the stretch is way more intense. He strokes in and out, watching every movement.

"Move your finger up more."

"Here?"

I direct him to my prostate, and the second his fingertip brushes over it, pleasure rushes through me. "*Here.*"

He tugs my hand out, stuffing two fingers back inside, breathing getting heavier as he watches me. He's having no problem finding that spot now, and I'm dangerously close to coming like this.

"Shit, you're leaking," he rasps.

"Yeah. You should, umm, probably stop. Definitely stop. Like … now." I grip the base of my cock and strangle it as Connor pulls his fingers free. My dick is oversensitive and aching, and I need him back inside me. Need something to feel full, for me to clamp down around as I come.

Connor rolls the condom on, then covers his cock in lube. I'm on PrEP, and he's regularly tested, but foregoing condoms is a talk we can have *after* we're both not so riled up.

I pull my knees back as Connor leans over me and presses the blunt head of his cock to my entrance.

"We good?"

"Yep. Just take your time."

His groans last the entire time he pushes inside me. "This feels so … so … fuck."

I squeeze around him, loving the sense of fullness, and Connor's eyes roll back.

"Gay sex is going to kill me."

I know he's joking, but I have Connor Kikishkin inside me, and I'm going to shamelessly revel in years' worth of unrequited lust coming to life. I wrap my fingers through his hair and tug his mouth to mine.

He kisses me like he's starving for it, and when he moves inside me, I'm already so sensitive my orgasm buzzes along my spine. It takes every bit of experience for me to hold off coming, though I'm not sure Connor is far behind me. He increases speed and pounds my hole while greedily sucking on my tongue. His arms are wrapped tight and secure around my back. I'm trying to move with him but can't do much more than take it because my fantasies didn't conjure up the man moving inside me; he's in complete control, a demon absolutely destroying me. All of me. Inside and out.

We're both sweating. Our kiss is sloppy. Deep. Desperate. Because he's always made me so fucking desperate.

So desperate to tell him to fuck off. To tell him to look at me. Notice me. Realize I'm goddamn worthy of him too.

Connor pulls out suddenly. "Get on top of me."

Ngh. Yes, yes, yes.

He rolls onto his back, and I straddle his hips before sinking down on him again. Connor's large hands cup my hips, urging me into a punishing rhythm.

I ride him hard, and he thrusts up into me, making every muscle in his chest and stomach stand out sharply. His eyes are glued to my dick, and I have no clue what thoughts are racing through his mind, but his tongue flicks out to wet his lips, and I decide to take that as a good sign.

"Fuck, Park …"

"Yeah, I know."

"I didn't know watching you take me could be this hot."

"You better be close."

"So close. Your ass is heaven."

The compliment makes me almost touch myself, but I'm holding out. Wanting him to come first. Judging by his panting, he's close.

"Who's hole is this?" His fingers bite painfully into my hips.

"It's yours. Only yours."

He cries out, pressing firmly against my ass as he empties his load into the condom. I feel him twitch through the whole thing, and when I go to grab my cock, to get myself off while he's still inside me, Connor bats my hand away.

He wraps his fist around my aching dick and I grind down onto him as he jerks me off. The warmth, the roughness, it's all too much.

"This is … holy shit, I *really* fucking like this." He glances up, and the flash of split-second vulnerability is what gets me. My balls tighten a second before I release. My cum floods his hand and leaks down onto his abs, and poor Connor doesn't know whether to watch my face or the way my cock is pulsing, judging by how quickly his eyes are pinging between the two.

When I come back from the high, I lean down with a smile and drag my lips over his. "Don't worry. We can do that as many times as you want."

He flips us quickly so I'm on my back again, and when his dick slips out, his fingers press back inside. "In that case, we better keep this hole nice and lubed, then. I'm just getting started."

CHAPTER TWENTY-EIGHT

CONNOR

Sex is awesome, but I'm quickly realizing that cuddling is the best. It turns out I'm a real cuddle whore. I can't get enough. Even if it fills my head with even more questions than before. Because if I'd known this about myself years ago, would I have done it with those random, empty hookups I had before Parker? Would the intimacy of it have made me want to be like this with them?

Waking up on a day off, wrapped around each other, after the best sex ever, without a care in the world?

Parker stirs, which only makes me hold him tighter. I haven't opened my eyes yet, just basked in the warmth of him pressed against me all night. "Five more minutes," I beg.

"I'm not going anywhere."

His voice lulls me back to sleep until I wake up at who knows what time, spooning a pillow.

That bastard.

I slip out of bed and trudge around his apartment looking for him. He's not in his bathroom, the kitchen, living room, or dining room, and I'm about to call out to him when I hear his murmurs from down the hall. He's probably talking to himself about gadgets and whatchamacallits, ideas for his latest tech venture. I haven't been into his office before, but I'm pretty sure I remember drunkenly stumbling past it when I was here with the guys.

I burst in there, naked as the day I was born, and put my hands on my hips. "You left me in bed—oh fuck."

His desk faces the opposite wall, and on his computer screen is the red face of an older, graying man. I didn't realize tomatoes could grow hair.

Now would be a great time for me to turn around and run, but instead, I'm frozen. With my bits out. *Fuck*. My hands at least fly to my junk to cover myself.

"I'm so sorry, Gary," Parker says and turns to me and mouths, "What are you doing?"

Finally, my feet listen to my brain, and I back out of the room real fast.

I should've known when I heard him talking that he might have been on a call. I just didn't think it would be over *video*. And now, I'm the dumbass who overstepped boundaries, and I have no idea who he was talking to, but I'm really hoping it was no one important.

Because now someone else knows about us, and it's my fault.

I go find my sweats and put them on, then land my ass on his couch and run my hand through my hair, trying to think of how to do damage control.

I was so good at this when it came to Easton, but saving my own ass? I'm blank. I've got nothing. Other than quitting hockey, changing my identity and how I look through cosmetic surgery, and then starting over as anyone but me.

Dramatic? Me?

Parker finds me only a minute later, and I can't think of anything else to do but slink to my knees and apologize.

"I'm sorry. I'm sorry. I'm so sorry. I didn't think, and now whoever that guy was knows, and if we're hoping to keep this thing quiet, I really shouldn't be allowed out of your apartment. Or in your office. You should chain me up to your bed and leave me there forever."

"Now, there's a nice idea. Will you be naked too?" Parker's face breaks into a wide smile before a laugh escapes. "Come on, get up." He helps me to my feet, and then he wraps me in one of his hugs that has a hold on my heart. "He didn't see anything."

I pull back. "What?"

"He saw your cock but not your face. To him, you were a random hookup, and it's not news that I'm gay. I do feel like I might need to look for a new financial advisor though. Gary was so flustered he either ended the call in disgust or accidentally hit the disconnect button when he saw how big your dick is."

I bury my head in his shoulder. "Can I go die of embarrassment now?"

"Nope." Parker rubs my back. "Because you're way too cute to die."

"Cute?" I exclaim and pull away again. "I am not cute. I'm big and strong and—"

"Impulsive?"

"That too. I really am sorry. I don't think I can be trusted with our secret. All I want to do is tell everyone you belong to me, but that comes with big consequences, so I understand not doing it, but I'm finding ways to fuck it up anyway. Telling Tripp your name, walking in on a business meeting *naked*—"

"I agree your stealth needs some work, but you want to know why I'm not mad?"

"Because you secretly want me to ruin your life for a second time so you can hate me forever?"

Parker laughs some more. "Because the worst that could happen to me if it got out was I'd be forced to sell the team. I don't want to do that, but it's not like hockey's my life. Not in the same way it is yours."

My brain trips over that assumption because … I'm not even sure of that anymore.

"Tech is my life," he adds. "And I want to show you something." Parker goes to lead me back down the big, scary hallway toward his office.

I stop in my tracks before we get anywhere near the room. "Is it a replay of my dick all up in your financial advisor's face? Because I don't want to see that."

"I wish I was recording that."

"You're going to have fun with this, aren't you?"

"Oh, you have no idea. Seeing Connor Kikishkin's humility is rather … cathartic. High school Parker is very smug."

"Does that mean we're even? I get a pass on the high school asshole thing?"

"Not even close. I'm just not holding it against you anymore."

Fair enough. If I were him, I'm not so sure I would've let me off the hook so easily.

"I want to show you what I'm working on." I'm not sure I've seen Parker this excited. Other than maybe right before we have sex.

"What is it?"

We walk back into the scene of the crime, and I push that image out of my head because Parker is endearingly animated as he sits in his ergonomic chair and brings up some program that looks like a whole bunch of letters, symbols, and numbers thrown together in random order.

"A few weeks ago, I kind of got the bug to start designing again. I've been at the rink so much lately, watching how it's run, how you do things, and I came up with an idea."

It's great he's getting his mojo back.

"Sounds like you're getting over that bitterness you had toward the tech industry."

He deflates slightly. "I will always hate that I was too late to help my dad, but that wasn't the industry's fault. It was cancer's fault. Fuck cancer. I'm happy to be getting ideas again. I thought I only had that one good one in me."

"So what's this new idea?"

"You know how you all watch hours of game tape so your coaches can try to point out what you did wrong, what other teams' weaknesses are, and how to use all the data to your advantage?"

I snort. "Yeah?"

"What if a program could do it all for you? It would be essentially the same thing but wouldn't take hours of studying the tape to figure it out. Like here ..." He types something into his computer, and a simulation pops up.

It's a cartoon overlay of footage of me where I fell because I changed directions too quickly and didn't have control of my skates.

I slow down, and the cartoonish me shows the path of how I should've moved. "That's cool." And it is ... But I bite my lip.

"You don't sound too enthusiastic." A worry line appears above Parker's brow.

I kiss it away. "It's amazing. And a great idea. But what about our game tape coaches? What would happen to their jobs?"

"Wait, you have coaches dedicated to game tape? Is that why there's so many coaches on this team?"

Now he's the one being cute.

"This won't replace their jobs, but it could assist them. I don't want to make programs that will take real humans' jobs. Just make it easier. And there are still kinks to work out anyway. Look." He hits some more keys, and when he hits Enter, the cartoon hockey player bends completely backward like he's in the Matrix or possessed by a demon or some shit. "I don't think that's a realistic maneuver."

"I'll try it for you next time I'm on the ice."

"Thanks, but I'd rather you not have a back injury." Parker stares at the screen a little longer, and I can smell the dejection.

I fall to my knees again so I'm at least his height. "Hey. This is an amazing idea, and I mean that. You should pursue it."

His smile is weak. "You really think so? I don't want to put anyone out—"

"I didn't mean it that way. Well, I did, but if there was a way to use this as a tool for coaching instead of replacing it, you could sell it to every single coach in the country. Just not … any other NHL teams." I wink.

"I would never. I still want to win that Stanley Cup. For Dad." The fire in his eyes, the excitement … I should be reflecting the same thing.

But I'm not.

Because as he says the one thing I've been telling myself for years—that the only thing that matters is the Stanley Cup—I realize something about myself I never saw coming. This is even bigger than my sexuality. Bigger than Easton pointing out I was an asshole. It's the biggest shock of all.

I don't give a shit about winning a Stanley Cup.

CHAPTER TWENTY-NINE

PARKER

It's been a long time since an idea has gripped me like this. Not only do I get to build the program from scratch, but watching games becomes research, and I get to fill the whole thing with math.

I'm giddy.

I'm also trying really hard not to repeat past mistakes. When Connor is home, I force myself to set it all aside and focus on him. What we have feels big and tenuous. I'm not getting ahead of myself, but I can't stop that sneaky little voice telling me that Connor is important. There might be a future between us, but it's too soon to know for sure, so I force all those hopeful little pieces away and focus on the now.

The now where he's in Canada, a whole other country, playing another Collective member, and I'm watching the game on my enormous flat-screen. I'm taking notes by hand, with my laptop open beside me. While this is good for planning, and I'm sure the game is probably over and I'm only midway through the second period because I keep pausing the TV, I miss being there live. I miss my big, lonely suite and the chill in the air.

With my resentment toward Connor gone though, I'm finally seeing what Dad saw in him. He's an amazing player, and when he and Easton are on the ice together, the opposition always looks on the back foot. Montreal's defensive side has been targeting Easton a lot this game, so he hasn't had a chance to score yet, and I can tell Connor's getting agitated about it.

I wish I was there waiting for him after the game. I *could* have been there. But we learned last time being on the road together was too tempting and too risky.

I toss my pen onto my notepad and run both hands down my face. What am I doing? Connor Kikishkin is one of the most high-profile players in the NHL, and here I am, hoping one day we can have a real relationship and ride happily into the sunset.

As his team owner.

I've lost all attachment to reality, I swear.

No matter how many times I go over the scenarios in my head, none of them have a good outcome for us. All people will care about is the serious power imbalance that exists between us. I own his career. There is absolutely nothing stopping me from exploiting the oldest Kiki brother, especially given our rocky past.

I know exactly what people will say about us, and *that* kind of speculation would move our relationship beyond hockey news and into the wider public. Telling people I'm a nervous wreck who's desperately trying to hold on to how much I loved my dad won't do a damn thing.

Telling people that Connor is the first person who's made me feel something other than anger, frustration, and deep-seated loneliness won't help either.

I pluck at my sweats, an option I'd thrown out once in passing coming back to me. I could sell the team. Move away from the hockey world, giving it time and space, and *then* we could go public. If we're even dating then.

Shit. What if I sell the team so we can be together, and then Connor decides he's done with us?

Then I'll be back to square one of having nothing in my life that makes me happy. Can I risk that on a possibility?

I only ever have these thoughts when he's not here. When my face isn't buried in work and a stray insecurity creeps in, it sends me down an endless spiral of what-ifs. People don't know our story, and unfortunately, no one wants the truth when drama and wild theories sell more stories.

My phone lights up beside me, Connor's name on the screen, and I glance back at the game that's only just wrapped up the second period. I must have gotten *really* behind.

"Hello?" I quickly answer.

"How fucking good was that goal?"

Ahh … I realize this is maybe one of those sort-of boyfriend moments that I probably should have been watching to see. "If you're talking about a goal in the third period, I might not be up to that yet."

His chuckle is so warm and comforting that I realize this is exactly what I needed. "You working?"

"Playing." It's not work if I'm not specifically on my laptop. At least, that's the lie I like to tell myself.

"My mistake. I won't ruin it for you, but someone scored the goal of the year."

"I can't wait to see how incredible you were."

"Oh. Not me." Something shifts in his tone that I can't place. "Easton. He was … that was … just watch, okay?"

"Promise."

"What are you doing now?" At least his voice goes back to normal.

"I'll finish watching, then probably work a bit and go to bed."

"Wish I was there."

"I know—"

"No. I really wish I was there."

"Con … are you okay?"

"I am, actually." He clears his throat. "Just sort of missing you."

This. How the hell am I supposed to walk away from something like this? Or hide it? Or lie about how amazing being with him makes me feel? "I'm a *lot* missing you. I hate not being there in person."

"Sorry."

"It's not your fault."

"It kinda is."

I laugh. "I also could have chosen not to get into a relationship with you, so you don't get to take the full blame."

"Fine. Be all logical." There are muffled voices in the background. "The team's heading out. Maybe, if you're up working late enough, I could call you when I get back to my room?"

Yet another reason why I can't regret our relationship, even as risky as it is. "I'll make sure I'm awake."

We hang up, and I'm left grinning. I put the game back on, absently sketching in my notebook, and when I look down, I find that I've doodled Parker Kikishkin and Connor Duchene all around the edge. I quickly scribble them out. I'm nowhere near thinking about marriage, and neither of us is close to thinking about it with each other.

My crush is crushing strong tonight.

I watch the game through until the end, and Colorado wins by one. It's a tough game, but there was no way for

Montreal to stop Easton's goal. He threw himself into the air, caught the rebound on the very end of his stick, and when the goalie went high, the puck slipped past his glove for the type of goal where every little thing had to go right for it to happen.

I skip back and replay over and over, slowing it down frame by frame to follow the exact flow of movement.

This moment would look incredible in my software.

I've been mindful of what Connor said about making sure that what I'm creating can't be a replacement for real people, and no matter how sophisticated the software is, it will still need human input.

My aim is to have the system preloaded with plays, natural movement from the players, which will mean doing body scans of them on and off the ice, and the ability for coaches to easily input new plays so they can talk their players through it. They should be able to overlay the game footage with the computer-generated players, then input commands for how play should have progressed. They can use this as a way to correct behaviors and moves, as a way to show the most effective way of playing against another team, as a way to introduce new lines and see how the players would work together ... the possibilities are endless.

I'm so excited to talk to Macklin about it and walk him through what I'm working on, but while I might have shared with Connor, it isn't ready for anyone else's eyes yet. My experience tells me that some people can only focus on what is in front of them rather than embrace the vision of what something could be. I need a workable prototype to get people as excited and on board with my plan as I am.

I want it finished quickly, which is why I'm throwing every waking minute into it, and when Connor's home, it's a real challenge not to give in to the urge to grab my laptop and tinker.

His handjobs and the way he fucks me are good distractions though.

He's still in his head about, well, *giving* head, but it's not something I need. Maybe he'll never get there, and that's okay. I've told him that, but I've caught him a few times now, starting in that direction and hesitating.

Would I love for Connor to suck me off? Absolutely. But I have exactly zero complaints about everything else we're doing, and there are so many other ways he makes me come.

Sex has never been a deal breaker for me. Affection is though, and luckily, Connor dishes it out constantly when he's home.

So I'm happy.

Really happy.

I'm just worried that it isn't going to last.

When my dry eyes come into focus a couple of hours later and see that it's 3:00 a.m., I scramble for my phone.

Four missed calls.

Fuck. They were two hours ago, so he'd have to be asleep by now. My gut sinks under the sludgy feeling that I've messed up, and as much as I want to call him and repeatedly apologize, waking him up will only make things worse.

So I'll sit with this unnerving feeling that I've screwed up before we've barely gotten started and call him first thing tomorrow.

Connor's Connor, so I doubt he's going to be angry. Mildly annoyed at the most.

It's me I'm worried about.

This is how it all started with my ex. The thoughtlessness. The single-minded focus on work.

I don't want to be like that again, but I'm worried it's impossible for me to be any other way.

CHAPTER THIRTY

CONNOR

The second the team arrives home, I don't bother going back to the house I now hate. I loved it not too long ago when I bought it, but it's the type of place I thought I should have, not what spoke to me.

I thought I was laying down roots, growing up, and doing what those who had their shit together did. But the spacious house only reminds me of what my life is now: empty.

Hockey isn't the same, things I thought I once loved no longer bring me joy, and according to that viral mantra by that lady I can't remember the name of, I need to rid it all from my life.

There's really only one thing that's keeping me going, and as unhealthy as it is to obsess over a new relationship to the point of finding everything else meaningless, being with Parker makes me feel like a brand-new person.

Maybe I need to see someone about it, but why do that when I can let myself into Parker's building and knock on his door to get the same validation?

Delusion? Hi, it me.

Yet, when he opens that door, all I get is a sense of … not home, exactly, but safety. Someone I can do or say anything I'm feeling, and he doesn't judge me for it. I've had more than enough judgment I can handle for one year from the very people I'm closest to—including myself.

Parker eyes me up and down. "Didn't even go home first, I see. Unless that huge suitcase means you're suddenly moving in. I'm loving spending time with you, but it's a bit soon for that, don't you think?"

"Way too soon." Though the thought of never going back to my house does fill me with happiness. "But I couldn't wait to see you."

I enter the apartment and set my suitcase down, closing the door behind me with my foot. My gaze roams over him, greedily drinking him in.

He's in a plain gray T-shirt that's too big on him and black sweats that hide everything I want to see. Everything I want to … maybe suck.

"Connor?" Parker asks.

I shake out of my blatant ogling. "Hmm?"

He smiles. "I asked if you wanted a drink."

He did? Eh. "Only if you're offering up a drink of you." I grab the waistband of his sweats and pull him toward me, all the while wincing. "That sounded a lot more smooth in my head than it did out loud."

Parker's good mood doesn't waver. "I don't care. You can be as corny as you like when you're saying nice things to me." He tilts his head more, leaning in and bringing our mouths so close I want to rush to press our lips together.

But not before I tell him this: "I missed you."

His eyes widen like he can't believe it, even though we said it on the phone to each other while I was gone. If he doesn't believe it because they're empty words, there's no way he'd be able to deny it's true when I surge forward and kiss him.

My mouth moves against his, firm and dominant, but when I push my tongue against his, it's nothing but slow and sensual. Because this isn't about our physical connection. It isn't about having an orgasm after days of being apart. I want to show him that I'm truly in this. That I want to be with him and that I might not know much about what I want when it comes to other elements of my life, but I do know I want him.

All of him.

And maybe he's right. It is too soon to be having these types of thoughts, but as long as I keep them as inside thoughts, we should be fine.

I don't want to scare him off, but I also don't want him to think that I'm only using him to explore my bisexuality. It's way more than that.

I'm serious about him, and I want to do what other same-sex couples do in relationships. All of it. Starting with this. I'm fucking terrified of doing it wrong, but it's not about me. It's about making him feel good.

I wrap my arms around his waist and hoist him up so that when I turn toward his kitchen counter, his ass slides across the marble effortlessly.

This probably isn't the best angle to give him a blowjob, but I figure it's better for my degenerating hockey knees if I don't have to rest on them.

Parker tries to grind against me, and I have visions of fucking him like this. His ass hanging off the edge of the counter, me slamming into him while he has to hold on to the edge so he doesn't fall backward into the sink. What's sex without a little core workout?

But that'll have to happen another time. I'm determined to suck Parker's cock and be good at it. Or at least not so horrible it ends with bite marks and an ER visit. I have to have realistic expectations for my first time.

I grip his hips and take a step backward, and he tries to follow, not letting our mouths break apart.

A laugh bubbles out of me, skimming across his lips.

He breaks away. "I need you."

"I want all of you," I reply.

I lift the hem of his shirt, and he helps me take it off, and then his sweats go next. He hisses when he settles back on his ass.

"Cold counter?" I ask.

"Little. Don't care." Parker grips the back of my hair and pulls me back to his mouth.

We go back to making out, and as eager as I am to get my mouth around his cock, I like this too. Tasting, teasing …

He captures my bottom lip in his teeth, and I groan.

I'd love to feel his skin against mine. I'm wearing way too many clothes, but I also don't want to pull away from him again.

I work open my pants and drop them to the floor, but I can't step out of them without nearly falling over because my head is swimming.

In the end, I have to give up kissing him, not only so I can get rid of the rest of my clothes but to catch my breath and compose myself enough to get the courage to do this.

It's way too tempting to pull him against me and rut until we both explode.

Even though our mouths have gotten sloppy and I can feel his saliva on my lips, my tongue is drier than the Sahara.

We're both naked now. Him on the kitchen counter, me standing between his widened legs, and as I stare down at his needy cock, his swollen head stretching his tight, velvety skin, I can practically taste his desperation already. I want to taste it for real. Have all of him—or at least most of him—in my mouth.

"Con?" he rasps.

I glance up at his gorgeous face, unable to connect the stunning man in front of me with the invisible guy I passed by every day during my senior year of high school. Was he always this good-looking? Had I noticed back then but never thought anything more of it? Or was I so in my superficial era that all I saw was what everyone else did? A loser computer geek with a dandruff problem. And that smile.

Yet here I am, standing before him, offering to suck his cock.

Oh, how ten years can change a person.

"What's wrong?" he asks. "You just … stopped."

"I want … I want to …" I stare down at his cock again and get the words out in a rush. "Use my mouth." Heat creeps up my neck. "But I don't know what I'm doing. I could do what I did when I was a virgin, which was pretend I knew what I was doing and give you the worst orgasm ever. Fuck, maybe I can't even do that. I doubt Jade Whatsherface got off back then. What if—"

Parker covers my mouth with his hand. "How about we don't talk about the people you hooked up with in high school?"

Right. Probably a great way to ruin the mood. He removes his hand.

"Sorry," I say. "I'm out of my element, and as much as I want to fake confidence, I can't with you."

He reaches for my face again, but this time, it's to cup my cheek. "You know you don't have to do anything, right?"

"I do. But I want to. I just want to make sure I'm good at it. For you."

"Then that right there is all you need," he says softly. "It doesn't matter if you're good at it or you suck—pun intended. You wanting to make it good for me already puts you ahead of any other man I've been with."

"What?"

He shrugs. "Well, mostly, the guys I've been with have been experienced. Or at least pretended to be like you said. When someone thinks they know what they're doing, it can be difficult to correct them, you know? Egos get involved. I'm assuming with you that if I tell you what I like, you'll listen because you don't have this past full of other dicks you've made come and assume it would be the same with me."

"That kind of makes sense."

Parker shakes his head, and his unstyled hair falls in his face. "I'm blabbering. I'm delirious with blue balls. At this rate, all you'll have to do is put your lips on me and I'll come, so …"

I smile. "It would make it a lot easier for me if you could do that."

"I promise it won't take much."

"And I promise I'll try not to bite your dick off."

His hand on my cheek freezes. "Okay, now I'm worried."

"You reckon old people with dentures give good blowjobs? If you think about it, if they take their teeth out, they'd be all gums. Maybe I should tell the team's dentist to stop giving me dental implants whenever they get knocked out on the ice from now on."

Parker blinks at me. "I'm starting to think you don't want me to come at all because with that visual in my head, it's really hard to keep, well, hard."

I bite my bottom lip. "I might be stalling."

Parker taps my shoulder and wriggles his butt off the counter, pushing me to get out of his way as he sets his feet down.

"Wait, what are you doing?" I ask.

"I'm taking the decision away from you. I'm not going to let you give me a blowjob. How about that?"

"Nooo. I want to."

"It doesn't seem like you do, and it's totally fine. I'm taking the decision out of your hands." He turns and ambles toward his bedroom.

"Where are you going?"

"I was going to go jerk off in the shower, but if you want to join me, I'll allow you to do it for me."

"No, I'm going to blow you."

"No, you're not."

I'm, like, two seconds away from stomping my foot like a child. "Yes, I am, and you can't stop me." My face falls. "Shit. Wait, unless you actually do want to stop me and are taking away consent, then of course I'll back off, but if you're doing this for me, don't."

He eyes me, trying to figure me out. Join the club, Parks. All I know is now that he's said I can't blow him, I want to prove that I can.

Stubborn streak? Apparently, it's an old Connor and new Connor trait. Check that off the list.

"I'm not taking away consent," Parker says. "I'm taking away the pressure. There's a difference."

I don't hear much after he says he's not taking away his consent. That's a green light, and I don't hesitate to pounce on him.

I put my hand on his chest and guide him backward until he's up against the wall right next to his bedroom door.

It's probably a good thing that he almost took my chance away because it only makes me want it more, and it gives me the courage to go through with it.

I sink to my knees—fuck the pain they'll be in later—and am maybe too overeager as I try to take as much of him in my mouth at once.

My gag reflex threatens to make me cough immediately, but I swallow that down. Nope, nope, not going to cough. The salty taste is also a shock to the system, but I'm not letting that get to me either. Holding everything back only brings water to my eyes though, and Parker pulls out of my mouth himself.

"How about we ease into it first? Go slow and only put the tip in your mouth while you use your hand to cover the rest."

Glancing up at him through my lashes, I lower my head and try again, only taking the round mushroom head of his cock past my lips. When my thick fingers wrap around the base of his cock, Parker's eyes roll back in his head.

"That feels so good."

His encouragement is what gives me even more motivation. But I don't allow myself to jump ahead this time.

Slowly, I lower my head, taking more of him in my mouth and then pulling back up. I suck on his tip while using my hand in the opposite direction. My lips meet my hand over and over until I get used to having him in my mouth.

Parker's moans are loud, only spurring me on. His breath quickens, he grips my hair loosely, and I know he's enjoying it because what he said is true. If he told me to change something up to make it even better for him, I wouldn't take it as an insult. I'll do whatever he wants me to so I can get him across the finish line.

The more I bob my head, the more of him I fit in my mouth, the more I get used to his taste. The saltiness comes and goes with each dribble of precum, and while I thought I wouldn't like how it feels, I drink him down greedily. At one point, there's so much I swear he's come without warning me, but nope. He's still going. He's still moaning, still looking blissed-out, and he's still only gripping my hair like he's cradling my head more than taking any kind of control over my movements.

The thought of him coming down my throat by surprise is actually really hot. So hot I have to use my free hand to take care of my own need.

Parker senses the movement and brings his chin down, those blue eyes watching me. I don't take my gaze off him either.

"You remember what I did to you the other day on the couch?" he asks.

How could I forget? My ass tenses at the thought, as if searching for that wandering finger again. I nod as subtly as I can.

"I need you to do that for me." He's breathing so hard now. "I'm so close. I'm so fucking close, and that will be the end of me. I know it."

As much as I'd love to see how far I could go, how deep I could take him, bringing him this close to the edge is too much of an accomplishment to drag it out. I want him to break. I want him to crumble, and when he's done, I want him to realize what I've been trying to deny ever since he waltzed into my life: He's it for me.

The second I move my hand from his shaft to behind his balls, giving his sac a light squeeze while circling his rim with my finger, his grip in my hair tightens, and then my mouth fills with his cum.

Surprisingly, I don't choke, though some spills out and down my chin. It could be my fault or his because in the next second, his cock falls from my mouth, and I'm suddenly on my back with him on top of me, his still-erupting cock rubbing all over me as he grinds against me.

His cum makes it slippery as fuck, and before I know it, my cum joins his, my orgasm hits, and my brain becomes a happy pile of mush.

Parker continues to move against me but slows until we're both spent. I close my eyes and bask in the post-gasm bliss. That is, until he starts laughing uncontrollably.

My eyes fly open. "Shit, I wasn't that bad, was I?"

He's still laughing. "No, no. You were … phenomenal. But … did you say you were a happy pile of mush at the end there?"

"That was out loud?"

"Yes."

Oops. "Eh. I said what I said. You do make me a happy pile of mush."

Just like that, he doesn't find it funny anymore, and I'm worried I've overstepped, or maybe that's too serious for him.

The longer he stares into my eyes without saying anything, the more self-conscious I become. I try to find words. Try to find something that will deescalate what

I've said. But all that comes out is, "I think I'm falling for you."

Fucking. Idiot.

That is not deescalating.

CHAPTER THIRTY-ONE

PARKER

I told myself to quit staring at Connor about a minute ago. Make that two. I'm … I … For a guy who's normally pretty smart, my brain is being very dumb.

"Parker?" he croaks.

My heart feels like it's on steroids, and I lean down to kiss him before stiffly climbing off his lap. He's falling for me? *Fuck, Connor, I've been unwillingly falling for you since we were teenagers*. All the self-loathing wasn't enough to make it stop, and all I ever wanted was for him to see me. Well, he sees me clearly now, and apparently, I'm freaking out.

Because you don't drop something like that after sex. You don't.

I leave him behind and head for the kitchen.

How the fuck am I supposed to know he won't regret it once the orgasm haze fades and he catches up to what he said?

To me.

No, I think the best course of action is to run far, far away and revisit this conversation in, oh … ten years? Surely he'll know by then if he means it or not.

"Parker?"

His voice from down the hall startles me. Guess I'm not running fast enough. "Ah, yes. Very good sex. Excellent work. Need milk. Back soon."

I'm not anywhere close to the door when Connor cuts me off. His large, naked body really should come with a warning label because I momentarily forget what I'm doing at the sight of it. It does remind me that I, too, am very naked and can't run out to the store like this. That could've been embarrassing. Though, not as embarrassing as facing my feelings right here and now.

"Very good excellent work need milk?" he repeats incredulously. "Was the blowjob *that* bad?"

Okay, now *that* cuts me out of it. In all of the feelings floating around, I completely forgot about his nerves, and now I feel like the worst person ever. "No," I hurry to assure him. "No, no, no. Con, when I say that was the best blowjob ever, I'm not being facetious. Yeah, you were clearly inexperienced, but that meant absolutely nothing because I've never had someone want to make it that good for me. That's worth more than years of experience."

"Let's pretend like I believe you … why did you run away?"

My face flushes hot, and I know it's a trick question. Doesn't Connor know that I'm doing this for *him*? So he doesn't get through this experimental phase and realize he's made a giant mistake? Even if we could come out and be together, how the hell would that look on social media?

I can see the comments from former classmates now.

THE hockey hotshot ended up with the douche?

Should someone remind Connor that it's not April 1st?

He's really slumming it now.

Or worse:

I'd hook up with the douche too now that he's a billionaire.

My eyes close for a second, and I remind myself that Connor is not saying he wants to run out and tell the world. He's just … falling for me.

Holy mother of fuck, what is wrong with him? My eyes snap open, and I find Connor studying me. His expression leaves no doubt that he knows what I'm really freaking out over, but how can he not get it? Isn't he scared? Like, falling for someone is a lot, and what if he doesn't mean it?

His big hand comes up to cup my face. "I'm falling for you, Park."

"Don't."

He freezes. "Don't fall for you?"

"Don't say it."

He looks pissed. "What?"

"*Now*, I mean. Like, let's set an alarm. Try again in an hour, or—"

"You want me to tell you how I feel in an hour?"

"It's the orgasm talking. I don't want you to say something that you're going to regret."

His jaw tightens. "Why don't you trust me on this one?"

"Trust you? You just came! I'm usually delirious for a good three point four minutes after blowing my load, and here you are saying things you'd never … things you shouldn't …"

He groans, and it has a hard edge to it. His hands close over my shoulders, and he pulls me a step closer. "Out of the two of us, I think you're the one about to say something you'll regret."

"What do you—"

"I know I'm asking a lot when I say this, but you really need to give me some trust here. This wasn't a spur-of-the-moment thing. It's been creeping up on me since we first got together, maybe longer, and I'm trying really hard not to get offended that you think I'm too stupid to know how I feel."

"I'm really fucking it up."

"Little bit."

I take a deep breath and let it out. "I'm … scared."

"Scared?"

"It's possible that I've had this big-picture idea of who Connor Kikishkin is since I met you." I can't look at him, so I focus on his bare chest, which isn't much better. "Hot, confident, someone people are drawn to. I'm not convinced that my crush on you wasn't some kind of jealous hero worship, but no matter what it was, I've had feelings for you for a really, really long time. Then you went and screwed me all up."

"What do you mean?"

I risk a glance up at him, and thankfully, he looks more curious than annoyed now. "You're so much better than I ever imagined you were. All that superficial stuff? It's nothing compared to how you treat me. How you love your family. How you're okay with being vulnerable while you find yourself. Sometimes I wish we'd never had … *this* because when it goes away, I know I'll never find it again."

"When?"

I sigh, but it's more the energy seeping out of me. "How do you see this working? Us? It … it can't."

"Do you want it to?"

It's maybe the most ridiculous question he's ever asked. Do *I* want to make it work with the most gorgeously sweet man I've ever met? No, I want an asshole. "If you leave me—"

"That isn't what I asked you."

I guess I can add determined and stubborn to my list of Connor qualities. "Can't you let me crawl away into my avoidance cave and—"

"Answer the question."

"Fine. Yes. I want it. I want us to work out and be end goals and keep making each other happy. I selfishly want *the* Connor Kikishkin who I built up in my head to be mine and the real Connor to be even more mine. I want you to keep looking at me how you always look at me, and I want to keep being there for you while you find the best version of yourself. I want it all too much, and that's why it scares me."

One corner of Connor's lips tilts upward, and he gets that look in his eyes. That one he doesn't hold back that makes me all tingly and high.

"Then let's try this again." His voice has deepened, and when he steps forward, I step back until he has me pressed up against the wall, his fingers hooked under my chin so I have no choice but to meet his gaze. "I have feelings for you, Parker. I'm falling for you. I want all of those things and more, and from this point forward, you're mine. Not only in the claimy, possessive, caveman sex kind of way. In *every way*. Got it?"

My brain has gone stupid again. Never, ever in my life have I felt as wanted as I do in this moment. "You won't regret it?"

His grip on my chin tightens. "Got it?"

"Yes. Got it. Want it. And you're … you're mine too. Right?"

"Exactly."

A smile splits through his intensity, and his lips crush against mine. His tongue fills my mouth with the lingering taste of my cum, and when his body presses against me, I wish desperately that I could get it up again. Apparently, the poor thing needs more than a ten-minute breather.

He pulls back, forehead resting against mine, and I let myself hope for a moment that this really is something.

A loud yawn rips from Connor that breaks the tension.

"You need a nap?" I ask.

"I shouldn't. Actually, you know what would be perfect?"

"What?"

"Can we crash on the couch, watch a movie, and maybe order in food? All I want to do is spend the day with you and recover from this grueling schedule we're on."

"Deal, except for one thing."

"Yeah?"

I run my hand down his chest. "We're staying naked, so instead of ordering in, I'll cook us something."

"Careful, I might just let the L word drop."

That makes me laugh. "Then I really will know you're still cum-drunk. You get some blankets, and I'll put some pasta on."

I turn to head into the kitchen when arms circle my waist and Connor's lips come down on my shoulder.

"Are you okay now?" he murmurs.

Am I? The whole confessing feelings thing has me raw in a way I never would have picked coming. No matter what he says, it really will take me time to trust that we're the real thing, especially since we can't be together publicly. There's too much at risk for the both of us, and that's before we cover the whole Connor not being out thing. I'm more than happy to stay a secret in order to keep him and protect both of us, but I don't think there will ever not be a small part of me that worries when it will end.

I never had that with my ex, and I'm starting to worry that maybe I wasn't as in love with him as I thought. Sure, I forgot about the phone call with Connor, but now he's here, I haven't had the urge to reach for my computer once.

That doesn't mean I won't fuck things up.

But hopefully, it means I'll be more conscious of how I treat him.

Dad would have loved him for me.

"I have one regret," I say, turning toward him. "I regret Dad never got to see us together. He was a big fan, and I know if he saw what a good boyfriend you are that he would have loved you even more."

"I'll just have to be the best boyfriend ever. To make Pappa Duchene proud."

I blink quickly. "Stop it. You'll make me cry."

"Wait until I meet your mom. I'm going to have her planning our wedding from hello. She's going to be all 'ex-boyfriend who' because she'll know that no one is good enough for her son but me."

I'm cautious as I ask the next question. "And … will I meet your parents? As your boyfriend this time? One day?"

"Of course. With my parents as my managers though, it's a tricky one. I know they'll support me, but I also get the feeling it's going to be all calculated and PR mode rather than something I can enjoy and—" Something crosses his expression. "And … exactly how I reacted to Easton and Lachie. I get it, universe. I can really do without all the shitty reminders now, thanks."

It's my turn to comfort him. "Stop beating yourself up. From what I've seen, Easton is enjoying himself now. So are you. Maybe your parents will be clinical and business-first, but that doesn't take away that we get this. Nothing does. Take whatever time you need because it's not like we can be public whether you're out or not."

"True. I really hate that we have to hide this."

"It's either we hide it or have nothing. I'm comfortable with our decision."

Connor opens his mouth but very obviously changes his response at the last minute. "Me too. But I think I need to talk to my brother."

CHAPTER THIRTY-TWO

CONNOR

Parker and I watch brainless movies while snuggling on the couch the whole day, lazily making out, talking about unimportant stuff, and letting the heaviness of the morning fade away.

I don't regret telling him what I was thinking. It might have come out in the heat of the moment, but I meant it. I do regret *when* I told him because he thought it was an empty confession, only brought on by an orgasm. It's easy to see why he assumed that, but it wasn't my intention to make him retreat inside his head.

There's something else I want to tell him. Something that is life-changing and will turn everyone's world upside down. But I'm keeping it in my back pocket for now. My figurative one. I've been naked all day.

It's bigger than me coming out publicly. Bigger than telling my parents it turns out they have three queer sons. It's … it's something I never thought I'd do this early, and the only reason I haven't jumped on it immediately is because I'm worried I'm confused. That it's a phase.

Fucking hell. I'm talking about quitting hockey the same way bigots talk about people's sexualities.

These thoughts have been niggling at me for a while and are only growing stronger. But it turns out I still have some old Connor in me after all because I know how difficult it would be to come back if I left now and regretted it.

But as Parker brings me a glass of water and then curls back up into my side under the blankets, I don't see how I'll ever get to a point where I'll regret it. Letting go of hockey would also mean I'd be able to give us that real chance to be together. Publicly.

It's why I want to go talk to East. Because he's been in my position, and even though I don't deserve to ask him for advice on this when I was the one holding him back, I'm hoping what he said in Vegas is true. I hope he can see how this conflict has the potential to tear me in two. But is it really a conflict when the answer seems like an easy one?

"What are you thinking about?" Parker asks.

"Huh?"

"You look like you're trying to do math."

"I'm good at math, thank you. Twenty minutes to a period, broken up in one- to two-minute shifts, divided by three defense teams of two equals—"

"Do you know any math that doesn't involve hockey?"

He's got me there. "Sure. You plus me equals one now?"

Parker melts against me, and I tell myself to focus on here and now, but the thing is, I can't enjoy it. Not fully. Not without talking through some of the thoughts running wild in my head. And I can't talk to Parker about them because what if I decide it's a bad idea? What if I tell him I'm retiring, he gets his hopes up, and then I crush his heart?

I need to be sure, and to be sure, I need to talk to East. Or Knox. Hey, now they're together, I get two for the price of one.

I shift so I can look Parker in the eyes when I say, "Do you mind if I head home tonight? The more I think about coming out, the more I want to talk to East about it. About how he thinks our parents might handle it and all of that."

"I'm not going to hold you hostage if that's what you mean."

"Is it really hostage if I'm here voluntarily?"

"I mean, I could tie you down so you never leave. You said you were mine, after all." Parker rolls on top of me. We haven't come again since this morning when I arrived on his doorstep, so he knows exactly how to play me.

"You win, but after orgasms, I'm leaving to see Easton."

I don't go see Easton.

-

It's one of those times where we have a couple of days between games. We still have practice, and I still have to do my exercises to keep warm and loose, watch game tape, and prepare ourselves for our next match-up, but it's not as packed a schedule as usual.

Which means that as I pass my brother at our weights facility and he asks me to spot him on the bench press, I take that opportunity to talk to him about all the stuff I haven't gotten the chance to yet.

I'll wait for the right time though. That's what I tell myself anyway, but I find my mouth blurting, "What do you think Mom and Dad would say if I retired?"

The bar drops so fast, the weight of it pinning Easton's chest and knocking the wind out of him.

"Shit." I'm quick to help him lift it off.

He breathes hard, rubbing his sternum as he sits up. "What did you say?" He's so loud others in the room have glanced our way.

"Uh, maybe we shouldn't have this conversation here."

"You think?" His chest still rises and falls in an exaggerated way. "Broken ribs were not on my bingo card for today."

I cock my head. "Are they ever on your bingo card?"

He stands, seemingly recovered. "Every game day. It's a possibility."

"Fair enough. Can I come by your place after this?"

His brow furrows. "Fuck that. We're talking about this now. I can work out later."

Now that people are staring, I glance around. "Okay, but not here."

Here at the practice facility, we don't really have a lot of places to go to be in private, so we end up sitting in Easton's new car in the parking lot. We used to carpool until I moved away, so he never bothered upgrading his beat-up old one until recently.

"Still smells like new car," I say, running my hand over the smooth leather interior of his G-Wagon.

I should get props for keeping my mouth shut about dropping two hundred K on a ridiculous car with all the bells and whistles being a frivolous expense, but with wisdom and growth also comes perspective. I spent four million dollars on a house I don't even like being in.

"Stop stalling and spill. You want to retire? Like, retire retire. Did you hit your head? Do you have a fever? I'd ask if you'd been overseas anywhere you could've gotten a parasite that eats your brain if I hadn't seen you two days ago."

"And you say I'm dramatic."

"This *is* dramatic." Easton's arms flail, and then his face falls. "It's not because you're worried about the backlash of being bi, is it? Oh, Con—"

"It's not," I say quickly. "It's not my sexuality or how I identify. It's who I'm with that's the issue. Could you imagine everyone finding out I'm seeing the team's owner? How Parker could come under scrutiny with the power imbalance? You saw how Oskar and Lane's relationship played out. Lane got fired because he was Oskar's PR manager. There were rumors of how ethical it was. I don't want that for Parker."

"Retiring isn't the answer though," Easton says. "Even if you do retire, it's going to come out that he owned the team, and depending on when you tell people you're a couple, they could speculate it's why you're quitting early when there's no injury, no reason to quit, and you're one of the best D-men in the league."

I realize I'm making the Parker factor bigger than it really is. "It's not only that. If I'm being honest ..." Fuck, why is it so hard to say out loud? *Hey, turns out I'm bi* is easy. *I'm no longer in love with hockey* isn't.

"What? Is it because of our thing? Because I told you to back off? I told you, we're cool now, but if it's still too hard for you to butt out, you could ask for a trade? Hell, I could still ask for one. Knox can move with me, and if I get on a team on the East Coast, there'd be less travel for him, and—"

"I don't even like hockey," I yell.

The car fills with silence.

"W-what?" Easton eventually asks. "You *are* hockey."

"No, I'm ... naturally talented at a sport our dad enrolled us in when we were little. I played hockey because it was our parents' built-in babysitter while they were at work. I feel like every decision I've made about hockey and my life has revolved around what has been expected of me, and now that I'm out on this ledge all by myself, trying to figure everything out that I should've had figured out as a teenager, I'm realizing that everything I've done has been because of expectation. Not because I love it. I thought I did, but … maybe I don't."

Easton goes back to being at a loss for words. He stares out the windshield.

Shit. "You're not taking this as well as I thought you would. And if you, of all people, are freaking out, I don't want to tell Mom and Dad now."

"No, no, I'm … fine."

"Mm. Seems like it."

"No, really. It's a shock, but if you're adamant about it, then I'll support you. No matter what. Just like you have always been there for me. Even sometimes too much." His lips twitch. "But when you say you think you only play hockey because it's expected, I tried to think about a time where I ever thought that. Or didn't want to play. Or God forbid if something happened on the ice and I was forced into retirement, how I'd feel."

"And?" Maybe I am reading into all this. Maybe my love of the game will come back to me.

"Honestly, it would feel like my life was over."

There goes that idea.

"You should tell Mom and Dad," he adds. "They'll be as shocked as I am, but you know they'll be there for you. You did everything for them when you got your first big paycheck from the NHL. You owe them nothing. You owe Lachie and me nothing. It'll be weird though. Not having you on the ice with me."

"You asked for a trade during preseason to get away from me!"

"Yes, but you still would've been playing. I still would've seen you on the ice, even if instead of protecting me, you'd be the one shoving me into the boards. It'll be an adjustment, but you have to do what makes you happy. No matter what. And I'll stand behind you."

Easton is a better brother than I ever was to him.

"I'm sorry I wasn't that person for you. The one who'd say I'm there for you no matter what."

He shoulder bumps me. "You were. You just added a caveat at the end, saying, 'Even when you do things that I deem dumbass mistakes.'"

"And I shouldn't have added that. I'm thankful you're not a spiteful asshole. You could tell me the exact same thing, but you haven't."

"They're your mistakes to make," he says. "And who knows, maybe you'll retire and regret it immediately, or maybe it's the exact thing you need to be your authentic self. It's hard to know which way it'll go."

It's not so hard for me. Because now more than ever, I know it's what I want.

CHAPTER THIRTY-THREE

PARKER

Things with Connor are amazing. The team is on a winning hot streak, and because of the recent stint of away games, it means that I've been able to get my software to a workable level. My CGI characters are no longer matrixing or needing an exorcist, so I'm taking that as a good sign. I'm planning to show it to Macklin and get his endorsement before taking it to the coaching team. They'll be the ones to give me notes on what they can use it for, along with what plays might be beneficial to add into the system today. If they're interested, it won't be long before we can move it to uploading actual player data, which will be the real game changer.

"Wish me luck, Conishkin," I tell him as I return him to the cage. I'm still not convinced I'm a pet person—even the cleanest animals are too dirty for me—but I do love that he keeps me company while Connor and Mom are away.

Maybe I should sign up for a friend app? Do they have those? There are dating ones, so friendship ones shouldn't be too much of a stretch.

Conishkin gives me a motivational squeak before climbing into his wheel and running like his life depends on it. The voluntary cardio goes to show he's far more like his namesake than me.

Even with all the work I've put into this program, I'm not convinced the coaches will want it. It's a weird thing, putting so much time and energy into something I'm proud of, only to find out all that time, energy, and pride was misplaced. It happened with some of my earlier designs before I hit on my last success, and even with that huge sale behind me, I feel like I'm starting from the ground floor again.

My guts are queasy with nerves, and all I hope is that they keep an open mind and look for the potential to make their lives easier here. Being resistant to change is a natural human emotion, and that's amplified by superstitious jocks when they're on the hot streak of their careers.

I know how good this will be though. I want our team to dominate.

Because at the end of this season, I want that Stanley Cup.

I want the marker that buying this team was the right move for me and that the universe will reward me with the ultimate sign that I've made Dad proud.

Keeping the Kiki brothers together—as misguided as that was—felt like kismet, and this is the next stage in my plan.

With the brothers and this software working together, I really think we're in with a chance.

I can feel it in my bones.

That's not me trying to diminish the rest of the team either. They're all working together like it was meant to be, but I've noticed how their energy changes based on how the brothers are playing. The rest of the team looks up to those two, especially Connor. If Connor is playing his heart out, the rest of them match that dedication.

Dad was right.

Connor and Easton were born for this.

Part of me wishes that Lachie also played for Colorado, but I'm not about to get greedy.

It took me four outfit changes before I felt ready to leave the house this morning. As much as I'd love to wear a suit and hide behind my camouflage, I'm also overly aware of what Macklin said about being approachable, and if there was ever a time for needing that, it's now.

The sweatpants and hoodie are too restrictive though. Sweet baby Jesus, my palms are sweating.

The whole drive to the practice facilities, I tell myself that it's okay. I know what I'm talking about, and when I get going about something I love, I'm good at getting other people excited too. My prototype is behaving and will give them a good idea of what my vision is.

And I will make it clear there are no layoffs. By … giving them a pay raise? Is that too drastic? I'll have to brainstorm it later, but the first thing to do is to get them to believe in me the way I believe in them.

I take a moment to get out of my anxiety brain and into work mode before I grab my laptop and get out of the car. I'd considered emailing Macklin ahead of time to give him the heads-up, but I didn't want him thinking this was a "we need to talk" scenario, so I'm going to blindside him instead. Perfect plan. Foolproof way to win someone over.

Fuck.

I get inside, find his office empty, and make my way out to the ice. The whole team is there running drills, with Macklin calling out things from the side. I'm sure they are very important things, but I've never attended a training session before, so this is all new to me.

My gaze finds Connor on the ice, and I watch him for a moment, mesmerized by the way he moves out there. He's so strong. So confident. Like he was born for hockey.

I chuckle to myself as I remember all those games in high school I'd go to and watch, completely obsessed with hating him while not able to move my eyes away.

I remember how excited Dad would get. "Look at the way big Kiki read that pass and little Kiki was ready for his intercept. They're like one brain out there. Phenomenal hockey!"

I'm ready to agree with you, Dad.

If only I'd had that chance when he was still around to hear it.

I wait for Macklin to turn back to making notes on his clipboard before approaching.

"Hey, Coach."

"Mr. Duchene. What can I do for you?"

"First of all, Parker is fine."

Surprise lights up his eyes. "Here to watch training?"

"Actually, I was hoping to run something by you. It's something I've been working on that I thought could help the team."

He checks his watch, then calls out to Dion, one of the assistant coaches, to take over. "Want to do this in my office?"

"Actually, I've got everything with me," I say, sliding onto one of the benches around the ice. It's freezing in here, and I'm not so sure my fingers won't go brittle and snap off, but in a choice between warmth and getting this over with, I'm committed now.

"I've been thinking a lot about what I can bring to this team since I bought it," I say.

"Money." Macklin eyes me. "I think you're underestimating how important the funding of a team is. You're paying my wages, that's all I care about."

"Sure, and that's great and won't stop, but it's not me. I'm not someone who can sit around throwing money at something. I want to feel like I'm making a tangible contribution."

"Again. You are reeeeally underestimating the role of money in a franchise."

I open my laptop. "Fine. Yes. Money. It's important. I get it. So let me spoil you and give you something else as well."

His eyes narrow a little. "I'm listening."

My fingers fly over the keys as I open the program and punch in the commands for the trial run. "I've been working on assistance software for the video coaching team. Something specifically to help with game tape, but I'm open to ideas to expand it. Maybe generate new plays you want to run, that kind of thing." I open the footage I preloaded into it from one of the games a few weeks ago. Munter sent a rogue pass to New Jersey that they were able to score off. "Please remember, we're looking at a prototype here. If there are any glitches, roll with it. This is my vision." I hit Play, and the footage rolls; then once it starts a second time, I slow the footage down and have my generated players take over and position themselves into the play it should have been. "I want to be clear and state up front that this isn't being created to take anyone's jobs. I want to make things easier. More visual. Instead of talking through it and having random arrows to try and convey how things should have run, you can actually show them.

And if it's something you're on board with, we can really drill down and make it as sophisticated as we want. You and your coaching staff can give me all the requirements they need. I'll show you how to generate new plays into the system. We can do full-body scans of our team so you can have lifelike Kiki brothers skating around on here. It'll learn how they move and what they're capable of…" I trail off, not wanting to scare him with how far these possibilities can go but too full of excitement not to keep rambling about all the what-ifs.

Macklin doesn't talk at first.

"It looks complicated."

"It isn't," I promise him, quickly navigating to the menu. "Here is the footage I've uploaded. It takes a few seconds to do. Then you can click on whichever one you want. This toggle here is the plays I've preloaded. We'll have a list of all our players on the other side, and then when you're reviewing the play, you'll have the ability to switch out players to see how, based on statistics, any other player would have reacted in any given situation. That'll give you flexibility with the lines. Across teams. The uses really are infinite."

The shell-shocked look he's giving me makes it clear I've gotten ahead of myself again.

"But let's focus on the basics. For now, why don't you take some time to go through it." I hand the laptop over. "You can click on anything you like. It won't break. And if it does, I'll know how to fix it. Don't be scared."

Because that's a big thing with technology. People are always scared. Learning something new and different can be overwhelming at first, but I've created this with the user in mind, and from everything I've seen in those game tape meetings, the user is short on patience, high on results, and wants to be more practically than theoretically focused.

After a couple of minutes of testing out the functionality, Macklin glances up at me. "This … you can guarantee no one will lose their jobs because of this thing?"

"Guarantee it. There are a lot of automations, but it still needs the human factor to upload and make sure the data being presented is correct and—" Do not overwhelm the man, damn it. "No one will lose their jobs."

"In that case, this could be a game changer."

The tension I've been clinging to all morning slowly releases. "Yeah?"

"If you can make it do all the things you say you can, it really will be something else."

"I'm so relieved. I was worried you'd think I was overstepping."

Macklin cuffs my shoulder. "What's the point of having a tech genius with us if we don't get to reap the benefits?"

"Nerds and jocks unite."

He holds out his fist that I tap with mine. "What's our first step?"

"We take this to the coaching staff so I can get all the notes together, then I start work."

"Excellent." He glances over at where the team is leaving the ice. "I better get to it. Set a meeting, and I'll make sure we're all there."

He walks off, and I smile at a few players as they pass. Connor is one of the last off, which I'm sure was on purpose because he hangs back by the seat I'm sitting on.

"Fancy seeing you here."

I'm too excited to go back and forth with him. "Macklin liked it," I whisper-shriek.

Connor's face lights up. "I knew he would."

"I'm so relieved. So fucking relieved."

Which, of course, he knows because I've been stressing to him over it all week. "You shouldn't doubt your genius."

"I'm trying hard not to get excited and jinx us."

"What do you mean?"

This is a lot to admit, but I trust Connor more than I trust anyone. If we're being real in this relationship, he's going to know all of me, even the weird parts. "You know why I bought the team."

He nods.

"Ever since then, it's like everything has been exactly right. The way we've connected, the way the team is gelling, the way staying home for away games has spurred this idea. Everything feels like it has perfectly built to this moment, and I … I think …"

"What?"

"Please don't hate me for saying this." I'm grinning hard. "I think this is where I'm supposed to be. Here. Developing this while you dominate out there. Between you on the ice and this software hopefully doing what I think it can do … this might be it."

"*It*?"

"You're gonna win me that Cup, Connor. For Dad."

CHAPTER THIRTY-FOUR

CONNOR

I've been checked into the boards so many times over my career that I've lost count of how many hits I've taken. I've given just as many. But none of them hit as hard as the pressure Parker's put on me.

Win a Stanley Cup for his late father. Hockey players chase that Cup for their entire careers. We're taught to live and breathe for the day we're allowed to touch it because everyone knows if you haven't won it, you don't get that honor. And if you do touch it, you're doomed to never hoist it above your head after a Championship game.

Everything I've spent the last couple of months to change comes rushing back to me, old Connor filling my mind and trying to take over.

It's too much responsibility to put on my shoulders. Last season, I would've said, "Let's do it," and be eager to fulfill his wish. But also, last season, I probably would've punched Parker that day in the locker room, gotten fired, and I wouldn't have to worry. I also wouldn't have him now.

It figures the minute I decide to give up hockey, the next second is someone asking me to be great at it for them. No, not them. Their dead father.

How am I supposed to say no to that? How am I supposed to say, "I'm sorry, I would rather be unemployed than try to win you a Cup."

It has nothing to do with Parker. If I could, I would go out and win it for him this very next game. But that's not reality. The reality is more players walk away without their name on the Cup than with it, and the idea of sticking around until I can possibly pull it off makes my stomach churn.

Parker's still rambling about his software program and how great it's going to be, and I have no doubt, but I'm stuck on the amount of pressure he's dumped on me. The expectations.

"I'm so excited." Parker's voice breaks through the fuzz in my brain.

I force a smile. "I'm so happy for you." Everyone else fucked off to go shower and go home to rest up for our game tomorrow. We'll have a morning skate, then some downtime, and because it's Pride night, we'll be showing up extra early to sign some jerseys and interact with the fans. Which brings me to another depressing thought that feels way too much like a tourniquet around my chest.

It's Pride night.

And I can't show off Parker on my arm like I want to.

While I'm playing hockey, I never will be able to. Unless I sign with a different team. But then if I do that, would there really be any point in continuing this with him when we'd be in two different cities?

"You okay?" Parker asks, snapping me out of my inner freak-out again.

"Yeah. Fine. I should go shower though. Rest up." Go hide under a blanket fort and never come out.

I want to be me. I want to be out. And most of all, I don't want hockey to get in the way of that.

Yet, with only one sentence, Parker has made sure it will. I may claim to be a new person, but all I am is old Connor: someone tied by responsibility. I could tell Parker the truth, or I could make it easier on him by shutting up and doing as he expects.

Only problem with that is I could do everything in my power to win and still miss out.

I could see what will happen if I try to play the shittiest game in all existence. Maybe that will be able to lower his expectations when it comes to me and this team.

-

Pride nights have, unfortunately, always been a source of contention within the sport of hockey. Sure, the league can say it's an issue with all theme nights as it detracts from the point of hockey itself, but it seems to only be when it's Pride. Military nights, cancer awareness themes, they're okay. But Pride always brings out the worst kind of people and comments.

From those who think it's shoving sexuality in people's faces to the players who refuse to wear rainbow anything, I can see why they once tried to ban rainbow-themed jerseys and gear. Not because the NHL as an organization has homophobic policies but because of the backlash it caused. That was long before Easton came out, and I'm thankful that allies in the league stood with those of us when we boycotted the ban and used rainbow tape anyway.

But not everyone did.

And one of the most defiant players is here tonight, playing for LA. He's next to me as we sign jerseys, hats, and anything else that a Sharpie can mark up.

Radimir Novicov, affectionately known in the league as Novi, is a great hockey player. One of *the* greats, even. And even though he was drafted at twenty, is now pushing thirty-eight, and he's been in the States that long, he still refuses to participate. He cites Russian anti-LGBTQ laws as the reason. He's never come right out and said he believes in those laws, but seventeen years here and he has no wiggle room?

Still, I'm not going to throw the homophobic label at him. It must be hard being from a country where laws are so extreme you can't show support for a cause in fear of repercussions. Maybe he's an ally, maybe he's not, but with how uncomfortable he looks as he signs a jersey for a fan—a fan who is wearing overtly queer-focused apparel—I have to go with he's not someone I need to be friendly with.

I almost feel sorry for the kid, who's probably sixteen or seventeen, has bright eyes, and is obviously obsessed with Novi. The jersey he's brought with him is Novi's, and even though he's getting everyone to sign it, Novi doesn't even acknowledge that this fan is there for him.

He's never been a big talker to begin with—in interviews and as a reply to the countless chirps thrown his way during games, he says in perfect English, "I don't speak English," or "I don't understand," when it's obvious he does—but he barely makes eye contact with this kid. Doesn't say anything. And with every passing moment, I see the brightness in the kid's eyes dim.

I finish up with the fan in front of me and move on to them, smiling wide. "Am I allowed to sign too, or do you really have that bad taste you have to root for LA?"

Novi scoffs and walks off.

The kid pulls out a Colorado jersey from the backpack at his feet. "I've got that covered."

I emphasize my fake disappointment. "Novi and my brother's jersey? Who hurt you?"

It's a joke, but when his face falls and he looks around, I realize the answer to that might be "everyone."

"I'm joking," I say. "My brother is awesome, I'll give him that. But it's not going to stop me from doing this." I take the jersey and sign, "Number 91 Kikishkin is better," and then my signature.

The kid smiles. "I like your playing too. But Easton is out and an inspiration and—"

"Say no more. I get it. I really do." More than he could know. More than I'm allowed to say. "Do you play?" I ask.

He hangs his head. "Yeah."

"You going to try to get drafted?"

"My team isn't very good."

"You still have time to hone your skills."

"I was on a different team, but then they found out about, well, all of this …" He waves a hand over his "love is love" rainbow shirt. "Let's just say the locker room was no longer a safe place for me there."

"That's horrible. What's your name?"

"P-parker."

Of course it is. I almost look up and ask the universe what they're doing to me because I can't help flashing back to the day I shoved Parker against the cubbies in our locker room. How I threatened him in high school. And as adults.

I was part of the problem this kid is facing now, and in the ten years since I was his age, it seems nothing has changed. Sure, I never attacked Parker for his sexuality, but that doesn't make what I did any different to what the kids of today are doing to this Parker.

"I wish things were different for you," I say.

I wish things were different, period. I want to fix this for him, but how can I do that other than going to his old team and tell them to shut the fuck up. Hey, maybe they'll listen to me. I am a Kiki brother, after all.

"Thank you for this." He holds up the jersey when I hand it back.

I need to move on. There are more fans here to see.

"You're welcome. And remember that no one deserves to hold you back from who you are."

No one.

Not even the guy you're falling for who has unrealistic expectations of you.

I don't want to hide who I am. Or who I'm with.

I can't wait as long as it takes to win a Stanley Cup to follow my own advice. So I have two choices here:

Push hard and try to take out the Cup in my last contractual season or lose spectacularly to stop giving Parker hope.

I should try for the former, but the pressure and expectation makes me opt for the latter.

From here on out, forget technique. Forget skill and proper form or the aim to do nothing but score. I'm going to go out there and wing it. Foolproof plan. I love it.

Losing, here we come!

CHAPTER THIRTY-FIVE

PARKER

My jaw is on the floor.

I can't believe this.

There is no goddamn way I'm seeing what I'm seeing.

Is this a hockey record? Because I think it might be a hockey record.

Two periods in, and we're up by seven. LA hasn't been able to find the net, and it's like every time Connor hits the ice, magic happens. If I were the type of guy to make loose and fast bets, I'd put my billions down on this being the game of Connor's career.

I'm also ninety percent sure Macklin has given him more ice time tonight than he saw in the playoffs last year.

I'm not going to lie, seeing the way his large body shoots up and down the ice, commanding every play, slamming against other players so hard he almost sends them through the boards … my very basic instinct, my primal brain, is attracted to him more than ever.

It's the first time all season I'm glad for my very big, very empty suite because no one can see me getting inappropriately hard in these pants.

I felt bad about saying all that win the Cup for Dad stuff yesterday because, first, hockey players are superstitious as hell, and second, it's not fair to put that kind of pressure on him, but it doesn't look like he's melting down over it.

No. It's doing the opposite.

I actually jump to my feet and scream when Connor shoots for goal and the puck sails right past Dotrosky and into the net. Eight-nothing. We're up eight zip.

Music pounds, and the crowd roars along with the lyrics.

I'm so swept up by how excited I am—for the team, for Connor, for myself—that I barely notice the buzzer signaling the end of the second period.

The team funnel off the ice, and I'm hit with a stupid idea.

A really messed-up, don't-do-it idea.

I need to see Connor.

Maybe it will fuck with his mojo, or maybe he'll be thrilled to see me, but I need two minutes of his time before I creep back up to solitude. Celebrating isn't as fun when you're doing it alone.

Especially when something feels off with your boyfriend.

He didn't stay over last night, which I think might be a first for us. We're deep in the season, and there's more pressure put on every game, so I understand that he'd be tired. Obviously. It has to be the exhaustion thing and not being sick of me. Has to be. I don't even think we've been together long enough to be sick of someone, but Connor is breaking all his records tonight, so he might as well be breaking that one too.

I'm just so proud of him. A little bit in awe. A lot in feelings. Ever since Connor said he was falling for me, it's like my heart went, "Perfect, hold the parachute," and launched itself out of a plane. Being with him is the sweetest kind of pain. When he's not around, it's the worst kind.

I might have done a super-sneaky, kinda creepy lurk earlier while he was signing those Pride jerseys, and I wasn't prepared for how my mood would dip knowing that Connor wasn't doing it as his full self. Is he playing like he is because of it being Pride night? Is it a coincidence? Does he wish that he could come out, and if he isn't, is it because of me?

I jog down the stairs into the lobby and move as quickly as I can to the back. I text Connor, hoping he'll see it, but if he doesn't, I'll have to make do with addressing the whole team and giving him puppy dog eyes while I do it.

I'm panting by the time I reach the hall to the locker room, sweat building under my suit, and it's not the most attractive way to be seeing him, but it'll have to do.

I'm giving myself a minute breather before going inside when Connor steps out into the hall. He's wearing his pants and socks, with base layers on top, and even half-dressed and kinda disheveled, he looks good enough to lick.

"Hey," he whispers. One corner of his lips kicks up, and he goes to reach for me before stopping himself.

But his eyes hold a hint of worry, and this isn't the greeting I'm used to from him.

I swallow hard. "You are … you're doing …"

"Yeah." The response is so short I don't know how to reply. I'd been expecting Connor to be bounding out of his skin, but my scruffy, overenthusiastic puppy of a man doesn't even seem happy.

"I thought you'd be more excited."

"No, I am."

"You're having an amazing game."

He huffs but doesn't reply.

I blink up at him for a moment. "Are you clenching your jaw?"

"No."

"You are."

"I'm *not*."

"Is everything okay? You seem …"

"It's fine, Parker." He glances around like he's suddenly paranoid. "Just playing the game that I love. So much. So, so much."

"Then why are you being so snappy?"

"This isn't snappy. I'm focused. Now I need to get ready to go out there and win a game. For you."

"Con, that's not what I—"

"I'll see you later." He turns on his heel and storms back inside.

I have half a mind to follow him, to drag him out here and make him talk, but this is not the time.

Even if I desperately want it to be.

That one night apart could be dismissed. Connor's schedule is insane. But considering how well he's playing and that he seems mad at it … at me … The insecurity I was keeping at bay over Connor not spending the night develops into full-blown panic mode. Because it's obvious something is wrong. If he was playing badly or the team was losing, I could put it down to that, but this … No. There's definitely something up with him, and I can't help assuming it's me.

How did I fuck it all up so quickly? How the hell am I supposed to go another whole period without knowing where I stand? How am I supposed to sit there and cheer for him around this lump building in my throat? I'll go back up there, to the very empty stands, to my very empty suite, and be reminded of everything I don't have.

The team doesn't need my software; they're winning enough games on their own. And Connor doesn't need me. Not like I need him.

I'm heading back to that dangerous headspace I was in a month or two ago, and I'm determined not to have that happen again. I can't rely on Connor to be the only one filling that loneliness inside of me.

So instead of dwelling on the what-ifs and the maybes and placing all this pressure on him and our relationship, I square my shoulders and head for the main arena.

I spotted three people in the stands earlier tonight, who were all there to cheer for the Kiki brothers. It takes me a second to get my bearings without the high viewpoint I normally have, but it doesn't take long to spot the tall man with strawberry blond hair halfway up the stands.

"Knox?"

It takes him a minute to hear me, but when he does, his face splits into the kind of smile I was expecting from Connor.

"Hey, Parker!" He shuffles sideways along the row and pulls me into a quick, one-armed hug. "What are you doing down here?"

"Coming to see if you and Mr. and Mrs. Kikishkin want to come up to my suite." I'm holding my breath, almost scared he's going to say no.

"You have beer up there?"

"Uh … yeah."

"Fucking awesome." He yells out to Connor's parents. "We're going to see how the other side lives."

And while it might be the beer luring them up with me, some of the anxiousness building in my chest settles.

I don't have to be alone. Maybe these people are linked to Connor, but after tonight, I'm going to make more of an effort with people. People outside of the team and Connor.

Because if his attitude earlier was any indicator, I'm worried I won't be able to rely on him forever.

I'm trying not to dwell on it, trying not to get too far ahead of myself, and I'll deal with that conversation when and if it happens.

Unfortunately, being logical doesn't help lessen the pit in my gut.

"Wow," Mr. Kikishkin says as we walk into the suite. "You have this every game?"

I shift awkwardly, reminding myself that I'm interacting with them as the team owner, not their son's boyfriend. "Yeah. You, uh, as you can see, I have a lot of spare seats, so if you ever wanted to be up here … like, for every game …"

Knox helps himself to a beer and passes one to Mr. Kikishkin. "Oh, we'll be taking you up on that. Look at the view."

The two of them move down into the seats, and Mrs. Kikishkin lingers.

"This is a very generous offer," she says.

"Not really. The seats might as well be used."

"That's true …" She hesitates, and I can tell she has something else to say.

"We're on a night off," I say, holding up my hands. "Just enjoying the game, no need for professionalism. No owners or agents up here."

There's something about her expression that's so much like Connor. "I got the feeling that the last time we met, you didn't like my son much."

Way to get straight to the point. "You were right," I say carefully. "I don't know if you knew that we went to school together. We had … a difference of opinion. But we talked and sorted it out."

"I'm glad to hear it. I was worried for a minute that any friction between you might impact his career."

Her choice of words does *not* make me feel comfortable. There's still plenty of *friction* between us, the explosive kind, but it could impact his career in an even worse way. "I would never let something personal impact the team."

"Good." She swaps her bag to the other side, and the professional mask slips. "Was he a good kid in high school? Not mean to anyone or …"

She's not asking me as his agent. Mrs. Kikishkin is obviously a smart woman, and I think she's put together what some of our issue was about. She wants to know if her son was a bully, and it takes a brave person to face the truth.

The me who bought this team would have been fast to tell her that Connor was the worst. To blame him for how shitty my schooling years were. And no, he wasn't a saint. There were a lot of ways he could have pulled up his team and held them accountable, but he was also a kid. High school dynamics are the fucking worst, and maybe I understand now some more of the pressure that Connor was under.

So the current me has it in him to be gracious.

"I didn't have it easy in high school. I was the nerdy, gay kid, and there wasn't a lot I could do to hide that." This is where I pick my words carefully. "Unlike some others on his team, Connor never targeted me over it. He was focused on hockey and looking after his brothers.

That was it." I manage a short laugh. "Everyone in school knew that if you started on one of the little Kikis, you'd end up with the big one. You raised a very loyal brother and a pretty okay guy. You should be proud."

I'm not sure if she buys it, but she thanks me and heads down to her husband.

Even if Connor could have done more, I stand by what I said. He's an incredible, big-hearted person now, and focusing on the past won't help anyone.

Including me.

Having those three seats filled is already doing a lot for my mood, even if I can't count on keeping it up after how I left things with Connor.

He has something on his mind. Something most likely related to me. Or that's what my insecurity is telling me anyway. And this period cannot go fast enough for me to see him and talk it out.

If he wants to end things, I'll respect that. I'll be confused as hell because everything was so good between us, but I won't force him to be with me.

If it's something else, I'll be there for him too.

Connor needs to start learning that he doesn't have to do everything himself. We might not be public, but I'm his partner now.

For once in his life, he has someone on his side.

CHAPTER THIRTY-SIX

CONNOR

Me: I'm going to stop giving a shit about how I'm playing. I no longer care if I win or lose because this will be my last season in the NHL.

My body: Sweet, let's have fun and have the best game of our entire career.

It's almost as if the universe has heard me and won't allow me to let go of the game. Because two goals and four assists when I'm not even trying? What the fuck?

I shouldn't be reading into it because it's making me doubt my doubts. And doubting my doubts is doubtfully doubty out here. And now the word "doubt" has absolutely no meaning anymore.

Parker's right that I should be over-the-moon ecstatic with how I'm playing tonight, but all it's doing is making me angry. It's like no matter what I do out on that ice, the puck finds a teammate's blade, and they flick it in the net. So then I decide to start aiming for the net, and I fucking score.

Maybe if I'd stopped caring about winning a long time ago, I'd already have a Cup to my name, and then I wouldn't feel the seed of resentment that's already beginning to grow.

Parker came to see me during the break to congratulate me, and the only thing I was focused on was his expectations of keeping it up. Of going all the way.

My resentment isn't only at him though. It's at my parents. At myself. At everything. Because I finally decide what I want to do with my life—sort of. Okay, I've decided what I don't want to do with my life—and everything else is pushing me back toward it. Old Connor would've sucked it up and gone with it. New me, I can't. I just fucking can't.

There are murmurs around the locker room to get the puck to me this period. Everyone wants to see me turn my two goals into a hat trick, not unheard of for a defenseman but not expected, and there everyone goes throwing expectations on me again.

Do I suck it up and go for it? Or do I dig my heels in and do what I want?

When we get back out onto the ice, I decide to do neither of those options. A petulance I never knew I had—one that would rival Lachie's—takes over my body, and I hit even harder. My anger drives me, and at one point, I catch the speed of one of my slapshots and begin to worry for Dotrosky's life in the net.

Yet, no matter how many times I tell myself to calm down when I'm back on the bench, I somehow only manage to reach new levels of pissed off. And when I see Novi on the ice and I'm sent out for another shift, I can't help picturing the way he avoided teenage Parker tonight. How he looked so uncomfortable, didn't seem to want to be there, and refuses to wear anything Pride.

Instead of focusing all my anger on those it should be directed at, I let it all flow out irrationally toward Novi.

Like he's the reason I can't quit hockey. Like he's the reason I can't come out. Like he's the reason I finally know what I want and can't have it.

I practically chase him down on the ice, waiting for my perfect chance to check him without getting a penalty, but it seems being so far behind has made LA as fired up and frustrated as me because it all comes to a head when Novi and I run into each other so hard we both go down.

The whistle is loud as it rings in my ears, and it's not until I sit up and get dizzy that I realize I must've hit my head on the way down.

But as I stagger back to my feet, I almost lose my footing again. Not from the knock to my head but from Novicov punching me square in the fucking jaw.

I've gotten in fights on the ice before—where warranted. This could go either way, and I'll have to wait and see the replay before knowing who was in the wrong in the first place, but with the way my mind is in sabotage mode, calculating risk is not something I'm up for. So instead of skating away or letting the refs separate us, I go all in.

The gloves are off, and I give the people what they want. Hell, this is what I want too.

Novi might be my proxy for everything else happening in my life, but I don't care.

I land a jab to his pads, probably hurting my hand more than his ribs, but the sharp hit does make him cradle that side, opening up the left side of his face for a perfectly executed hook that comes next.

We're literally that meme: "I went to watch a fight and hockey broke out."

The crowd is deafening, the refs don't even try to pull us off each other, and we just keep throwing fists. I'm not sure which of us is angrier. It's a struggle to keep upright on my skates, but all I'm concentrating on is hitting as much as possible, and judging by the way fists keep flying at my head, Novi is doing the same. His breathing is as heavy as mine.

Novi eventually goes down, and I know I need to stop. When a man hits the ice, you don't go for more. But I'm not done.

Not until I land another punch, and the refs finally realize I'm an unhinged fuckhead who won't stop unless they stop me. It takes two of them to pull me off Novi while another helps him up.

I'm breathing hard, regret setting in almost immediately but also the urge to cry too.

Yesterday, I was uneasy about letting hockey go, even if I wanted it, but I had a sense of hope, a bright outlook on the possibilities of what I could do.

Today, I suddenly hate hockey so much I'm willing to do anything to throw it away.

I'm halfway to the penalty box when the ref and linesman on either side of me stop me. I figured I'd be getting a five-minute major, but no. The other ref skates to center ice, where he makes the announcement that we're both being slapped with ten-minute misconducts and are ejected from the game.

Fun times.

I deserve it though.

-

Disappointment and guilt follow the adrenaline crash, and it sets in pretty fast.

I shower immediately, not caring about properly cooling down, even though I'll feel it tomorrow, and by the time I'm getting dressed into my suit, I'm defeated.

Completely and utterly defeated.

I told the guys outside that I don't want anyone coming in here. No coach, no PR person, no parents, and, in particular, no Parker Duchene. Not that security could ever make Parker stay out. He owns the damn place. Well, he owns the team, not the arena, but same difference, practically.

That's why, when the locker room door opens, I don't even look up. It's probably him.

"I don't want to talk about it," I say.

Only where I'm expecting Parker's sweet voice laced with "What the fuck were you doing out there?" I get a faint Russian accent in return.

"I'm sorry."

My head snaps up to find Novi in his suit, a nice bruise down the side of his face and murder in his whiskey-colored eyes. His face doesn't match his words.

"You are?" I ask, making sure he didn't come in here to, in fact, kill me.

"I don't normally let the game get to me like that, but … Fuck, give us the puck every now and then."

I huff. "Fair. And I guess I should say I'm sorry too. I … I might have used your face to get out all my personal frustrations."

His murderous eyes don't falter, but I swear he almost *smiles*. "I could say the same thing." He approaches me and sits on the bench next to me in front of Easton's cubby. "It's difficult not to hate you two, you know."

"Us two?"

He points to Easton's name. "Gay brother. Big protector."

"I really hope this is a language barrier and you're seriously not telling me you hate my brother because he's gay. Because I have news for you. He's not the only queer Kiki, and I can easily punch the other side of your face so your bruises will be even."

Novi laughs deep and slow, almost sounding like one of those over-the-top Russian James Bond villains. "Calm down. I … I didn't have that growing up. No support. Lived in Russia where being myself was not an option. I—"

I pull back. "Wait, what?"

"I have waited seventeen years to be able to get the rest of my family out of Russia before being able to live my truth, and now that I have permanent residency and I worked out how to get my family visas in Canada, my sister refuses to leave our homeland. It feels like she's doing it to hold me back." He eyes me. "What is holding you back?"

When he puts it like that, the fact Parker and I can't claim each other in fear of some stupid, untrue comments online feels weak.

"What makes you think I'm talking about me?" I ask defensively but quickly slump. Because why bother?

He cocks an eyebrow at me.

"Okay, yes, I was talking about me, but it's complicated. Not fight for my life kind of complicated but fighting for some kind of life. One I want. One the universe doesn't seem to want me to have."

"I don't know what any of that means, but speaking as someone who has put off his personal life for his entire career, don't let it make you bitter."

I hang my head. "I don't want to play hockey anymore."

At some point while talking with Novi, someone else entered the locker room, but I didn't hear them.

I hear them now though.

"You … what?"

I tense at Parker's croaky voice, and when I lift my gaze and meet the blue eyes of my boyfriend, my heart breaks at the betrayal reflected back at me. "I … I …" I look to Novi for help, but he doesn't give me any.

Instead, in the thickest Russian accent that clearly isn't his usual voice, he says, "Uh, this not visitor locker room. I don't speak English." He's out of here so fast I could swear I see smoke trailing behind him.

I guess our bonding session hasn't quite sealed a lifelong friendship.

If Knox were here, he'd come to my rescue.

As if proving me wrong, Knox comes in next. "What the fuck, man?"

I have some explaining to do.

CHAPTER THIRTY-SEVEN

PARKER

It's lucky Knox is here and talking because all I can do is stare. It feels like Connor has socked me in the face.

There are too many questions trying to come out first, from how long has he felt this way to why didn't he tell me?

Though I have a sneaking, horrible feeling I know the answer to that one.

Did I really tell a man who doesn't want to be here that he needs to win the Stanley Cup for my *dead father*?

What the fuck is wrong with me? Scratch that—the list is too long to stew on, but my lack of social skills really isn't an excuse here because who the hell says that? Who gets so caught up in their own life that they don't realize when someone they're supposed to care about is struggling?

Knox takes a hesitant step forward while Connor watches him, expression tight. "You don't want to play?"

Connor's stormy eyes flick toward me for a second. "No."

"But … but … Out there. The way you play …" Knox says.

He shakes his head. "Just because I'm good at it doesn't mean I like it."

"Since when?" My voice is still croaky when it comes out, like I'm not sure I should be speaking yet.

"It's been coming on gradually. All season. When I stopped focusing on my brothers and started focusing on myself, it opened my eyes to a lot of good things but also a lot of shit I didn't want to deal with."

"And one of those things was hockey?" Knox clarifies. "But you've always loved it."

"No, I've always been good at it and worked to be even better because I saw how much my parents sacrificed to get me there."

A still silence stretches through the room.

This wasn't a spur-of-the-moment decision. Apparently, this has been on his mind for a while, and he didn't talk to me about it, for whatever reason. I've talked to him about so much, every insecurity, every past experience that I struggled with, so why did he feel like he couldn't do the same with me? I'm trying really hard not to look too deeply into it and make this about me, but it's hard not to ask where the gaps are in our relationship for me to only be hearing about this now.

"You didn't say anything," I finally manage.

"I was still working through it."

"I'm a constant work in progress, but I don't keep any of the big stuff from you. I want to be your partner, Connor, not some guy who you talk to once you've already made a decision."

"Then maybe you shouldn't be guilting me into doing shit."

Aaaand I was right. I'm an idiot. "I'm sorry." The apology might be automatic, but I mean it. "I thought you loved the game. You've been playing incredibly this season, and I didn't say it to put pressure on you. I was excited. I never would have said anything if I knew."

Knox takes over. "You're under a lot of pressure, but this feels really sudden, man. First, you discover you're queer, and now, you don't want to play? Discovering yourself doesn't have to mean that you turn into a totally different person."

"That's not what this is," Connor snaps.

Before Knox can get frustrated, I take over again. "Then what is it? From our side, this is really sudden. You've gone from loving your job and being one of the best to being ejected from the game of your career." I force my feet to unstick from the floor and cross over to sit next to him. His gaze that meets mine is wary. "I know you're used to doing things yourself, but you don't have to. You've got me, Knox, and Easton."

Connor sighs. "I think I hate it."

I'm not expecting that. No one else is either.

Knox actually sounds like he's choking. "The fuck?"

"There's so much pressure to be the best, and I've felt it since I was young. I hate who I become so that I can play. First high school, ignoring the way my team bullied people, and now I can't even come out for fucking Pride night and be goddamn proud of my boyfriend and our relationship."

That sounds like the complete opposite of getting bored of me. I slide my hand into his, and Connor squeezes tight.

"I know that I can come out, but people still can't know about me and Parker. And that's messed up. It's … it's not worth it anymore. The training, the travel, not being able to give my relationship my all, and knowing that if I do come out, it's going to add even more attention and pressure to not only me but Easton and Lachie too. At what point does it become okay to say that I've had enough?"

Knox crouches in front of us. "Why the hell did you keep all that bottled up? That's not okay, Con."

"I … I told East."

"You did?" Knox looks as confused as I am. "He didn't say anything either."

"Yeah, because he's my brother first, dickhead." Connor lightly shoves Knox, who thankfully doesn't stand up and punch him, even though I'm waiting for it.

I'll eventually get used to insults equaling love.

"Good." I squeeze Connor's hand back. "I'm glad you talked to someone."

"It should have been you."

As much as I wish it had been, that's not fair. "No, it should have been whoever you wanted it to be. I'm just glad you knew you had someone there."

"Parker's being way too nice," Knox says. "I'm mortally offended that you didn't talk to me. Your best friend. Of a billion years. Dick."

"You'll get over it."

And just when I think Knox is going to finally follow through and punch him, he swamps Connor in a hug instead. "I love you, I'm proud of you, and you know I've got your back for anything."

Connor hugs him back, and it's one of those moments where I'm unsure if I'm supposed to go and let them have this, but then Knox makes my decision for me.

"I'm gonna go and let you two talk." Knox makes his exit, and now I'm left with nothing but confusion and Connor looking so damn depressed.

"I don't know what to say," I start with honesty.

"Yeah ..."

"I support you too. Obviously. I think I might need to say it though."

He slides closer to me on the bench, warm thigh pressed against my leg and fingers still linked between mine. "Even though you really want that Cup?"

I do. That part hasn't changed. But while it's all well and good to honor Dad, he's gone. Connor is sitting right in front of me. The man who's the best part of my day. Who helped me heal. Who hopefully won't be going anywhere anytime soon, and he matters. He matters more than a Cup. "It's lucky I have an entire team out there who all want the same thing I do."

His expression is full of skepticism. "You're not at all disappointed? Really?"

"Of course I'm disappointed that my team will lose a star player and I won't get to watch you skate anymore. But disappointed in you? No way. Besides, if the team is one person, it isn't much of a team. If we can't do it without you, we probably don't deserve to do it at all."

He expels an enormous breath and leans forward to press his hands to his face. "I feel like I'm letting everyone down."

"Here's an idea," I say, rubbing his back. "Why don't you let the rest of us worry about us, and you worry about yourself for a change."

He glances up at me, eyes tinged red. "I don't think it's that simple."

"It's exactly that simple."

Somehow, that gets a tiny smile out of him. "This is why it sucks that I have to keep you a secret. I'm sorry it took me so long to work out how amazing you are."

I'm not sure about all that, but it's nice he sees me that way. At least for this moment.

"You got there eventually" is as much as I'm willing to acknowledge his compliment. "As for hockey … what are you going to do about your contract?"

"I haven't thought that far ahead yet, but I might need to do something I've been dreading since the thought of hockey started to make me annoyed."

"What's that?"

"I need to talk to my parents."

I think of Mr. and Mrs. Kikishkin, and while they have their own version of my professional mask, it's clear they love their sons. "They're in my owner's suite. I can take you up there if you want."

"Maybe."

"You can do this."

"Will you wait for me?" he asks. "I want to come home with you tonight."

Finally, that relationship angst that I'd bottled up in my chest releases. "Of course. I'll wait outside all night if I have to."

CHAPTER THIRTY-EIGHT

CONNOR

Parker holds my hand all the way up to his suite, and I'm so busy thinking about going in there and talking to my parents, telling them about everything, that I realize something.

I stop walking right before Parker can open the door. "My parents are in your suite."

Parker's lips turn up in the corners. "They are. So was Knox. I figured I have all of that space and no one to share it with. It should be put to good use."

I put my hand on my heart. "Little Parky Parks is making fwiends."

My man laughs and playfully shoves me. "Stop stalling by making this about me."

I take his hand. "I know I asked you to stay out here until I was done, but … could you, I mean, uh—"

"You want me to leave?"

I grip his hand tighter. "No. I … I want you to come in with me. I want to tell them about you. We may not be able to tell everyone, but you welcomed them into your space, and I don't want to keep you from them."

"I'm here for whatever you need. If you're ready, I'm ready."

I step closer, closing the gap between us, and I kiss his lips softly.

We're broken apart by Dad's deep voice. "Did we walk into some kind of alternate universe or what? Connor's getting into fights, ejected from games, and kissing boys, and Easton is the one with his head down, kicking ass on the ice."

Parker and I break apart, but I don't let him get far. And by the look on Mom's and Dad's faces, they're not really mad. Dad's just fucking with us. Still, I have some things I need to get out in the open.

"Mom, Dad. We, uh, we probably need to talk about a few things."

Dad snorts. "No shit."

Mom backhands him in the chest, and even though it's not hard, Dad makes an exaggerated "Oof" noise.

This conversation is going to be fun. For him.

We head into the box, and even though there are only a couple of minutes left of the game, I can't help noticing the score. We were up to eight nothing before I got ejected from the game, yet somehow, LA has managed to come back to only a four-point deficit in the sixteen minutes I've been gone.

Jesus H. Christ.

I turn to Parker. "You were saying something about the team not being about one person? I'm out for one period, and we choke."

"Always with the ego," Knox comments from where he's sitting in the front row out on the balcony part.

"Oh, hon," Mom says. "The team isn't falling apart because you aren't playing. They're falling apart because their most levelheaded defenseman lost his temper and got thrown out of the game. They're frazzled and wondering what's going on with you, and so are we."

"Would we call Connor levelheaded?" Knox asks, still not taking his eyes off the game. The traitor.

Mom turns, and her tone is exactly like it would be if she was talking to Lachie or Easton. "I said the most levelheaded. Not that he was levelheaded. Though he usually is when it comes to business decisions."

"I think that's my problem," I cut in.

"What is?" Mom asks.

"I've always seen hockey as a job. As something I had to do. I saw keeping Easton and Lachie in line as my job. My responsibility."

"We've been over that." Mom's hand lands gently on my upper arm. "We're sorry we made you feel that way. It wasn't our intention."

"I know, but … it's only been since Parker walked into my life that I've realized everything I've done, I've done for everyone else, and …" This is the hardest thing I've ever had to say. "It's time I choose myself."

"W-what are you saying?" Mom asks.

Dad's gaze ping-pongs between us. "I have a feeling this conversation is going to need drinks."

"Yes, please!" Knox calls out.

"Get your own," Dad snipes back.

Ah, families.

"Come sit with me." Mom drags me to the back row of seats, but Parker hangs back near the bar with Dad. "Talk to me like I'm your agent, not your mother."

"That's just it. For this … I need you to be in mom mode."

She takes a deep breath. "Okay."

My words come out rushed, hurried, and not so much intelligible. "I don't want to play hockey anymore."

"Tonight?"

"*Ever.*"

Mom pulls back. It's as if the world stands still for a brief second, but then the final buzzer of the game sounds, the crowd roars and cheers, and suddenly, the world around me is deafening.

After goalie hugs, the team heads down the chute to the locker room, and I should be down there with them. Reporters will fill the locker room, there'll be a press conference, and there's no way my scuffle with Novi won't be brought up. But I can't bring myself to go back down there and face everyone.

Dad hands Mom a glass of wine, and she throws it back like it's a shot.

"I know I'm disappointing you," I say.

"No." Mom is confident as she throws the word at me. "You're not disappointing me. You're surprising me, and it will take a bit to swallow that, but you're not a disappointment. If anything, I wish you'd figured this out sooner, or … you could've told me sooner how unhappy you were all these years."

I rub my hand over my head. "The good thing about that is I didn't realize I have been unhappy. Not until …" My gaze drifts to Parker in the background. If he can hear us from where we are, he pretends he can't and does something on his phone.

"Parker," Mom says.

I nod.

When Dad sits, he's on the other side of me. "Have you always known but felt the need to hide it? I don't really understand why you would when you know we support Easton and Lachie."

I stare down at my hands. "The truth is, I didn't know. I had no damn clue until Parker came waltzing into that locker room and took over the team. And I think the reason I never figured it out is because I haven't had the chance to get to know myself. It's why all of this is happening. I've tried to ignore the niggling feeling at the back of my mind, the one telling me I'm going through something and it will go away. I'll find my love for the game again. But … it's not happening. And if I keep pushing myself, keep fighting to stay, I'm only going to resent it more. Especially when it means I can't be with Parker."

"I've never heard you talk about someone like this before," Mom says. "You've always put hockey above anyone and anything else."

"I know, and that's where my problem lies."

She pats my hand. "We support you, no matter what. You're up for a contract extension at the end of the season. We were already in early talks with management, but you don't have to sign anything. This can be your last season."

I'm relieved but also frustrated because now that I've decided … Now that I've got the ball rolling … I want it now. Selfishly.

"What will you do with your mortgage?" Mom asks.

"So, funny story." I rub the back of my neck again. "I kinda hate that house too. I bought it to fit the mold of what I thought I should want. I'll sell it, and—"

Knox, who's obviously been listening in since the ice is now empty but he hasn't moved, swivels in his seat to face us. "Wait, you're selling it? But it's so pretty."

"I think I'm more of a penthouse kind of guy."

I'm more of a Parker, ugly-ass rat Conishkin, and the cozy living room and fireplace kind of guy. That's what I want. I'm not sure if I'd feel differently about my place if Parker was there with me, but I love his apartment. I want to move in there. If he'll have me. And when it's safe to be a couple in public.

"Can Easton and I buy it?" Knox asks.

"Go for it."

Mom's sitting next to me, her lips pursed. I can tell she wants to say something else but is holding back.

"What are you worrying about?"

"I know I'm supposed to be in mom mode, but can I please put my agent hat on for one minute?"

"That's fair." Even if I know I'm not going to like the next thing that comes out of her mouth.

"I'm only going to ask this once, and I realize how bad it's going to sound, but I want to double-check. Are you sure this whole wanting to quit hockey thing isn't a phase?"

I laugh hard because I had the exact same thought. "I think you're parenting wrong. Aren't you supposed to ask that of me being with men?"

Mom waves me off. "Eh, we've had practice with our sons coming out to us. You're good there. I just don't want you to regret this decision. I'm not going to stop you, and I support you, but I don't want you to throw away your life on a whim. There. I've said my piece."

"And you were allowed to say it. But I'm sure. I'm more than sure. Do I know what I want to do with my life instead? No. But I also have the funds to take my time and figure it out."

After talking to teenager Parker yesterday, I got the faintest idea of possibly motivating kids. Those who are being bullied, those who are LGBTQ and feel like they don't fit in. I could go around the country and talk to schools about how in high school, I hurt people because hockey was my only goal. From a sideline bully—someone who saw injustices but never did anything to stop it—to realizing what I did was wrong. It might not make a huge difference, but if I change one kid's life, it might be worth it.

Parker has stopped fiddling with his phone, and he approaches us. "So, I've been chatting to our GM."

"What? Why?"

"You said you want to quit, and I thought I could ask how to hypothetically release a player from their contract early … if that's what you want."

"And?" I tell myself not to get my hopes up.

"We know they wouldn't release you because of the optics of it all, but how do you feel about injuring yourself so badly you have to be put on long-term IR so your salary frees up some cap space until your contract lapses?"

"They'd let me do that?"

"They will if I tell them they will."

I stand. "I love being injured!" But I don't want backlash to hit him in the face because of this. "Are you sure you're okay with doing that for me?"

Parker steps closer to me. "Oh, sweet, loveable Connor. I'd do anything to make you happy."

Guilt over thinking he was pressuring me to keep playing hits like a fucking freight train, but it's not the only thing I'm hit with. I'm also hit with the overwhelming sense of experiencing something I never have before. Sure, I love my family, my brothers, Knox, but this type of love?

It's completely brand-new and something I never, ever want to lose.

"You make me so happy," I say.

"Then I guess you're stuck with me."

Good.

CHAPTER THIRTY-NINE

PARKER

I wake up, inhaling the smell of Connor's skin, wrapped around him for the third day in a row. He really is a snuggler, and I'm an affection whore who can't get enough.

Today is his first official game day on the injured list for an apparent upper-body injury. There's a very small part of me worried that he might regret walking away, but at least this option gives him the freedom to change his mind if need be, and no matter my insecurities, he's making this choice himself. I need to trust him.

"Good morning," he rumbles, still half-asleep. His arm tightens around me, and I love how wanted and claimed he always makes me feel.

My face buries into his neck as I slide my hand down his chest. "Tell me where the poor, injured hockey player hurts."

"Huh?" He's immediately awake. "Uh … further down."

My hand skims his abs.

"Yeah … keep going, almost there."

I slip my hand under the waistband of his boxer briefs and wrap it around his already hard cock.

Connor moans, husky and deep, as he involuntarily thrusts into my grip. "There. Right there."

His desperation sends a shiver of delight to my balls, and Connor's large hands close over my ass. He grinds me against his thigh as I jerk him off until we're both spilling into our underwear.

I slump against him, kissing my way up his neck until Connor's mouth is on mine. I'll never get over the possessive way he kisses. Slow and in control. It makes my toes curl pleasantly.

"Now it's a good morning," I say, grinning as I pull away.

His smile is also stretching across his face, and it's still hard to wrap my head around that I made him look that way.

He reaches down to kick out of his underwear and helps me do the same, then does the best job he can cleaning the mess off us. We'll still need to shower, but at least we don't have to do it right now.

"Come here." Connor opens his arms, and I climb into them, half-draped over his chest. "I'll never get sick of waking up to this."

Me neither. We lie there in a lazy silence, soaking in each other's body warmth. Connor has nowhere to be, and I technically don't either, even though I'm planning to spend a lot of time with my coaching team while I develop my software.

Connor strokes his thumb over my cheek, pulling my attention back to him. "No, Park, I … I won't get sick of this. Ever."

"This?"

"Us."

I go all melty inside. Connor swallows roughly, and I realize more is coming. "I'm selling my place. Knox and East want to buy it, and I hate being there."

"Where will you live?" The words are barely out of my mouth when I catch on to where this is going.

Here.

He wants to live here.

With me.

"Yes," I say, so fast that he hasn't got a word out.

"Umm … yes?"

"Yes, you can move in here."

A laugh barks from him. "How did you know that's what I was going to say?"

"Even if it wasn't, I want you to. Will you? Move in?" It's the type of serious move that might be too soon for some but feels exactly right for us. I'm going to go back to traveling with the team to a lot of games, and knowing that I get to come home to a man I'm confident I've fallen for sounds like a dream to me.

"I *can* find another place," he says. "No pressure. I just really don't want to."

"Then don't. Let's live together."

"Fuck, I like the sound of that."

I'm swimming with nerves and excitement, and for the first time since we first hooked up, I can see it. Us having a life together.

"We'll have to be careful though," I remind him. "We're not going public about us for a reason."

"I know, and that won't change. With me more or less out of the sport, no one will give a shit where I'm going home to, and if my brother buys my place, I can keep that address as mine on paper. Then, once my contract has ended and enough time has passed that it won't bring heat on you, we can relax about it."

I'm dying for that day to come, but while Connor might be happy to walk away from hockey, I'm not. I love the sport. It might have started with a need to spend time with Dad and then keep that closeness once he passed, but the games are fun to watch, my team is hardworking and dedicated, and with me finding a more active role in the franchise, I'm getting that hit of belonging, of being part of something, and I've always craved that.

Connor respects that as much as I respect his need to distance himself from it. For Connor, he's never been able to be his own person, and I'm so proud he's taking that chance now.

"Any idea of what you want to do next?" I ask.

A contemplative look falls over his face. "Yeah … I don't have all the details, but I thought I'd give public speaking a try."

"Really?"

He shrugs. "I'm good at it. The media always comments that I'm easy to interview because, unlike most of the other guys who grunt, I can actually string a sentence together."

"Shocking with how many hits to the head you've taken."

He pinches my side. "Okay, brainiac. But I thought the first step could be to reach out to our old high school. Maybe have a practice run and see how it goes?"

He sounds nervous about it, and that only proves this could be a great step for him.

"What are you going to talk about? Hockey? Queer men in sport?"

"Definitely a bit of that." He pauses. "And also … bullying. How you can easily be a bully by not saying anything at all."

"Connor—"

"Nope. Don't let me off lightly. Having the perspective of a few years makes it a lot easier to know that if I had said something to get the team to lay off, most of them would have done it. They looked up to me. As captain, it's not only how you are on the ice that the guys pay attention to, and while there'll always be the outliers who don't give a fuck, I could have made a difference. So I figure if I can get through to one kid, just one, it'll all be worth it. You're such an incredible person, Parker, and you didn't deserve any of what happened to you."

My eyes get all misty. I know I accepted Connor's apology, and I know he meant it, but this feels like … like validation. Like he's looking at me and he's understanding. Knowing that he wants to bring positive change even though he's not that person anymore is all a bit too much emotion for me to handle.

"Thank you." I brush his lips with a kiss. "But I don't want you to do this for me. I want you to do it for yourself."

"I am." Those two words fill me with relief. "And for them. The past mes who still have a chance to be better."

Knowing he has a plan for what he's working toward makes it so much easier to get out of bed and get ready for my day. We shower together, cook breakfast together, take Conishkin out for a play and to explore together, and it's this brief little glimpse of what our lives could look like once he moves in that makes me excited for the future.

Connor Kikishkin finally sees me, and more importantly, I see him. The real him and not some fantasy dream man who I had built up in my head.

The reality is better anyway.

Me, Connor, and our little rat baby.

Who he finally held the other day.

Cup or no Cup, I know that getting to see me like this would make Dad proud.

He only ever wanted me to be happy, and for the first time ever, I actually am.

EPILOGUE

CONNOR

"Queer Collective is taking over the owner's suite!" The loud, booming voice comes from the entrance, and I don't need to look to know who it is.

"You're going to regret letting Ezra Palaszczuk into our space," I mutter to Parker.

I'm getting used to the Collective guys. Slowly. They're a lot, and they go against every PR-trained thought I have, but they're not my problem. They have their own PR managers and agents for that.

Parker smiles. "One, I love that you call my suite *our* space now, and two, look at me, I have friends now."

And I love that for him.

If it were anyone else in the league, I would question their motives behind their move to be friends with him—not because Parker isn't loveable, but as he even admits himself, he's not good at the friend thing. Something about trust issues from when he was a teenager. Have no idea what he's talking about with that. But while the Collective are a lot of big personalities, they're a great group of guys underneath all of that. The entire reason they got together in the first place was to make sure queer players in the league had a support system.

Parker turns to Ezra and Anton. "Welcome. Help yourself to food, beer, whatever you want."

They both glance around the suite, from the large table of food in the center to the fridges and counters around the sides to the tiered seating below, and Ezra says, "Can I fuck our owner to get my own box like this?"

"Question," Anton says. "Theoretically, if you fuck our owner and get a suite … when will you use it, exactly? You can't watch the game and be on the ice at the same time."

"Don't ruin my fantasy with logic. Maybe I could live in it. Turn it into our sex den. You don't know. Or maybe I could be like Con here and reti—" Ezra gags. "Retir—" He gags again. "Nope, can't even joke about that." His icy blue eyes meet mine. "I don't know how you did it, but it looks good on you."

It feels good too. Though the whole not coming back hasn't been announced publicly yet. Coach and I have had a lot of talks about it, and while I know he hopes I'll change my mind, he also respects if this is something I need to do. "No idea what you're talking about. I'm injured. So, so injured."

"I heard," Ezra says. "What injury is it? Upper body, lower body …"

"Yes. All of them."

Anton puts his hand on Ezra's lower back. "I'm getting food. You want anything?"

"Sure."

I expect Ezra to go with him, but he doesn't. He stays standing in front of me, arms now folded, and I get the impression he's waiting for something from me. He studies my face but says nothing.

"What?" I ask.

"You're an anomaly, and I think you should be studied. Like, in a lab. Or a zoo."

See? Supportive all the way …

"You're a peculiar kind of grown-up."

"He's not a grown-up at all." Oskar, another Collective member, joins us and pats Ezra's back.

"And why should I be studied in a lab?" I ask.

"Oh," Oskar says, "if that's what you're talking about, then I agree with Ezra."

"What? Why?"

"The official story is you're on long-term IR because Novi hit you so hard you had a ruptured spleen or your brain flew out of your head or whatever lie it was, I can't remember, but we all know the truth. You're not injured at all. You wanted out. And now, here's your team playing in the Stanley Cup Final, and you could technically be back out there and get your name on that Cup. Yet, you're up here. With us. Instead of on the ice with your brother."

I bite my lip because that same thought has crossed my mind many times over these playoffs.

Even though I played on the team this season, I didn't hit the qualifying forty regular games to be included on the Cup should they take it out. I'd only have to play one game in the final to qualify, which is why I've been thinking about it, but when I really assess why I'd want to be out there, the reasons don't hold enough weight for me.

I'd be doing it just so I could say I'm a Stanley Cup champion. To almost prove that doing as I was told for decades was somehow worth it because my name was on a trophy. That's not enough for me. There's a reason I wanted to stop playing.

"I didn't like the person I was when I put the whole importance of my existence into hockey, so I don't want to be rewarded for it." It's as simple as that, but apparently, it doesn't appease them.

"I will never understand," Oskar says.

"Does not compute," Ezra adds.

I look to Parker to defend me.

All he does is shake his head and say, "Hey, I'm with them. I think you should be playing."

He does, and I know he's trying to be supportive, but the thought of going out there and not winning? Not getting him that Cup that he so desperately wants for his dad? I can't do it. I can't be a part of his disappointment. Maybe it's a superstitious thing or a self-preservation thing, but I'd rather not have that hanging over my head for the rest of our lives.

Instead, I'll be by his side to reassure him it will happen next year or the year after that, and I'm certain of that because there's one thing I'm sure of, and it's that Easton Kikishkin has Stanley Cup champion written all over him. I know it'll happen for him one day.

I just hope today is that day.

"And I told you that Easton has got this." I wrap my arm around Parker and kiss the top of his head.

Anton comes back with some food for him and Ezra, and his gaze snags on us. "Wait, are you two out as a couple? Did I miss that?"

The entire Collective knows about Parker and me, thanks to coming out to them at Easton's birthday party, but we're still on the DL when it comes to the team. Though kissing his head where there is an arena full of staff coming and going in the suite probably isn't the smartest, sometimes I can't help myself. I release him and put a gap between us. Reluctantly.

I want Parker by my side always. "We're not out yet. But soon. I'm announcing that I'm not coming back during the off-season, and we figure next season sometime, we can start being not so careful."

Ezra turns to Anton. "If we weren't allowed to be together, would you quit for me?"

Anton's eyes practically bug out of his head. "Umm …"

"It's not love if you don't quit your job for your partner," Oskar says. "Lane did it for me."

"Would *you*?" Anton asks Ezra.

They stare at each other, neither willing to admit that, no, they wouldn't, and I feel the need to step in.

"The good news is, neither of you have to, and neither did I. I didn't quit so I could be with Parker. I was going to be with him either way. I left because of my own shit. I walked away myself."

"Gun to my head …" Ezra says. "Yes, I would give up hockey for you." His delivery needs some work because it totally sounds like he's lying.

Anton swallows hard. "Same."

"But we don't have to do that, right?" Ezra looks so scared it's almost comical.

"Hell no," Anton says.

"Good. We should, uh, not talk to Connor anymore. He makes no sense and scares me into thinking thoughts I really shouldn't."

"I'm really feeling the Collective love here," I say dryly as they walk away from us.

Oskar stays.

"You don't want to run away too?" I ask.

"Nah, I get it. Expectations, playing, retirement … sometimes I think it would be easier if I retired after my contract too."

Thank fuck there's no one else around us to hear that. I could see the dramatics now. It's surprising, but there comes a time in every athlete's life where they have to reassess their priorities.

"You're thinking about leaving?"

"Maybe. I haven't decided yet. But you know what they say, once these thoughts start popping up, it doesn't take long for them to take over."

I scoff. "Understatement in my case. Once I thought it, I was on board."

"Don't let Ezra and Anton make you second-guess yourself," Oskar says. "I think they're going to keep playing until no one wants them anymore. They'll be in their eighties with walking frames in front of a cardboard cutout crowd with a three o'clock puck drop so that they're in bed by the time the real game starts."

"That sounds like them. But they're not getting to me at all." It's the opposite even. Because while they're acting like retiring is the worst thing in the world, all that's going on in my head is wanting to ask them if they're aware it is literally *a game*.

I won't though. Because being thrown off this suite's balcony is low on my bucket list.

But my point stands. Despite what I was told growing up, hockey doesn't hold much meaning to me. Winning doesn't hold the honor they think it does.

Making a difference in the world is what I want to do.

And while the Collective and everyone in it is doing their part—they're out queer athletes in the public limelight—I want to be more involved than that. I want to see the results firsthand by working with future generations.

I haven't started yet, but I have a plan. It will involve traveling all over the country and even Canada, and for most of it, Parker will be right there by my side. There will be some times where he'll need to be with the team to work on the glitches in his new training program. I might be done with hockey, but he isn't, and he doesn't have to be.

He does it to feel closer to his father, and I will never deny him that.

More Collective guys arrive, as well as Knox, who looks more nervous than Parker. He so desperately wants this win for Easton, and so do I.

The team made it so far last season, but not this far. And for it to be a game seven, the stakes are so high tonight. The series has been going one for one until Tampa led into game six. Our guys fought tooth and nail to win the last game, and now, here we are.

For some reason, I'm eerily calm about it all. I'm confident. For whatever reason, the pit in my gut tells me Colorado is going to win this one. Or maybe I'm merely hoping for it for Parker's sake. For his dad.

While the suite fills with Collective members and their partners, I'm reminded of how close everyone in this group is. It reiterates to me that no matter what I end up doing with my life, Easton will have these guys watching over him.

He may hate my overprotective side, and even though I've tried to shut it down, it turns out being protective of what's mine is a true Connor trait. I have learned, though, that not every protective move or thought needs to be said out loud. I can worry about my brothers, but I have no right to try to run their lives. I understand the balance now.

"Is Little Kiki coming?" Dex asks me.

"He's here, but he's sitting with Mom and Dad."

Tripp frowns. "Because he's still not technically out, and they think hanging out with us would be bad for his career or what?"

Tripp is almost as overprotective of my brothers as I am because of what our parents and I put on them, and I think he always expects me to be defensive over it, but I'm not. Because in the end, both Tripp and I want the same thing—for my brothers to be happy.

I smile. "Nope. Lachie chose to sit with Mom and Dad because, in his words, he can't trust himself not to screw up by offering to get on his knees for anyone in this room. Apparently, you're all too hot or whatever. I personally don't see it, but …"

Tripp ignores my dig at him. "Just because he offers doesn't mean we'd take him up on the offer."

I can see now how the overprotective thing can get annoying. For the millionth time, I send up silent apologies to my brothers.

"Did someone just offer a blowjob?" Oskar calls out from where he's now sitting and watching warm-ups.

Tripp points in Oskar's direction. "Okay, he might take up that offer, seeing as Lane is still in California."

"No, I wouldn't! I would watch though. I'm allowed to do that." Oskar says this so proudly and without shame.

I guess Lane can tame some of that man's old ways, but not all of them. I think about Parker saying shit like that, and it makes me want to hold on to him and never let him out of my sight. Connor Kikishkin doesn't share.

Even if it's only voyeurism and Parker wouldn't do anything but watch. Nope. Fuck that noise.

He's mine.

And as if proving how perfect he is for me, Parker leans in close and asks quietly, "Are people actually okay with being watched? Or being the watcher, for that matter? Do you keep eye contact? Do you pretend you're not blatantly staring at two people having sex? I'd be so self-conscious I'd probably have my hands up the whole time like 'I'm not doing anything with my hands.'"

I laugh. "Good thing we will never have to worry about that because there's no way in hell you're going anywhere near other couples having sex."

"Thank God." The tension leaves his shoulders. "Wait, and no one will ever be allowed to watch us?"

I growl. "No one gets to see you naked but me."

Parker smiles. "So possessive."

"You love me this way."

He doesn't falter. "I do. I love all of you."

"I love all of you too." I didn't know this kind of love existed. The kind that has the word forever floating around in my head. The type of love where he not only makes me a better person but is supportive in whatever I want to do. Where that feeling is reciprocated and not just taken.

We're in this thing called life together, and I never want that to change.

I so badly want to lean in and kiss him, but we still have to be patient about that. Soon, it won't matter if we're seen together, and I can't wait for that day. Until then, we'll have to settle with being side by side, looking like we're friends and nothing more.

"Pregame is starting," someone says while, at the same time, Westly Dalton arrives with his husband, Jasper, and brother Asher. Asher and Jasper greet us but move on quickly to get food and drinks. They seem close for brothers-in-law, and I can't help picturing a day where Lachie or Easton will be like that with Parker. Pouring him a drink. Grabbing tongs and putting a salmon puff on his plate.

We'll never have to worry about that kind of thing with Knox because he's already like one of our family. But I want that for Parker. I want my brothers to be his brothers, and even though he has a mom, I want my parents to be like a second set for him. He's been alone for way too long. There's nothing wrong with that if he wanted it, but he craves affection and closeness. He just never got the chance to let himself be vulnerable with anyone.

"Good luck tonight," West says to Parker. "It's nerve-racking even for me, and I have no skin in this game."

While West talks, Novi walks into the suite.

"Did I miss puck drop?"

"Hey, you made it," I say. "You're here."

"I am." And even if he looks like he's about to shit a brick, this is a big step for him.

Parker and West continue with their conversation.

"Maybe you're still recovering from your own Frozen Four loss," Parker says. "That's why it's so nerve-racking for you."

West throws his head back. "Don't remind me. Colby Kessinger is way too good a coach to be stuck coaching D1 hockey."

Novi's head swivels so quickly in West's direction I'd worry it would fall off if his neck wasn't so thick. For a forward, he's built like a defenseman. No, a linebacker.

For a hockey player in general, he's bigger than average, yet even at thirty-eight, he's still fast out on the ice.

"Uh, did you say Kessinger?" Novi asks, his voice thick and raspy. Almost like he's trying to talk around a swollen tongue or dry throat.

"Yep. Though rumor is he's been offered a job in the NHL." West cocks his head. "For your team, I believe. Do you know something we don't?" West's eyes light up. "Please tell me he's your new coach and he's leaving college hockey? My guys might have a shot of actually winning next year if that's the case."

I want to point out that a coach doesn't make a team win or lose, but nope, no more being that "*Actually* …" guy. No one likes that guy.

"I goddamn hope not," Novi mumbles under his breath. I don't think he wants any of us to hear it, but we do anyway. Or, at least, I do. When he sees we're still staring at him to elaborate, he says, "We used to play in the AHL together. Back when we were first drafted."

"Ah. So you've met the 'I'm so confident it's borderline cocky' guy yourself."

"Met him? I roomed with him on the road. He was a top ten draft pick back in the day, you know. Want to know how I know that? He'd tell me. All. The. Time."

West laughs. "That sounds about right, but hey, look where you are and where he is. Did he even ever play a game in the NHL?"

"No. I got called up before he did, and then …" Novi pauses. "I don't know what happened to him after that."

I get the feeling there's more to the story there, but I'm not going to be the one to ask for more from Novi.

He really is the most terrifying man I've probably ever met. If it hadn't been for all the anger and adrenaline passing through me that day on the ice with him, I never would've thought fighting him was a good idea. But I'm glad I did because since then, we've kind of become friends.

When I'd invited him here, I told him there was absolutely no pressure, especially considering outside of his family, I'm the only one who knows he's gay, but he's doing it.

"You want to get a drink?" Parker asks West. I'm so proud of him for putting himself out there like he is. Yes, deep down, he's still that insecure guy from high school, but he's masking it well. He'll be exhausted later from all the socializing, and if it was my choice, I'd be happy to be up here by ourselves with only my family, but he wants this. It's like he's had a taste of what a vast support network looks like, and now he can't get enough.

The introvert inside him hates him for it though.

I'll be sure to give him an all-body massage later to help him relax and get over the people exhaustion.

With those two getting drinks, it leaves Novi and me standing somewhere between the entry to the suite and the seats where everyone is getting ready for the puck to drop.

"Are you okay?" I ask him.

He shifts his weight to his other foot. Glances around like he wants to make sure no one's looking at him. I'm guessing the answer to my question is a no.

"You want to meet everyone or—"

"I know everyone. I kick their asses on the ice every day."

I snort.

"Novicov?" Ezra asks as he walks back from the bar area with another drink. "Are you lost?"

It's not judgment in his tone, more confusion, and I get it. To outsiders, it would look like Novi wouldn't want anything to do with the Collective.

"Palaszczuk." Novi gives him an up-nod.

Ezra's eyes soften, and he places his free hand over his heart. "I don't even care if you're lost. Your perfect pronunciation of my name means we're already best friends."

Novi leans in closer to me. "Do I want to be best friends with him?"

"That depends on how much attention you want to bring on yourself."

"I'm right here, you know," Ezra says. "Besides, that's a common misconception. When I walk into a room, it doesn't matter who's with me. Everyone's eyes go to me."

Somehow, I think *that's* the misconception. They're all probably wondering how in the hell Anton got slutbag Ezra to stop sleeping around and what's wrong with Anton to want to be the guy on Ezra's arm.

"Maybe I shouldn't have come here," Novi says.

It's slowly but finally sinking in with Ez.

"Oh. Ohhhh. New blood. Nice. Umm, okay. Wow. Okay …"

"You'd think he'd be used to this moment by now," Novi says. "Isn't he captain of this queer … what does Little Dalton call it? Babysitter club?"

I'm sure Asher Dalton is off snickering into his drink if he can overhear us. I also love how when Novi wants to be snarky, his Russian accent comes out thicker, and he thinks no one knows what he's doing.

He's been in this country for seventeen years. He knows the English words for things. He just pretends he doesn't so he can get out of awkward situations.

I'm not bitter about it. Just jealous.

Meanwhile, we've been so busy talking the three of us miss the puck drop. And the first entire minute of the game.

"Easton scored," Tripp yells out.

Only a minute and twenty seconds in and little bro has already scored? That's amazing, but the team can't get complacent. A one-goal lead is good, but it's so easy to have it go bye-bye. Parker appears back at my side. "We're missing the game."

He pulls me away from Ezra and Novi and drags me to the front row of seats where Knox is sitting.

I watch as my brother and former teammates fight like hell to widen the lead. They spend almost all their time in our offensive zone, and Tampa's poor goalie looks like he's already exhausted.

I turn to Parker. "I bet your dad is looking down on us, so fucking happy for you."

Parker slaps his hand over my mouth. "I thought hockey players were superstitious."

I pull his hand away. "In the words of Michael Scott, I'm not superstitious, but I am a little stitious. Besides. I'm not a hockey player anymore."

"Still. Don't jinx my team, dude."

"Aww. *Dude*. *Team*. Next thing you'll be like Miles and Bilson calling everyone *bro*." I run my hand over Parker's neat hair and mess it up. "My little jocky dude bro."

"Shut up."

"Easton scored again," Tripp yells out.

What the hell?

We turn our gaze back to the ice and the giant screen above the arena.

The camera zooms in on Easton, and he looks right up at us and gives Parker a salute.

Smart-ass.

"He really is going to do it," Parker says.

"Now who's jinxing them? We're in the first period and only up by two. Anything could happen."

"Nah. I feel it. Like you said, Dad's up there watching. It's going to happen. But even if it doesn't, just getting to share this with you, being in a place mentally where I've never been happier, where I'm moving in the right direction with my software, with the team … Cup or no Cup, I'm where I'm supposed to be."

I nudge him with my shoulder. "And that's with me, right?"

"With you is where I belong."

"Damn straight."

Parker nudges me back. "Or not so straight."

I want to lean over and kiss him so badly, but I'll have to settle for the shared smile instead.

I've never felt something so right.

That is, until Colorado dominates all three periods, and I watch my brother hoist that Cup over his head.

Okay, now everything is right.